MADDY MADRIGAL MYSTERIES BOOK 6

MAJOR MAGIC

DEBRA CASTANEDA

SHADOW
CANYON
— *press* —

ISBN: 979-8-9994829-7-6
Edited by: Lyndsey Smith, Horrorsmith Editing
Cover design by: Jacqueline Sweet

To my brilliant beta readers, Allison and Lydia. Thank you for spotting the bumps and glitches.

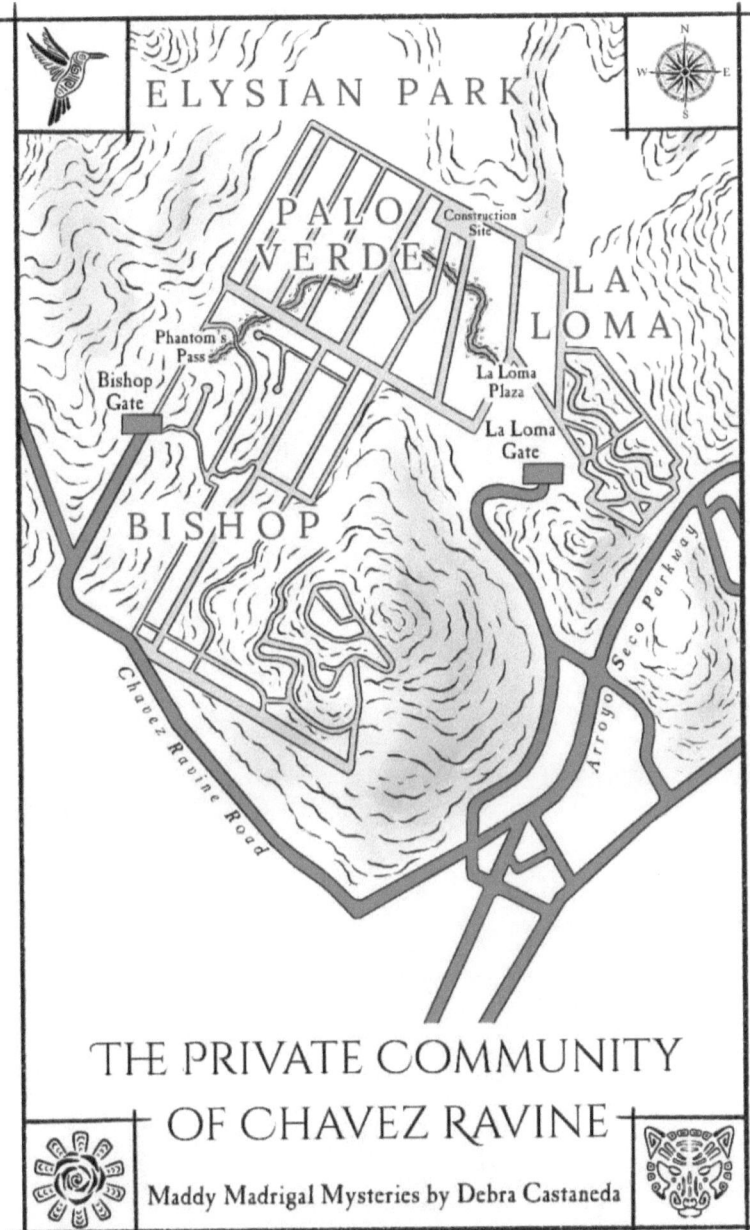

ELYSIAN PARK

PALO VERDE

Construction Site

LA LOMA

Phantom's Pass

Bishop Gate

La Loma Plaza

La Loma Gate

BISHOP

Chavez Ravine Road

Arroyo Seco Parkway

THE PRIVATE COMMUNITY
OF CHAVEZ RAVINE

Maddy Madrigal Mysteries by Debra Castaneda

Chapter 1

The vibration intensified until my bones quivered like tuning forks. Whatever was causing it lurked on the edge of the patio at Olga's Cantina, where minutes before our table had been covered with plates of steaming chicken mole and flickering sugar skull candles for the Dia de los Muertos dinner.

Stu, Clare, and I had spent a fun evening touring the Day of the Dead altars that had gone up around Chavez Ravine and afterward met our friends Julia Suarez and Ben Tomas for dinner at Olga's Cantina. We had just finished our street tacos and mezcal flights when a strange buzzing came from the edges of the patio.

Moments later, Augustina Paz called from the command center with alarming news: the heatmap was blowing up, which meant we were dealing with an entity emergence. *Multiple* emergences, if all the pulsing red dots on the heatmap were accurate.

There was no time to waste.

I herded everyone inside the restaurant, then dispatched Stu to secure the entry points. Not a simple job. Olga's Cantina sprawled like a maze, with dining rooms and hallways branching in every direction.

Clare lunged after her father, but I caught her arm and pulled her back. "Stay with me," I said, watching Stu yank a machete off Olga's wall.

It was one of those rustic Mexican farm tools she had collected over the years. The blade appeared dull, but it was better than nothing. Stu might have owned one of the top security firms in LA, but whatever waited outside wasn't some garden-variety, human threat. We didn't know what kind of entity was about to announce itself, but I wasn't about to let Clare find out the hard way.

The noise, like a million angry bees, made it hard to think straight. I pressed my palms against my temples, trying to focus and not having much luck. My job as head of security for Chavez Ravine meant I needed to figure out how to neutralize whatever nightmare was materializing on that patio.

My hands began to itch, and when I glanced down, a faint red glow was pulsing beneath my skin. Great timing: my magic had decided to wake up. That was a relief. And a problem.

Most of the terrified diners had no idea their security chief occasionally handled supernatural threats with inherited magical abilities. Shooting crimson energy from my fingertips in the middle of Olga's Cantina would almost certainly result in emails demanding answers to questions I preferred to avoid. I crossed my arms and tucked my glowing hands under my armpits.

Clare's fingers dug into my arm. Julia and Ben stood frozen beside me. The bar crowd had surged into the room, drawn by that hellish thrumming, with Olga Sanchez at the front, her face drained of color, knuckles jammed against her lips. All eyes locked on the chaos beyond the glass.

The patio looked like a war zone: chairs sprawled on their sides, a server's tray upended, and glass shards glittering among food scraps. A neon pink sugar skull centerpiece stared up at me from the Saltillo tiles.

I wanted to call Augustina Paz at the command center, where she had been monitoring the heatmap that tracked entity activity, to hear her soothing voice, to let her businesslike demeanor keep me focused. But that would have been selfish. There were more eruptions than the one on our patio, and she would be swamped coordinating our security response.

Augustina had dealt with entities from the beginning, back when she was with the LAPD and the first wave of entities started turning Los Angeles upside down. She knew what to do, and I needed to leave her alone to do it.

Julia let out a sharp cry when she peered through the plate glass window. "No, no, no. It's so ugly."

Clare leaned forward, squinting. "Where? Where are you looking? I don't see anything."

"I don't either." Ben sounded bewildered.

That made three of us, but I didn't doubt Julia. Not for a moment.

She pointed with a trembling finger at a rock wall across the patio. "There! Don't you see it?"

A collective gasp rippled through the crowd. A landscaping spotlight cast an eerie glow across the pale stone. I stared at the gathering darkness. Tiny black specs fluttered about, coalescing into a shape that pulsed and quivered. Its throbbing synchronized with the bone-jarring vibrations hammering us from every direction.

"Make it stop!" Clare shouted.

And just like that, it did.

Despite whatever horror was about to reveal itself on the other side of the sliding glass doors, my body relaxed slightly. The pounding in my head ceased when the buzzing cacophony abruptly ended.

"What the hell?" Stu said in my ear.

I jumped a little, then latched onto his arm, my fingers digging into his sweater. Relief coursed through me. He had made

3

it back safely. Words didn't come. I slowly turned my head, mesmerized by the thing taking shape on the other side of the glass.

"You see it now, yeah?" Julia whispered.

I managed a strangled, "Yeah."

The thing materializing before us looked like a Camazotz, but it was huge and as dark as coal, with a frosting of silver-tipped fur, glittering black eyes, and a snout like a dagger. Bits of pulsing and undulating flesh flanked its nose. The creature's short, broad skull bulged beneath leathery skin. Bat ears crowned its domed head.

Ben groaned. "Oh man…that's not a Camazotz, is it?"

"Looks like one." I swallowed the ball of panic rising in my throat. "But it's too big. The one that showed up at the equipment yard was a fourth its size. Jesus."

The crowd behind me erupted in panicked cries and shouts of alarm.

"Oh my God, what is that thing?" a woman cried. "What's it doing here?"

"Just another entity," a man said.

"We're not supposed to *have* entities here!" another man objected. "The neighborhood is supposed to be entity-free. My realtor told me so."

"We had those vampire birds," the woman said. "But this thing could eat those for breakfast."

A bit of an exaggeration, but point taken. Definitely not the time to tell people they were looking at a super-sized Mayan demon bat.

"All right, everyone." My voice came out steady, calmer than I felt. "Let's keep things quiet, please, and I'd like everyone to leave the room. Nice and slow. Entities don't come inside buildings, so there's nothing to worry about." I tried to sound matter-of-fact, even casual. "But it's always best not to antagonize them either."

I gestured toward the door to an interior dining room, hoping the calm would catch on. Stu tried to steer a small group of stragglers out of the room, but they pushed him away, determined to stay and watch.

The sliding glass door was locked, but the calculated way the enormous creature was observing us made me double-check the latch. The mechanism seemed secure, but I wasn't about to test it further. The monster's bat ears twitched.

Stu gripped my arm. "I think you should move away from the door."

The monster's ears rotated toward us, like satellite dishes locking on a signal.

I slowly began backing away. "No reason to get excited there, big boy."

A moment later, I wished I could take back those words.

The effect was immediate. The demon bat hurled itself at the glass, hard enough I thought the whole thing might shatter. Behind me, chaos. Screams and pounding footsteps while people stampeded down a hallway. Stu's voice, calm and steady, called for Ben to get everyone to the bar in the center of the restaurant, away from the windows.

The Camazotz appeared stunned after its encounter with the glass but quickly recovered. Something emerged from its left wing. A hairless forearm as skinny as a chopstick. Elongated fingers began pawing at the window.

Not good.

In all my time dealing with entities, I had never seen one try to enter a building. Now those spindly fingers were probing the lock like a burglar determined to get inside. Even knowing the door could only be unlocked from the inside, I held my breath.

Stu waved his hands over his head, planted his feet wide apart, and stomped. "Go on. Get! Shoo! Get away."

It was almost comical. My perfectly reasonable boyfriend with advanced security training was treating our otherworldly intruder like a raccoon rooting through the trash. A sharp laugh escaped my throat.

"It's not funny." Stu shot me a look of exasperation and continued to wave and stomp.

I ran a hand over my face. "Sorry. I know."

The creature's face contorted, its ugly-as-hell snout wrinkling in an expression of pure contempt.

A vibration against my hip made me jump, but it was just my phone. Stu whipped around, his blue eyes wide. Augustina was calling from the command center.

"Here's what I know," she said calmly. "The heatmap recorded eighteen eruptions in Chavez Ravine. Eight of them in Palo Verde, six in La Loma, and four in Bishop. We've got four reports of entity sightings, all large bat-like creatures. There are a couple of brown ones, but most of them are gray. Steve Zhou is trapped at Muertos Café and says it's a Camazotz, although the one he's seeing is bigger than anything he's processed before. And he says the bats do not appear to be suffering from typical entity disorientation."

My heart, already in overdrive, beat a little faster. "Steve's here? In Chavez Ravine?"

"Yes. Lucky us. He scored a ticket to Muertos Café's festival dinner, and he's there with his girlfriend. Also from OA research, in case you're wondering."

That explained Steven's recent makeover.

"Does he have any equipment that might come in handy?"

Augustina groaned. "He does, but the gear's locked in the trunk of his car, which is clear across the parking lot."

"Any reports of casualties?"

"Not so far."

A voice called out in the background.

A moment later, Augustina said, "Ron's here. So's Justin, his wife, and the baby. The boys are taking calls coming in on the emergency line. I'm seeing six Camazotz total. One popped up outside the church during an evening service, and another showed up near the market across the plaza. Could be the same one that went after Justin and his family, but we're not sure yet."

I took a deep breath. "What do you mean, 'went after Justin *and his family*?'"

"Everyone's fine," Augustina said. "Nothing to worry about. Oh, and Steve said your mom and her boyfriend are with him at the café, and they're fine too. I'm sure he would have called you, but he's been busy trying to keep everyone from panicking." She cleared her throat. "There's one more thing. The Camazotz are trying to gain entry to buildings. That's a new one. Any thoughts about how we should handle this?"

I wanted to smack myself upside the head for not stashing anti-entity weapons all around Chavez Ravine. The Camazotz had left extra-large emergence holes throughout our gated community, but we had never tracked them down. And I finally understood why. They had filtered up from the earth as teeny tiny creatures and had been hiding out somewhere, gathering strength and biding their time. And I had missed it.

There would be plenty of time for self-blame later. If I didn't pull myself together, the chorus line of should-haves, would-haves, and could-haves would paralyze me. I had to devise some kind of logical response to a situation none of our protocols covered.

Only twenty minutes had passed since the first alert. It was just a matter of time before the other entities took shape.

Augustina waited patiently for my response.

"I'll send out a community alert," I finally said. "Everyone is on lockdown until we can come up with a response plan. You, Steve, and I need to put our heads together and document everything we know about these things. I need to get to the command—"

Somewhere in the restaurant, someone screamed. Stu turned on his heel and sprinted out of the room.

"Augustina, I'll call you back." I followed the distressed cries down a hallway and into the main dining area. It was a large, beautiful room with a wooden ceiling, chandeliers crafted from white ropes, and a long row of French doors that opened to another patio.

Outside, the charcoal-colored Camazotz was hunched before a narrow, glass door, a claw wrapped around the handle, twisting and pulling. When it didn't yield, the creature sidestepped to the next door and repeated the motion. Ice flooded my veins. His movements were precise, intentional.

"It's trying to get in!" someone screamed.

The monster's domed head snapped up, and the fleshy bits around its nose fluttered. Its mouth parted, revealing an impressive row of teeth and a pair of long, yellowed fangs.

If there were any question about what sort of entity we were dealing with, its predatory gaze made it clear: we were its prey.

Chapter 2

Stu had never worked for Occult Affairs, but he had dealt with plenty of entities in his security business, so I was glad to have him at my side while I pondered my next move. We huddled together in Olga's tiny office, downing cups of coffee to counteract the lingering buzz from the mescal we'd had with dinner.

The enormous demon bat had flown off after systematically trying every door and window at Olga's Cantina. Its intelligence and determination left me reeling.

Augustina, Justin, and Ron were busy fielding calls from panicked residents. Steve Zhou wasn't picking up his phone, and neither were my mother and Hernan—all were trapped at Muertos Café. None of my other team members had been able to take my calls either, so I had no idea where they were or whether they were okay.

There was much I didn't know about these new entities, but one thing was clear: it was up to me to get rid of them.

I called Cora Bernal, the HOA president. She had gone to sleep early, exhausted after the successful Dia de los Muertos festival, and hadn't heard a thing. I gave her the headlines.

"But you put up a protection spell around Chavez Ravine! It stopped the entities from coming in."

"They're not normal entities," I explained. "So whatever spell I created didn't work on this bunch."

Cora paused, then whispered, "Entities 2.0. They're real, then?"

"Maybe. Probably. I don't know. But they're here, and they're huge, and they've got some really scary teeth. I'm trying to get ahold of Jo at the command center, but she's not picking up. Cora, we're going to need help from Occult Affairs." I paused to let that sink in.

"Don't you have enough people to handle this?" Cora's voice had a sharp edge, the same one I heard whenever we talked about allowing the LAPD into Chavez Ravine.

The community had a long and complicated history with the department and had a strict no-outside-law-enforcement policy. Which was why the HOA had its own security force. If uniforms started showing up, it would be obvious we had a problem we couldn't take care of ourselves, and residents would start wondering whether my team was worth the expense. But if entities started appearing, that could cause home values to drop.

I had no good options. "Based on what I've seen, we don't have enough people, and we don't have the expertise we need," I admitted. "At a minimum, we're going to need OA researchers to help us figure out what we're dealing with and how to combat them."

"You don't need to combat them, Maddy," Cora said briskly. "You just need to get rid of them."

I was trying to figure out the difference when I realized I had blasted the woman from a deep sleep and she needed time to process the bad news.

"Yes, we do need to get rid of them. But these things are showing some unusual and concerning behavior. You know I have an excellent security team and they've come through in some dicey situations, but they're not experts in entity behavior and containment."

Cora sighed. "Can't you just use your magic?"

"It's not that easy. I don't know what I'm dealing with yet. I can't just wave a wand and banish the things, as much as I'd love to." The lack of wands in brujería continued to be one of my biggest disappointments in learning the craft.

"All right," Cora said reluctantly. "You can bring in Occult Affairs, but just the minimum. Only the researchers. I don't want swarms of uniformed officers running around."

That was exactly what *I* wanted. Lots and lots of OA officers jumping out from behind trees, hurling Smoke Bombs, and shooting anti-entity elixir from their oversized squirt guns. Show those big bad Camazotz they were facing an army, not just a small security team. But I knew better than to argue with Cora. She was a great and supportive boss, but she had a blind spot when it came to outside agencies.

We ended our call, and I tried Steve again. Still no answer.

I was mulling over my limited choices when Stu squeezed my hand.

"Those things are bats, right? They're probably nocturnal. Which means all we need to do is wait it out until daylight, and then you can make your next move." He made it sound so easy. His blue eyes gazed at me with complete confidence.

"Stu, do you think I should evacuate everyone?"

"Evacuate! The board will never go for that. And that's a hell of a message, isn't it? Things are so bad people need to leave their homes?" He paused, lowering his eyebrows. "Are you serious?"

I drained the last of my coffee. "Not really, but I'm tempted. I just don't know how bad it's going to get." I sat up straighter. "But first things first. I need to get an accounting of where the residents are and how many we need to escort home. If you're right, we should be able to do that after sunrise, when these things go hang from trees…Or whatever they're going to do."

Stu nodded. "Do we have access to any anti-entity weapons?"

We, he said. I had a very nice boyfriend.

"We do. Steve Zhou has a trunk full. That's one of the first things we need to do: grab that stuff and see how it works on the Camazotz. Hopefully, it'll be a one-and-done blast, and then OA can come in and cart the suckers off to the dump, but I'm not counting on it."

I fell back against my chair.

"It's making me crazy not knowing where everyone is and what they're doing. I hope they're okay."

Stu took my hand and rubbed a circle on my wrist with his thumb. It was surprisingly soothing. "I'm sure they're fine. They'll be in touch as soon as they can." He jerked his head toward the door. "I'm going to go see how people are doing."

As soon as he left, I called Jo at OA's command center in downtown Los Angeles. That time, she picked up.

"Looks like you've got quite the situation on your hands," Jo said.

"What took you so long to answer?" I snapped.

"We're in the midst of an entity 2.0 outbreak. What do you *think* I've been doing? It's been one constant conference call with Steve and the other researchers."

"Have they popped up in LA too?"

"Chavez Ravine *is* in Los Angeles," Jo said. "As much as you people over there don't like to admit it. But no. So far, the outbreak is confined to your hood, and that's how we'd prefer to keep it. Honestly, Mads, there's something little…off…about that place. If it's not one thing, it's another. Have you ever thought about that?"

I glanced at a framed painting of Frida Kahlo. Under that famous unibrow, the woman's dark eyes stared back at me, as if daring me to dig deeper into Jo's question. "Yes, but can we talk about that over a bottle of wine once we get these things out of here?"

Jo gave a short, dry laugh. "Oh, suddenly it's 'we.' Can I send my people in? You've always resisted my offers of help before. What's changed?"

"Mayan bats with an unhealthy interest in entering buildings, for one thing. Look, I'm not asking for officers, but I could use a few more nerds to help us figure this out."

"You've already got Steve and Dria." A pause followed, one long enough to make me steel myself for whatever Jo was going to say next. She cleared her throat and continued. "Okay. So, here's the deal. Given the gravity of the situation and the unknown level of threat these things present, we want to make sure they stay in Chavez Ravine, where they originated."

I pressed a finger between my eyes. "What's that supposed to mean?"

"It means I'm sending officers to surround the community to make sure they don't try to get out. We're deploying nets along the trees at the border with Elysian Park to help deter them, and we'll use some new echolocation guns that will hopefully disrupt their flight patterns. And some drones, but they're still in the early testing stages."

I felt my eyes bug out. "Are you kidding me? How long have you had all that stuff?"

"It's brand new," Jo said calmly. "And you know how it goes with nerd tools. Sometimes they work; sometimes they don't."

"Well, how about you let me test those drones up here?"

"No way! It cost about a million bucks to develop those things, and each one costs a boatload to manufacture. There's no way I can loan them to someone on the outside."

I got up and pressed a hand into my aching lower back. "So, what you're telling me is you're sealing us off. We're...quarantined."

"Pretty much. But not to worry. I'm sending in some supplies. They should be there by daylight." She lowered her voice. "And, Maddy...If I could do more, I would. But you know how the chief is. He's always resented the way Chavez Ravine treats the LAPD, and then Augustina quit, and you gave her a job. And that really, really pissed him off. You know how he is."

I certainly did. How the man had gotten his job was one of life's biggest mysteries. He was a lousy manager, an egomaniac, and a petty, vindictive human being. The second biggest mystery was why the perfectly nice Augustina Paz had ever married the man.

After we hung up, I joined Stu in the main dining room, where he was sitting in a club chair. Olga and her staff had passed around serape throws, and people used the blankets to make nests on the floor. Julia and Ben covered the windows with the white kraft paper the restaurant used for its tables.

I fell into the chair next to Stu, and we held hands while waiting for the sun to rise.

Chapter 3

When the sun came up, my phone started buzzing, and I was finally able to breathe a sigh of relief. Every member of my team was safe and accounted for. Even my mother had checked in. She and Hernan were fine but anxious to get home after a long, uncomfortable night at Muertos Café. Just like at Olga's, a Camazotz had repeatedly tried to get inside, except their giant bat had been a strange carob color. My mother tried and failed to establish a connection with the creature.

"It's certainly not like the other entities," she said with a sniff, as if she had been personally insulted.

According to Hernan, there wasn't much in the historical record about the Camazotz, and I trusted he would know. The retired professor of mystical studies was a treasure trove of information about the supernatural, but all he could do was confirm it was an ancient demon from Mexico.

I was worried about my cat. As far as I knew, Sam was where I had left him: safely locked inside my house. He had some unusual powers, but they didn't extend to opening cans of Salmon Delite. If he was hungry enough, I was pretty sure he could get into the pantry and tear into a bag of kibble. He might also have had to use his kitty litter box since I wasn't there to let him outside to do his business.

The morning was just getting underway, and there was a long list of things to do, starting with keeping everyone where they were while my team ventured outside to verify if the Camazotz were indeed nocturnal. Liam volunteered to make a run for his truck, then come pick me up so we could survey the neighborhoods.

I was making notes on my tablet about who needed to be escorted home and who on my team was available to help when Rory Tuck called. The cranky real estate developer demanded to know what I planned to do about the latest invasion of monsters.

"First those damn vampire birds, and now these bat things. We had one flying around all night, and the fucker even tried to get into the houses!"

Rory's construction company had made a killing selling luxury houses at the end of my street, just below Elysian Park. After a rough start that began with his Bengal cat running away and moving in with me, I had actually come to like Rory, rough edges and all. And while he had a quick temper, he had turned out to be a decent guy.

"We're on it," I promised, then hung up before he could ask for details.

I texted OA researcher Steve Zhou to ask what he thought about Stu's theory that the Camazotz were nocturnal.

That makes sense to me. I mean, they look like bats, right?

I held out my phone to Stu. He squinted at the screen.

"Oh, come on. That's his expert opinion?"

I snorted. "Right?"

I bit my lip and tapped out a response to Steve: *Are all bats nocturnal?*

Bubbles appeared, and then a response.

No. Caution advised.

Thank you, Mr. Obvious. But I kept that comment to myself. Steve was a good guy, and I was in a bad mood.

Amazing smells were coming from the kitchen, where Olga and her staff were making breakfast burritos for everyone. My stomach grumbled, but I knew better than to risk a chorizo, egg, and potato burrito. Running from monsters was hard enough without carrying a food baby.

In the bathroom, I washed my face and touched it up with makeup from my purse. Not that the Camazotz would care, but I wanted to look put together and portray confidence in front of the residents, and nothing said confidence like winged eyeliner.

Stu slung an arm around my shoulders while we waited for Liam inside the front door to Olga's Cantina. Clare, an early riser, paced behind us.

"What if they're out there, hiding?" she asked nervously. "I know you're head of security and everything, and you were in Occult Affairs forever and stuff, but they're really, really big." She glanced over her shoulder and, when she saw we were alone, added, "Don't you have any magic you can use against them?"

I shook my head. Forced a smile to my face. "Unfortunately not. I haven't had time, and I would need to know more about them so I can make something that will work. I'll be fine. Don't worry."

Her brown eyes widened. "Of course, I'm going to worry. They might still be out there. Don't do anything crazy. Please."

"I won't." I gave her a quick hug. Since meeting Clare, I had been doing a lot more hugging.

I opened the door a crack and peeked outside. A large SUV was turning into the parking lot. It didn't stop at the curb, but kept coming between the columns holding up the covered breezeway. The vehicle rolled across the red brick path as if it were a driveway, finally coming to a stop a few feet from the front door. Liam, Bailey, and her boyfriend, Malik, an officer with Occult Affairs, jumped out, crossbows in hand.

I gave Clare and Stu a final hug before opening the door just wide enough to squeeze through. A blast of chilly fall air greeted me, along with the grim faces of the security guards.

"We're here to bust you out." Liam jerked his head at the open passenger-side door.

I had never been so glad to see them. They acted as lookouts while I slid inside. The door slammed behind me, and moments later, Liam was reversing so fast I grabbed the chicken handle.

After clearing the parking lot without incident, we sped down the street and headed east toward Muertos Café. Palo Verde was like a ghost town. Not a single person outside. Most homeowners had taken my emergency alert advice and drawn the shades. Up and down the streets, sprinklers were on, soaking front yards.

"Someone thought water might deter the Camazotz from showing up at their house and then posted about it on the community page, and then everybody started doing it," Liam explained.

"Any sign of them this morning?" I asked.

"Nope." Liam kept his eyes on the road. "The last sighting was at four o'clock at the new development. The big bad bat went from house to house, trying the doors, which freaked everyone out and they started calling the hotline."

"Did you respond?"

"Several times," Bailey said from the backseat. "We tried Smoke Bombs. They didn't work. No surprise there. We tried hitting them with the last of the slingshot ammo with the magic paste stuff you made, but those fuckers are really good at evasive maneuvers—"

"Yeah, well…They fly like bats, right?" Malik said. "Totally erratic."

"One hundred percent," Bailey agreed. "We tried crossbows too. No luck trying to hit them."

No wonder no one could take my calls. They had been too busy trying to do their jobs, bravely doing their best to help and protect our residents despite the risks, and as usual, they had made me proud.

"You think those Super Soakers of Steve's will work on these things?" Liam asked.

Bailey drummed the back of my seat. "Oh man…I can't wait to get my hands on one of those. I hate the Camazotz."

I thought back to the time a smaller version of one had appeared in the Palo Verde equipment yard. "Did it go after your hair?"

Bailey had hair the color of bright copper pennies, and the Camazotz found it irresistible.

Bailey snorted loudly. "Hell no. I learned that lesson. I borrowed Malik's beanie."

I turned in my seat and glanced at the young man sitting next to Bailey. We had first met at Muertos Café, where he had been working as a barista. Malik helped us figure out how to dispatch a ghoul, and I had been so impressed by his smarts I recommended him to Jo at Occult Affairs. He ignored LAPD regulations and kept his black hair on the longer side, his signature swoop over one eye still intact.

Jo had made it clear she wouldn't be sending in OA officers as backup, so I had to ask. "Shouldn't you be going to work soon?"

Malik shook his head and grinned. "I took a few days off, so I'm here as a private citizen. At your service, ma'am."

Jo might be okay with that, but the chief wouldn't be. I couldn't care less what the chief thought, but there was no way I would allow Malik to do valuable, dangerous work for free.

"That would be great and much appreciated, but I'll want you to submit a freelance invoice when you're done."

Bailey laughed. "That'll pay for the moving van. Malik's moving in with me. His apartment is a shithole."

Not surprising, given the pathetic salary Occult Affairs paid its officers.

I stared out at the chaos on the streets: overturned Day of the Dead altars, toppled lawn skeletons, and broken pots of marigolds. Had people done that in a panic, or had the bats? Maybe both.

Liam took his eyes off the road long enough to glance in my direction. "Lucky it was so cold outside. Most people were indoors when they emerged—"

"They'd already emerged, remember?" said Bailey. "They assembled...or whatever."

"Yeah. What's up with that?" Malik asked. "Entities have never done that before, right?" He wasn't as familiar with the history of entities as his colleagues were.

"No, thank God," Bailey said. "Why do we get all the super weird shit here? I thought El Cucuy was bad, and then came the vampire birds. Now these things. And they're flyers too."

"Flyers are the worst," Liam said grimly. "But I don't know. The Cucuy boogeyman flipped me out."

"But he wasn't an entity," Bailey said. "He was a supernatural creature."

Malik groaned. "Oh man...I'm having a hard time trying to wrap my brain around all this. But maybe Bailey has a point. It *does* seem like Chavez Ravine over indexes on the weird shit. Any ideas why?"

Everyone was suspiciously quiet. Liam stared straight ahead, his mouth fixed in a straight line. The coincidence of my arrival in Chavez Ravine and the appearance of entities was hard to explain, and it was my least favorite subject.

"Chavez Ravine has a long history of supernatural activity," I said tersely. "My great-aunt Lencha Bantacorte dealt with a lot of it back in her day. There's no denying there's something unique about this place." I thought of the long stretch of magic-infused red clay on her property I had inherited. The clay had been the secret source of her power as a bruja, and I had only begun to explore its possibilities.

"I'm not complaining," Bailey said. "Just to be clear. I love it here. Weirdness and all. But I am curious."

Liam ran a hand through his rough, blond hair. "Well, you know what they say. Curiosity killed the cat. It's probably not something you want to start poking your nose into. That's why OA has researchers. Those questions are theirs to deal with it. We're just part of the containment crew."

Liam turned into La Loma Plaza. We had reached our destination.

I pointed at the red muscle car at the far end of the parking lot, away from the other vehicles. Steve must have been worried his new toy would get dinged.

"That's Steve's."

Bailey snorted. "You're kidding! I thought he drove something totally innocuous. Like him."

"Hey!" Liam protested. "He's a good guy."

"I didn't say he wasn't. I just thought he'd drive something a little nerdier."

"So, what's the plan?" Malik asked. For someone who had faced a flesh-eating ghoul, he sounded nervous. I didn't blame him. On the scary scale, the super-sized demon bats scored a ten.

"I'll go in and grab the car keys from Steve while you guys cover me," I said. "Then you'll do it again while I get the gear from the trunk of his car."

"Let me do that." Liam opened his door to get out.

I shook my head. "My turn. You guys had all the fun last night."

My chest was tight. Until that moment, I hadn't consciously felt dread, but sometimes the body reacted before the brain had a chance to process emotions. There was something about our colony of monster bats that plucked at my most primal fears. And we had yet to find out what they could do if they caught someone.

I shuddered, thinking of the huge fangs I had seen.

Liam rummaged around in the center console, pulled out a beanie, and handed it to me. "Okay, boss, but take this. Just in case."

I shot him a grateful smile and stuffed my hair inside the knit cap.

We got out, crossbows first, scanning the sky, the trees, the rooftops.

"Clear," Liam said, and I ran.

Chapter 4

My mother and Hernan huddled at a bistro table, sipping coffee. Steve Zhou and a young woman were seated closest to the sliding glass door, fixated on the patio. In fact, everyone was. Even the servers behind the counter were distracted from their work by whatever was out there.

I crossed the room, squeezing my mother's shoulder when I passed. She startled, causing Hernan to look up with a frown.

"It's about time you got here."

"Nice to see you too," I said, clapping him on the back.

Steve turned toward me and blinked. "You're here."

His companion ignored me and continued to stare at whatever was outside in the shadows.

My scalp prickled. "What's going on?"

Steve stood and pointed. "If you look hard enough, you'll see one of those bats is out there. At the opposite end of the courtyard, under that big tree. We turned off the patio lights last night after a few of them showed up. They went away at some point, but one came back. We didn't see it until the sun came up."

It was hard to make out, but it was there, all right. Attached to a tree limb and hanging upside down, perfectly still.

"It hasn't moved?"

Steve rubbed the side of his face. "No. I think it's sleeping. Most bats are nocturnal, but these aren't ordinary bats. It would be nice if these guys slept during the day. Give us a chance to, you know, take them out."

"Don't they sleep in caves?"

Steve's girlfriend stirred in her chair. I guessed she was around thirty. She had beautiful almond-shaped eyes and wore her hair in short twists.

"They do," she said. "They like dark, safe places. Caves, under bridges, attics, crevices…Anyplace away from light and safe from predators." She paused, then gave an awkward but friendly wave. "I'm Adriana, but call me Dria. Everyone does."

Her name was familiar. She was the OA researcher El Cucuy had tried to drag away in Phantom's Pass. Dria spent some time in an emergency room, getting treated for her wounds. Steve said she had put up a hell of a fight.

"Nice to meet you, Dria. I think those things are way too big to worry about predators. But I have a question…If bats like to hide away while they sleep, what's it doing out there?"

Steve shrugged. "Maybe like you said—they don't worry too much about predators."

Dria's hand shot up. "We named it. It's a Camazotz, right? Only huge. So, we named it Megazotz. Cool, right?"

"We were just messing around," Steve muttered. "It was a long night."

I studied the enormous gray bat, several times the size of the last Camazotz I had seen. "I like it. It's a good name, and besides, you two are the experts. Megazotz it is." I held out my hand. "Can I get your keys? And where's the gear? Trunk? Backseat? Both?"

Steve dropped the keys into my waiting palm. "Trunk. I've got two spray guns and a can of elixir back there."

That wasn't much, but it was something.

"Is there anything else I should know about those bats before I go out there?"

"Well," Dria said, "if they attack you, stay calm and try to avoid contact. Don't swat at it. It might provoke a bite."

I forced a smile to my face. Obviously, Dria hadn't spent much time in the field.

Steve shifted from foot to foot, looking decidedly uncomfortable. "Maybe try to lock and load as fast as you can, in case any of them show up?"

I shoved the keys in a pocket to keep my hands free, just in case. Hopefully, all the big bats in Chavez Ravine were getting their beauty sleep, and I could go about my business without having to worry about them.

While I crossed the dining room, someone grumbled about their HOA dues and not getting their money's worth. I ignored them, mostly because after the night I'd had, I couldn't trust myself to keep it professional.

Outside, the weak morning sun cast a hazy light over the deserted streets. I was hurrying toward the vehicle—Liam, Bailey, and Malik brandishing their crossbows—when a movement caught my eye. It was a Megazotz swooping down from the upper parking lot, its massive wings flapping while it hurtled toward me.

So much for the nocturnal-monsters theory.

An arrow flew and missed. Then another. The giant bat screeched and headed straight for me. Instinct kicked in, and so did the adrenaline. I flung myself to the ground and rolled, narrowly avoiding its sharp claws. After scrambling to my feet, I fumbled for the keys.

A Smoke Bomb flew overhead, with a cloud of purple rising into the air. The stuff didn't drop the Megazotz, but it hid me long enough to reach Steve's car.

"Let's keep this party going!" Bailey shouted.

More Smoke Bombs went flying. One smacked a nearby tree and exploded. The purple smoke was so thick I could barely see, but I managed to point the key fob at the trunk, and a satisfying snick of the latch followed. I grabbed the spray guns and elixir jug. Somewhere off to my right, the Megazotz screeched.

"Incoming!" Liam yelled.

My heart sank. The spray guns felt too light to hold much liquid, but there was no time to fill them. I had to find cover.

I tore around the side of the car, yanked open the passenger door, and pulled it shut behind me. Just in time. The monster bat collided with the vehicle with such force it rocked violently, throwing me against the center console. The bat's leering face emerged through the purple mist. Its claws scraped against the metal roof, setting my teeth on edge. It was the one from Olga's Cantina, unless there was more than one with silver-tipped charcoal fur. Liam and Bailey were shouting something, but their voices were muffled, distant.

I was trapped. Steve's car was roomy, and it felt solid enough. I certainly hoped so. The Megazotz threw itself against the vehicle over and over.

I took a deep breath, trying to calm my racing heart, and grabbed the plastic jug. There wasn't much weight to it. I unscrewed the lid and peered inside. My stomach dropped. Just a few inches left. Not even enough for one decent blast.

I had been counting on OA's new formulation and pump-action sprayers to neutralize the Megazotz. The stuff had sedated a harpy that attacked me in Elysian Park. Granted, the harpy hadn't been as big as the Megazotz, but it was large enough, and it dropped to the ground like a sack of rancid, rotting potatoes.

Jo was our only hope. She would do what she could, but it would ultimately be up to the chief, and he was impossible to predict.

Outside, the purple mist was clearing. The Megazotz dove toward the car again. I steeled myself for another jolt, but it landed on the roof, just above my head. Its claws scratched the metal while it moved around.

What the hell was it doing? Did it plan to peel back the roof like an anchovy can? I felt a moment of solidarity with the oily, salty fish.

A moment later, the Megazotz's upside-down face appeared in the windshield.

I did what any exhausted, self-respecting head of security would do.

I flipped it off.

It studied me with black eyes full of menace and something else. Curiosity.

Something moved beyond that horrible bat face. It was Liam, a distant dot creeping closer, a crossbow in his hands. The Megazotz's ears twitched. It knew something was coming up from behind.

I wanted to scream, to warn Liam the thing had clocked him. There was little chance he would hear me, so I had to keep the monster's attention on me.

I rapped on the windshield and yelled. "What do you want! Where did you come from?"

The flaps of skin on the creature's nose came to life and quivered.

Liam was closer now, his crossbow aimed at the monster's head.

I banged on the glass again. "Yeah, I'm talking to you. You've come to the wrong place. You and your friends can't stay here."

Liam had stopped and was taking aim.

I shouted louder. "How did you end up here?" Their presence felt intentional.

Liam was taking a long time to set up his shot. After what seemed like an eternity, he set the arrow on the ground and pulled another one from the quiver.

Movement forced my attention back to the windshield.

A chopstick-like arm slid from the end of a leathery wing. Five elongated fingers scraped across the glass, and a gray hand finally came to rest on the window. A finger tapped once, then pointed.

At me.

Several things happened all at once. An arrow flew toward us, the monster's leering face disappeared, and the car rocked when the Megazotz launched itself into the air.

I fell back against the seat, weak with relief. The thing was gone.

For now.

Chapter 5

My Megazotz wasn't the only one that had disappeared after Liam's crossbow attack. They *all* did. From the heatmap too.

That was unprecedented. Entities didn't just come and go. Once the heatmap picked them up, it followed them until they were contained, processed, and on their way to the refugee center out near Palm Springs. Then, and only then, were they manually cleared from the system.

The development rattled Augustina, who insisted on staying in the command center despite having worked the overnight shift. "It's all hands on deck," she said when I called for an update. "The only thing I can think of is our heatmap is malfunctioning. I ran a systems check, but everything looks fine. I filed a trouble ticket with the manufacturer. If I don't hear from them in the next fifteen minutes, I'll call them again, see if they can do some diagnostics on their end."

I called a meeting in the command center.

Augustina brewed a fresh pot of coffee and handed out protein bars from a stash of snacks she kept in a drawer. I was amazed at her ability to stay calm and cool and think about the rest of us, with all the madness going on outside.

Justin's wife and baby were asleep in the back room. We had to get them home. In fact, we needed to get everyone trapped in restaurants and other places home too.

We gathered around the screen displaying the heatmap. Not a single red dot anywhere in Chavez Ravine. The tension in the room was like a living, breathing thing.

"So, where did they go?" Bailey asked.

"Maybe they flew off," Justin said. "Decided to go where the pickings were easier."

Augustina shook her head. Despite the purple half-moons under her eyes, she sat perfectly straight in her chair. She reminded me of an off-duty ninja in her tight-fitting black turtleneck sweater. "OA wouldn't let that happen. They have us surrounded. Shoot to kill is what I'm hearing." She paused. "The bats, not us."

Augustina played some of the video our surveillance cameras picked up. OA officers surrounded the perimeter of Chavez Ravine, armed to the teeth.

The wilderness area of Phantom's Pass near Bishop had presented some serious challenges since the only way to get there was to hike in from one of the trailheads in Los Angeles. But a few hardy OA officers had managed to make it.

All eyes turned toward me.

"Shoot to kill? Is that true?" Ron Mendez asked, his voice rising. He wore camo pants and a black sweatshirt, his hair grown out and a little wild since its last buzz cut. The LAPD had avoided killing entities for lots of reasons, not the least of which was PR.

I nodded. "Unfortunately, it's true. They don't want these things getting into LA and causing widespread panic, especially because we're not sure if the nerds' latest elixir will take them out. The concern is that it won't work on Entities 2.0."

"If that's what they are," Bailey said. "They could be something else. Like the vampire birds and the Cucuy."

"Those didn't appear on the heatmap," Ron pointed out.

Bailey began pacing, arms crossed against her chest, copper hair still tucked inside a beanie. "What if they're some sort of hybrid? Like entities plus something else? Maybe there's something we can do. Something we haven't tried."

Liam's eyebrows came crashing down. "A hybrid…the next phase…the next wave…whatever. It doesn't really matter what we call them. I just hope the nerds can figure out how to neutralize them. We don't have the resources to do it on our own."

Malik shifted in his chair and darted a glance at Bailey. "Um, I agree. OA is equipped and funded for that, and we're not."

Bailey gave a long exhale. "Yeah, okay. I get that, but I don't understand why OA doesn't want to work more closely with us. We're on the same side, after all."

"I'm with you on that one," I said. "It does feel like we're sitting ducks until we get our hands on the new elixir and whatever else OA can send our way. Augustina, any word on those supplies Jo promised?"

Augustina grimaced. "No. Not a thing. I'm not sure what's going on. I'm still waiting to hear back from some old friends at OA, but I'm getting a bad feeling."

"You're not imagining things," Malik said.

That got everyone's attention.

Bailey's hands moved to her hips. "What's that supposed to mean?"

Malik tapped his phone. "It means I have a buddy who works in logistics, and he says they haven't received any requests for supplies." He turned to Augustina. "You worked at OA the longest. Is there another department that might be handling that sort of thing?"

"No," Augustina said firmly. "Occult Affairs is dysfunctional when it comes to staffing, thanks to he-who-shall-not-be-named, but it's very buttoned up when it comes to research and logistics because the chief put Edwina Wong in charge of those departments after the second wave of entities."

Liam gave a wistful sigh. "Love her. She wouldn't go out with me, though."

"Didn't stop you from trying and making a fool of yourself." Justin laughed and clapped him on the back.

Liam sniffed. "You know what they say. Nothing ventured…"

"Yeah, well, next time let me give you some pointers," Bailey said, coming over to ruffle his hair.

Bailey, Liam, and Justin had forged their friendship in the chaos of Occult Affairs long before joining my team.

"Oh, and we didn't tell you what happened last night," Justin said, with a sidelong look at Ron, who groaned.

I tipped back in my swivel chair and drained the rest of my coffee. Augustina made it strong, just the way I liked it. "Sounds like a good story. I'd love to hear it."

Augustina waved a hand as if swatting away a fly. "We have plenty of other things to talk about, like how we're going to get all those people back home. I was thinking—"

"No, no," Justin said. "I think it's important to give credit where it's due. Right, Ron?"

Ron nodded glumly. "Yes, yes. Fine. Augustina saved my ass last night. Okay. *Our* asses. Me, Justin, his wife, and the baby." He turned to Justin, his bottom lip jutting out. "There. Happy?"

"I'm not," Liam said, rubbing his hands together. "Let's hear the details, Justin."

Augustina rolled her eyes but said nothing.

"Well," Justin began, "my wife and I were in the neighborhood last night, dropping off some homemade pan de muerto to some friends, and we thought it would be nice to bring some to Augustina because she didn't get to go to the festival. Ron had the same idea and was bringing her a plate of food, and he got here just before we did."

"Technically, I was still on shift, so I was just taking a quick break," Ron said, with a nervous glance in my direction.

"And then, out of nowhere, this giant thing comes swooping down. We're halfway across the plaza. For a moment, I thought one of those vampire birds had come back, but it wasn't flying the same. Like, it was all over the place. So, we start running for the command center. And then Ron comes out, and he has his slingshot, but when he pulls out his ammo pouch…" His voice drifted off, and he turned to Ron.

Ron stared at the floor. "It was empty. I'd forgotten to reload it. So, I had the slingshot but no ammo."

Justin picked up the story. "And I'm thinking, that's it. We're toast. This thing is going to get my wife and baby in the middle of the parking lot. Except Augustina shows up, and she grabs Ron's baton from his belt and jumps on a bench and launches herself into the air and throws the baton at that pinche bat, and it smacks one of its wings. It starts flying in crazy circles, and we make a run for it. It was like Augustina was doing a movie stunt or something."

Augustina rolled her eyes. "You make it sound much more exciting than it actually was. Ron would have recovered if I'd given him a chance. I just saw it all going down on the camera feed, and I overreacted." She turned toward Ron. "I'm sorry. I shouldn't have stepped on your toes like that."

Ron flushed and pressed his fists into his thighs. "No, you didn't step on my toes, but that's nice of you to say. If you hadn't shown up, I don't know what would have happened." He glanced over at me, and his face went from pink to red. "It was so stupid. Me not restocking. Basic rookie move."

"We all make them from time to time," I said.

Ron kept his eyes on the floor while Augustina busied herself adjusting the heatmap for the tenth time. I figured Ron had learned a valuable lesson. The woman he had once said was too old to be useful in the field had shown him up big time. And his co-workers knew it.

Time to change the subject.

"All right, everyone. Any idea how many people we need to escort home?"

"Ron, Justin, and I have been working on a list," Augustina said. "It's close to four hundred. It was cold enough that most people didn't linger after the festival. We've got the restaurants and a fair number of people who were at their friends' houses for get-togethers or whatnot…and quite a few who got stuck at the gym."

I nodded. "Okay. Let's prioritize the people at the gym. It doesn't have a snack bar, so I imagine they're pretty hungry by now. Then the people at bars and restaurants. Let's leave the residents at friends' houses until last. We have one security vehicle big enough to withstand an aerial assault from the Megazotz, but we need more. Ben Tomas has a few landscaping trucks we can use. Maybe round up a few Hummers and large SUVs from residents willing to let us borrow them. We need to do it fast while the Megazotz are taking a siesta, or whatever it is they're doing."

Bailey held up a hand. "I can help coordinate that."

Liam got to his feet and rolled his massive shoulders. "All right. But I do have one question. It's about the Day of the Dead festival. I don't know a lot about it, but I got the impression people were not just paying their respects to their ancestors, but were calling them back for a reunion. Is there a chance there's a connection between the celebration and the bats showing up on the same night?"

My brain went blank. "I don't think any of us are related to the Megazotz."

"No," Liam said. "I wasn't suggesting that. But it's kind of weird, right? We have this big festival with all these skeletons and skulls and candles and stuff. Is there any chance they might have been…accidentally summoned? Like maybe the wrong ancestors showed up?"

I shook my head, but my thoughts were spinning in a dozen different directions. "It's not a summoning ceremony."

"I know, I know," Liam said. "It was just a thought. I got to hear a bit of Hernan Frias's talk at the community center. He was saying the celebration's roots in Mexico go way back, before the Spanish arrived. The Camazotz are Mayan, right? That got me wondering." He shrugged. "I'm probably way off track."

I swallowed, thinking of the way the Megazotz had pointed at me after I shouted, "What do you want?" through the windshield of Steve's car. Maybe it hadn't been the random movement of a spastic monster.

Maybe it had come for me.

Chapter 6

Operation Get Everyone Home was four hours of nerve-wracking shuttle service, driving people to their houses with one eye on the road and the other on the sky. At any moment, I expected my security truck filled with worried homeowners to be jolted in an aerial attack, but we managed to get through the rest of the day without incident.

I didn't know how long the Megazotz would be gone, though I desperately hoped it would be forever, and I would need everyone on the job when they returned, so I sent my staff who worked through the night home to get some sleep.

Most of my team lived in subsidized housing in Chavez Ravine. It was a perk of the job, but it was also a way of keeping people close so they could respond quickly to emergencies. The only member of my team who had chosen to live outside Chavez Ravine was Augustina Paz. She stayed in her cramped apartment in Pasadena because she needed to care for her aging mother and the apartment was close to her mother's facility.

And since Occult Affairs wasn't allowing anyone in or out of Chavez Ravine—"out of an abundance of caution," Jo had explained—Augustina needed a place to stay. That was easy enough to solve. I offered her my guest room. She protested, but I finally wore her down.

I planned to stay at Stu's place anyway, with Stu, Clare, my mother, Hernan, my friend Julia, her boyfriend Ben Tomas, Steve, and Dria. Stu's house was plenty big, though I doubted any house would be big enough for my mother and me. But it did mean I would have easy access to both her and Hernan. It was always possible their dubious skills would be useful, and Liam's suggestion that the Megazotz had been summoned had wormed its way into my head.

Besides, they were getting on in years, and Stu seemed to genuinely like them. Clare didn't have living grandparents, and she enjoyed their company too.

After Stu and I doled out room assignments, Ben drove me home to pick up Sam and whatever else I might need for the foreseeable future. Julia came along to help, and we stopped at her house too.

The later it got, the more worried I became. It felt like just a matter of time before our ancient Mayan friends returned, so I asked Ben to back into my long driveway and park with the van's rear doors opening onto the porch. I nocked an arrow into my crossbow and got out first, cautiously looking around, but we saw nothing more than several noisy crows flying across the sky.

I expected Sam to greet us with a string of outraged meows, but he didn't.

"Gatito!" Julia cried behind me. "Where are you?"

Julia still had on the outfit she had worn to the Dia de los Muertos dinner at Olga's Cantina, a 1950s-style black satin dress embroidered with red roses she had found at a vintage shop. After sleeping on the floor of the restaurant, the dress was rumpled, and she had swept her hair into a messy bun.

Sam loved Julia. That he didn't come running was a bad sign. Ben went straight to the kitchen, checking window latches and pulling down the blinds I rarely used.

"He's probably just pissed off," I said.

Sure enough, I found Sam in the living room, lounging on his ottoman. He lifted his head and blinked his green eyes, as if bored by the mere sight of me.

I rushed across the room and rubbed his head, but I knew better than to subject him to anything as emotionally aggressive as a hug. He only allowed those from Julia and my neighbor Leo.

"I'm sorry, Sam. I'm really sorry, but some Camazotz showed up. Well, we're calling them Megazotz because they're so big. And we all got stuck at Muertos Café, and then I had a bunch of work to do, and Leo and Toby are out of town, but even so, they couldn't have come over to feed you because I put everyone on lockdown. And Julia and Ben were locked in with me too."

Exactly why I needed to justify all that to a cat, I couldn't say. Maybe because he had proved himself to be more than an ordinary cat.

Julia knelt beside Sam and buried her face in his neck. "Oh, you poor little gatito. You probably thought we abandoned you, but Maddy was really worried about you, yeah? We all were. You must be hungry!"

"No, he's not!" Ben shouted from the kitchen. "He's had plenty to eat."

I hurried into the other room. "There's no way he was able to get into the Salmon Delite!"

Ben laughed and pointed at Sam's food bowl. It was perfectly clean except for a pile of chicken bones. The day before Dia de los Muertos, I had roasted a chicken and stuck it in the fridge. It appeared Sam had finished off at least half of it.

"Looks like your cat can open refrigerators," Ben said. "But I have to say, I'm not totally surprised."

The evidence was clear. "I'm not either. He can open cabinets, and he must have been starving."

Ben went into the pantry and came out holding a Palo Verde Market tote bag. "Want me to pack up his bowls and stuff? Should we take his kitty litter?"

"That would be great, thank you."

I turned to the refrigerator, remembering I had filled it with fresh fruit, vegetables, and meats for the week ahead. "Can you grab the stuff in the fridge too? We'll take it with us. Plus the rice and beans from the pantry. Stu doesn't have a lot of food in his house."

Ben nodded. "You got it." He opened the refrigerator, peered inside, and gave a low whistle. "Ooo, you got some Negro Modelo in here. Can we take it?"

"Of course," I said.

In the living room, Julia was folding some colorful throws and stacking pillows.

"What are you doing?" I asked.

She spun around, smiling sheepishly. "Stu's place is so bland, yeah? Kinda sad. If we're going to stay there, we need to liven it up. You don't mind, do you?"

I didn't, but I wasn't sure how Stu would feel about a home makeover. Between me and Clare, we could convince him. "Nah. Bring whatever."

In the guest room, I changed the sheets for Augustina, swapped out the blankets for new ones, and set out fresh towels. Julia cleaned the bathroom and helped tidy the house while I packed clothes and toiletries. Then I went to my workbench and placed my herbs and other brujería items into a sturdy box with a lid. I would need them if I decided to try to banish the Megazotz with a potion or spell.

If they came back. And I was sure they would.

Ideally, I would be able to use my great-aunt Lencha's shed, which Ben had so beautifully refurbished. It was where Lencha had practiced her brujería, and it was in her backyard filled with magical red clay. I wasn't sure how I would get to the shed safely if the Megazotz returned, but I would figure something out. If I needed to, Stu had said I could work in his mudroom, whatever that was.

The clay figurine of Lencha watched me with disapproval. I grabbed a soft cloth and brushed a speck of lint from the top of her head.

"I think you should come with me. Just in case. What do you think?"

Lencha didn't come to life or glow or do any of the other things she had done before, so I was left to decide on my own.

"Fine. You're coming. I can't imagine doing anything magical without you anyway."

I found bubble wrap in a closet and bundled her up, hoping I wasn't smothering her in the process. Certain I was forgetting something, I looked around, went into my office, and shoved my laptop into a tote bag.

The nagging feeling persisted. I slowly turned around, taking inventory. My eyes eventually landed on the fireproof safe, where I kept Lencha's notebooks. In them, she had written instructions on spells, hexes, cures, rituals, cleansings, and other things she had learned in her practice. If I needed to concoct something to use against the Megazotz, I would need those notebooks, so I added them to my box.

Finally, I returned to the sunroom, unhooked strings of dried herbs and chili, and dropped them into plastic bags.

I was as ready as I would ever be.

Chapter 7

Sam sat on my lap while we drove the few short blocks to Julia's house. He pressed his nose against the window and stared up at the sky with fixed concentration. If the Megazotz returned, I was sure Sam, who was highly attuned to intruders, would spot them first, so I allowed myself to relax a bit.

At the bottom of the hill, we had to wait for a convoy of trucks to pass. I recognized the drivers: Liam, Justin, Bailey, and Malik. They should have been catching up on sleep but instead had returned to work early to escort residents back home. They slowed down when they went by and waved.

At Julia's, we sprinted the short distance from the truck to the house. I carried the crossbow while Julia held Sam. Once we had made it inside, I checked in with Augustina at the command center and made arrangements for Ben to drive her to my house. Julia bustled around, gathering clothes, art supplies, and several floor pillows she insisted on bringing, and off we went to Stu's house.

Stu had borrowed his neighbor's Hummer to take my mother and Hernan to pick up their stuff. My mother brought the contents of their refrigerator, along with the statue of Santa Muerte. A half dozen Spanish swords from Hernan's collection were lying on the dining room table.

I picked up the skeletal Mexican folk saint of death, put it on a shelf in an alcove, then lit a votive candle to welcome her to her temporary new home. Santa Muerte had come to my aid when the murderous El Cucuy stalked Chavez Ravine, and I liked to show her my respect. I made a mental note to ask Ben to bring some flowers from one of his forays. One couldn't be too nice to Santa Muerte.

Stu's beige and brown rug had been replaced by a fringed black one with orange, yellow, and teal diamonds.

Julia clapped her hands when she saw it. "Oh, I love it! It's beautiful!" She turned to Stu in surprise. "Where did you get it?"

Stu cleared his throat and gestured toward my mother, who was busily fluffing the pillows from my house. "Malena brought it over. I think Clare complained about my decorating choices." He turned toward me. "Looks like Maddy had the same idea."

I grimaced. "Sorry. Do you mind?"

"Do I have a choice?" Stu came over and kissed my temple. "I'm just kidding. It's fine." He looked around the living room and grinned. "It's looking a lot less beige in here, that's for sure."

"Thank God!" Clare said, entering the room, bringing with her a waft of coconut fragrance. She had changed since I last saw her in the restaurant and was now wearing a sweatshirt and black leggings, her brown hair damp from a shower. Clare glanced at the rug. "Oh, that's awesome. See, Dad? It doesn't look like a cheap motel here anymore. And nice! Maddy brought her pillows!"

Stu seemed like he was trying hard not to laugh while he took in the number of boxes and bags we had brought from home. "Should I be nervous? Are we settling in for a siege?"

Ben snorted. "It's a Mexican thing. You should see the amount of stuff we take with us to the beach or a picnic."

"Fair point," I admitted, knocking my hip into Stu's. "We may have overdone it with the packing, but since we have no idea how long we'll be here, you know the saying: hope for the best, prepare for the worst."

"Well, whatever happens, we'll be well-fed and in good company," Stu said.

While my mother and Julia unpacked the groceries, Sam inspected the house, and Stu showed Hernan around. I freed Lencha from her bubble-wrap cocoon, placed her on the counter in the mudroom, and went to greet our latest arrivals, Steve and Dria.

Both appeared exhausted, so I showed them to a guest room on the second floor. The other guest room had gone to Julia and Ben. The four would have to share a bathroom, but Clare said Julia and Dria were welcome to use hers. Clare had set aside some clean clothes for Dria since I thought they were about the same size.

Dria sat on the bed and looked around the room with wide eyes. "This is practically the size of my studio apartment. This house is, like, seriously huge."

Steve peered out the window facing the front yard. "Where do you think they are?" he asked over his shoulder.

I knew exactly what he was talking about. The Megazotz. "No clue. Are you hearing anything from Jo? An update on the supplies, maybe?"

Steve turned toward me, his shoulders drooping. "Not anything good. The last I heard, the chief canceled Jo's supply order, and the two were arguing about it, and Jo was threatening to go over his head to the city manager. She's trying, but you know how he is."

"He's an asshole," Dria said, flopping back on the bed.

She wouldn't get an argument from me. We would just have to make do until Jo finally won that battle. But even then, there was no guarantee the elixir would work against the Megazotz.

"Steve, when I went to get those new spray guns out of your car, I didn't see any other equipment. Any chance you still have those sonic tools you poked into the emergence holes?"

Dria propped herself up on her elbows. "Tell me he didn't do that."

"Oh yes, he did." I flicked on a table lamp. "Was he not supposed to?"

Steve rolled his eyes. "It's not fair. The two of you ganging up on me like this."

"Get used to it," I said with a wink, clapping his shoulder. "This party is just getting started."

Steve sighed. "It's ridiculous. The probes have extenders. Why have them if you can't use them? Dria doesn't get out into the field much, so no offense, but we only got meaningful data once we started sampling at lower depths."

"I was wondering what changed," said Dria. "How can we be certain you didn't make things worse by poking into the emergence holes? Maybe you made them coalesce…Maybe you pissed them off. We'll probably never know. And offense taken, by the way. That was a pretty condescending thing to say."

"It was. I'm sorry. I should have told you how I was gathering the data," Steve replied in a low voice. "I hope I didn't stir things up."

All the color had drained from his face.

Steve and I now had that in common: we both thought we might be responsible for the Megazotz. But handwringing and regrets weren't going to help us get rid of them. We needed supplies from Jo and more data.

And sleep.

"Look, we don't know how long we've got before those things come back, so we need to get some sleep while we can. There are fresh towels in the bathroom down the hall, and if you're hungry, all you need to do is step foot into the kitchen, and my mother will rush in to make you something. I know getting stuck in Chavez Ravine wasn't on your bingo card, but I'm glad you're both here."

And with that, I asked Stu to drive me in the Hummer to the command center.

When we arrived, Stu disappeared into the back room to return some work calls while I met with my staff. As head of security, I had more to worry about than just entities invading Chavez Ravine. The residents were a major concern. Keeping them safe was the top priority, but there would be hell to pay with the HOA board if residents were unhappy with the way we handled Operation Get Everyone Home. If that were the case, I needed to get in front of it and do some damage control. So, I wanted to hear how things had gone while the memories were still fresh.

Liam arrived first and sprawled on a chair with a groan. "Man, that was a long-ass day," he muttered.

Justin nodded, his face white with exhaustion. Ron entered the room, shoulders drooping, and stretched out on the floor with a yawn. Bailey fell into a chair next to Malik, her head on his shoulder.

Augustina made a fresh pot of coffee, but given the late hour, everyone appeared past the point of needing caffeine. Liam solved the problem by digging a flask from his backpack and pouring whiskey into everyone's mugs. No one objected.

Augustina sipped hers and gave a tired smile. "Wow, I needed that, and I wasn't even driving all day."

"So how did things go?" I asked.

Ron's eyes snapped open. "Fine. Until I picked up my mother and grandmother at their friend's house in La Loma, and then I got an earful all the way home. I tried telling them I was following the pickup schedule I'd been given, but they seemed to think they deserve special treatment because 'mijo' is on the security team."

"Poor mijo." Justin managed a half-hearted laugh. "At least you didn't get stuck with Eileen Simpson. She'd been at a party up in the new development, and things got kind of wild there, with those bats flying around. She was totally freaked out. I practically had to carry her to the truck. And then she kept asking what we were doing to get rid of them and demanding we do it immediately. Everyone else at the party was doing just fine until she started making a big deal of how she's on the board and needs to crack the whip, and then all of a sudden, people are saying they shouldn't have to put up with giant bats, not with the dues they're paying. I should have taken everyone else home and then gone back to get her."

Typical Eileen behavior. She never could pass up an opportunity to throw me and my team under the bus, no matter how many times we had proved ourselves on the job. Some people were like that. Luckily, board president Cora Bernal had my back when it came to Eileen.

"I'm sorry you had to deal with that," I said.

"No worries." Justin shot a dark glance in Bailey's direction. "Bailey's the one who did me dirty. She put Eileen on my list."

Bailey snorted. "For good reason. She thinks you're cute. If it had been me, she would have torn me apart."

"She doesn't much like me either," Ron muttered.

I turned to Liam, who was now flopped back in his chair and rubbing the back of his neck. "How about you? Any complaints I should know about?"

He shook his head. "Nothing special. Everyone was tired and cranky and worried." He sat up a little straighter. "Oh wait…There is one thing. There was this older guy, Latino, I picked up at a house in Palo Verde and dropped him off in that neighborhood with the funny circular streets, in Bishop. He's friends with Ron's grandmother, and she told him that you're one of those Mexican witch types and that's why the HOA hired you. Because you have special abilities that help deal with stuff like the bats and that's why he wasn't too worried."

My heart stuttered in my chest.

I must have looked panicked because Liam leaned forward in his chair and hurriedly said, "Not to worry. We were alone. The old guy was the only one in the truck. No one else heard him." He gave a sheepish shrug. "I just thought you should know about it."

"I'm glad you told me." My voice was faint. How many people had Ron's grandmother disclosed that story to?

Ron sat up and groaned. "I swear, my grandmother is the biggest chismosa."

"What's that?" Malik asked.

"Blabbermouth."

Justin shook his head. "More like a gossip."

Both worked. So did "busybody" and "meddlesome." Ron's grandmother wasn't about to change her ways. Once a chismosa, always a chismosa. And while she had talked about my brujería when I preferred to keep it quiet, she hadn't said anything bad about me personally.

Malik held up a hand. "Honestly, the people I drove were really nice about the whole thing. Very understanding. And appreciative. Not like the folks I usually deal with down in LA because they are so sick and tired of entities, and when they see you coming, they want to unload."

"I remember that," Liam said. "It used to drive me crazy."

Augustina stood, touched her toes, and straightened. "What a day…But everyone is back where they should be. And you will all be happy to know that I took quite a few phone calls from people expressing their gratitude for the rides home. In fact, I did not receive one single complaint."

With that, I declared our mission a success and ordered everyone home to get some sleep.

———·→·→· ⛩ ·←·←·———

At Stu's house, I headed straight to the bedroom, thinking of the king-sized bed just waiting for me.

When I passed Clare's door, I heard my mother's strident voice and stopped. Clare stood in the middle of the room, looking about as horrified as the day she had been surrounded by chupacabras.

My mother was on a cleaning rampage, snatching up crumpled clothes and throwing them into a laundry basket. "How can you live like this, young lady? It's a pigsty!" She picked up a mug from the nightstand and squinted at the contents. "Is that mold? Oh yes, it is. And all these beautiful clothes on the floor. Your father is a very nice man and all, but I don't understand why he lets you get away with this. I would never ever have allowed Maddy to let her room get into this state when she was your age. Every Saturday, she had to get up early and help me clean the house from top to bottom, and that included her room. Now I know I am just a guest in your father's house, but while I am here, we're going to get this room into shape, and I'm going to teach you how to do it because you cannot take these awful habits with you to college."

Clare's mouth opened and closed. If I hadn't been so tired, I might have found the energy to come to her defense. But my mother did have a point. Clare was a smart girl, but she was a hopeless slob. She was going to have roommates, after all, so I left them to it, slipped into the bedroom, and closed the door behind me.

Chapter 8

When my eyes snapped open, it was dark outside, and my heart was in overdrive. Had I accidentally silenced notifications?

I grabbed my phone from the nightstand. No missed calls. No sightings of the Megazotz. Nothing unusual.

I took a quick shower and pulled on a sweatshirt and joggers.

Almost everyone was in the living room playing cards. Everyone except Julia and Ben—who I suspected were still asleep—my mother, and Clare, who was in the kitchen chopping vegetables. Onion sizzled in a pan.

Since every dish I could think of started with onions, I asked, "What are we making?"

Clare spun around. "You're awake! Caldo!" She beamed.

I pecked my mother on the cheek. Soup was the ultimate comfort food, and we all needed it. Besides, it was hearty, easy to make, and fed a lot of people. "Perfect choice. What kind?"

My mother held up a can of hominy. "Albondigas. Hernan loves it, and I'd just bought some ground beef at Palo Verde Market. It was on sale, so I got extra. Can you find some rice? I'll need it to make the meatballs."

I crossed the room to the walk-in pantry. "How about I make tortillas? I brought the tortilla press."

"Yes, please!" Clare said. "But can we have flour this time?"

I nodded. Hominy was corn, so corn tortillas seemed like overkill. "Flour it is."

Stu poked his head in and offered the grownups glasses of wine, but I declined. If the Megazotz reappeared, I would need to be stone-cold sober.

My mother shook her head and sighed. "I wish I could, Stu, but wine at my age keeps me up at night. I'll have a ranch water instead, if you can swing it."

Stu raised his eyebrows. "Ranch water?"

I put down the tortilla press, went to the fridge, and pulled out a can of club soda and a lime. "Tequila and this in a tall glass."

"Ah!" Stu smiled. "I think I can handle that."

"Just a teensy bit of tequila, por favor. I'm not as young as I used to be," my mother added, dropping diced carrots and celery into the pan.

My mother seemed to be talking about her age a lot lately. She was fixed in my mind as middle-aged, not someone approaching seventy-five, and that tiny sign my indomitable mother was advancing in years made me uneasy.

After Stu set my mother's drink on the counter, we were alone again.

"So, those terrible things…" my mother said. "Have you figured out where they went?"

"No." I rooted around in a cabinet and pulled out a bag of flour and a box of baking powder. "They disappeared from the heatmap."

My mother sprinkled oregano into the meatball mixture. "That's unusual, isn't it?"

"Very. El Cucuy and the vampire birds never registered because they weren't entities. These registered, which means they're entities, but they don't behave like anything we've seen before. The holes they came out of are extra-large, and they skipped right over the disorientation phase."

My mother jerked her head toward the living room. "Can't Steve and his girlfriend come up with some kind of explanation?" she asked, lowering her voice. "They're awfully young. They can't even be thirty."

"Steve's one of the best researchers I've met at Occult Affairs, and Dria's been working on some critical stuff. The trouble is, there isn't much for them to go on. The bats haven't left anything behind for them to analyze. I think we're going to have to wait for them to reappear and go from there."

My mother formed the meatballs with quick, nimble fingers. She might have been worried about getting older, but she didn't have a touch of arthritis. "Would you like me to see if I can establish a connection?"

Clare gasped. "No! It'll rip your head off."

"That's what Hernan says the Camazotz do," my mother replied calmly. "Decapitate their victims. It's a terrible practice. I don't know much about them, but I don't understand why these are so much bigger than the ones in the legends or why there are so many of them. I had the impression there was just one."

"There's never just one bat, is there?" Clare asked, watching my mother while she worked. "My dad took me to Sacramento when I was little to watch the bats fly out from under a highway, and there were thousands of them. *Thousands!* So, it kind of makes sense that if there's one bat creature, there would be more of them." Clare frowned. "But you're not serious, are you? About trying to talk to one of them?"

My mother shrugged. "I'm totally serious. I do it all the time. In fact, I'm a little surprised no one has asked me yet." She cast a sidelong glance in my direction.

"This is different, Mom," I said sternly. "These aren't ordinary entities."

"It's *not* different. When I made my first contact with an entity, I didn't know how it would react. For all I knew, it could have killed me or at least tried to. But it didn't. And I think you'll agree…Things turned out pretty well after that. Nothing ventured, nothing gained."

She had a point. But while I kneaded the dough, all I could think about was what could go wrong. "I'm sure your first entities were still disoriented, but these guys are wide awake. I'm not sure they'll allow you to get close enough without attacking."

My mother's mouth flattened into a straight line. "Well, there's only one way to find out. Honestly, Maddy, if you don't take a little risk now and then, you won't be able to accomplish anything at all. The next time one of those things shows up, I'm going with you. Just like I did when you asked for my help with El Cucuy and we went into Phantom's Pass."

Yeah, my helpful mother had sensed the Cucuy's presence, turned around, and left. Though, to be fair, El Cucuy had been a powerful, supernatural being and not an entity, but still.

"Maybe," I said. "We'll see."

Julia stumbled in bleary-eyed, auburn hair a messy cloud around her shoulders. She yawned. "I hate naps. I feel like I was drugged or something. I can make dessert, yeah? What sounds good?"

"Mexican wedding cookies!" Clare said. "I love those, and I can help."

For the next two hours, Steve, Dria, and I traded theories and brainstormed ways we might try to subdue the Megazotz. At one point, Hernan joined us and said the creatures dated back to the time of the Mayans in ancient Mexico. They had believed a huge and bloodthirsty monster lived in a cavern in the hills and would kill anyone foolish enough to disturb its roost. He even had a Mayan pictograph showing the Camazotz as a fiend with outspread wings and a terrible grin on its face.

But there was one significant difference between the legend of the Camazotz and what we were dealing with now. Instead of just one demon bat, there were many, one for each of the eighteen extra-large emergence holes in Chavez Ravine.

Had Papa Camazotz wandered into another cave, met Mama Camazotz, and had giant-sized offspring?

By the time my mother called everyone to dinner, we had not had any breakthroughs, but it was comforting to share what we each knew.

Everyone gathered around the dining room table. Stu glanced down at his bowl of soup, looking crestfallen.

Clare noticed and laughed. "I think you can handle one meal without a steak."

Hernan spread butter on his warm tortilla, then rolled it up. "The soup has meat in it, Stu. It'll fill you up."

Steve sipped his soup, and his eyebrows shot up. "Oh, wow. It's delicious."

"So savory," Dria said, sliding a tortilla from the warmer on the table.

"Malena wants to go with Maddy if those monsters come back…to see if she can find out more about them," Clare blurted. "And I think that's a great idea."

The room went silent.

Hernan dropped his tortilla roll-up, a hand fluttering to his heart. "Not if I have something to say about it!"

My mother appeared distinctly pleased with the fuss. "Ay, Hernie. It'll be fine. If I sense I'm in danger, I'll turn back, I promise."

"You don't know what those things are capable of," Hernan said, his voice rising. "They are devils. Demon death bats. Killing is what they do. I don't want to say how they do it at the dinner table, but it's pretty darn tootin' unpleasant."

"I know. You told me."

Steve stirred his steaming bowl of soup. "It's not a bad idea, actually. Malena's been a big help with the other entities. Her presence might calm them down. Maybe she can connect with one and find out where they came from. What they want."

"That would be wonderful," Dria murmured.

Steve made it sound as if once my mother connected with the Megazotz, everything else would fall into place. The new stronger elixir would sedate them, OA would send in super-sized crates and cart them off for processing, and all we had to do was kick back and celebrate with margaritas.

"I think we need to take Hernan's warning seriously," I said. "These aren't trolls or chupacabras."

"But we've dealt with ghouls," Steve said. "And those are bad. *Really* bad. So was the harpy."

I used my spoon to slice a meatball in half but went in a little too hard. Soup sloshed over the side of the bowl. "But the harpy was just an ordinary entity, and I ended up in the hospital anyway."

Stu slung an arm around my shoulder and pulled me close. "With stitches in her head."

"That might not have happened if I'd been more experienced in the field," said Steve, staring down at his soup.

He looked so miserable I regretted mentioning my trip to the ER. "You did great. Really. And the most important thing is, you proved those spray guns actually work in the field."

Sam wandered in from the living room, jumped on the buffet, and stared at Ben Tomas, who turned toward my cat, set down his spoon, and said, "Damn it."

Sam swiveled his large red head toward me. His gaze was full of reproach.

"Sam, I just fed you! What's wrong?"

"He's not hungry," Ben said. "It's the gnomes. We forgot about the gnomes."

Chapter 9

My first call was to Ron in the command center. "Are you still seeing the gnomes on the heatmap?"

"Yes, boss. They're in Ben's equipment yard."

"Can you do me a favor and keep an eye on them? If you see sudden, frantic movement or if you see any of them…um…disappear, would you let me know immediately?"

We were still going by Steve's theory that the Megazotz were nocturnal, and it was too risky to send a crew to check on the gnomes at night. I crossed my fingers the little guys would be okay until morning, then told everyone staying at Stu's to try to get some sleep.

Which was my plan too, until I saw a press release from the city manager's office at nearly ten o'clock. It was all about an "entity-related incident" in Chavez Ravine and announced that, out of an abundance of caution, the LAPD was enforcing a "quarantine in the exclusive gated community."

I thought the release had a snarky, gleeful tone, but maybe I was just being overly sensitive.

As a result, I stayed up past midnight, fielding panicked calls from Cora, Eileen, and even the usually hard-to-rattle Charlie Perez, a real estate broker and investor who sat on the board. Afterward came the calls from reporters asking for comment. I sent those to voice mail.

When the board members' panic subsided, I called Jo, mostly to vent but also to ask when we could expect the supplies and the OA researchers she had promised.

"The city manager's office sent the press release against my advice," she said. "It doesn't really accomplish anything, but it does put a dent in Chavez Ravine's reputation. I don't know. Maybe that was the point."

I suspected that had been precisely the point. "Did the chief ask for the release to go out?"

"Yeah, it was his idea. And, Mads…I have some more bad news. The chief blocked my request for the nerds, and he was furious when he found out Steve and Dria were already trapped there by his stupid quarantine. I'm still working on the supplies, but the chief is fighting me every step of the way."

"You'd think he'd want us to subdue these things before they got out," I pointed out.

"He's not thinking." Jo's voice was edged with exasperation. "He's using his lizard brain—the part that still can't process his ex-wife leaving him and then getting a much better job with you."

The chief's former wife, Augustina, was now staying at my house and, the last I heard, enjoying a British mystery from my bookshelf while sipping the wine I told her to help herself to.

I sighed. "I don't know which monster is worse, the Megazotz or the chief. I just wish I didn't have to fight both at the same time."

We hung up, and I settled down for a fitful night's sleep.

———+·•·▸·⛩·◂·◄·———

At seven o'clock the next morning, not long after sunrise, we headed out. "We" included Ben Tomas behind the wheel of his landscaping truck, me, Stu, Sam, Steve, and my mother, not because I thought she could calm the Megazotz, but because she communicated easily with Beady and the other gnomes.

I wasn't exactly sure what I would say to them, but at least I wanted to warn them the Megazotz were hanging around. Maybe we would get lucky, and they would have some information from their home world that would help us.

There was no sign of the demon bats on our drive to Ben's yard in Palo Verde, but I did get a call from HOA board president Cora Bernal.

"Maddy, I know you're just trying to keep our residents safe, but I'm getting quite an earful about the lockdown. What can I tell people about when the lockdown will end?"

"I'll be honest, Cora…I have no idea. We still don't know exactly why these things are here or how to get rid of them, but we do know they're dangerous. And there may not be any place for people to go anyway. The LAPD has closed off our access roads. Occult Affairs is determined to seal off Chavez Ravine and keep the Megazotz—that's what we're calling these giant Camazotz—from spreading to the rest of the city."

Cora gasped. "They've never done that before!"

"No, but we've never had suspected Entities 2.0 before."

"But why here? Of all places, Maddy, why Chavez Ravine?"

I took a deep breath. There was no use getting snippy with my boss. "I wish I knew why they chose our neighborhoods. Hopefully, someday we'll find out. And, Cora, if you can, please let the rest of the board know what's going on. Eileen is bombarding me with texts, and I really can't take the time to hold her hand."

Eileen Simpson was not only an HOA board member, but also a luxury real estate agent specializing in Chavez Ravine's nicest homes. Anything that threatened to depress property values set her off.

When we pulled up to the equipment yard, Ben clicked a remote, and the gates swung open. He drove through the gravel parking area, between rows of potted flowers and plants, and toward the back of the property. We came to a stop in front of a large shed that served as the gnome's living space. Stu and Steve had agreed to play lookout and followed in the Hummer.

Beady must have heard us coming because he was already waiting outside, short arms folded across his barrel chest, eyebrows drawn together. Despite his worried expression, he was in one piece. I relaxed a little.

My mother got out of the truck. "Uh, oh. He doesn't look happy."

It was another chilly day, and my mother was wearing a black shawl over a red cardigan sweater, managing to look quite elegant so early in the morning. Ben and I were bundled up in coats. Sam jumped out of the car, swirled around Beady's legs, and began chittering away at him. Beady looked down, appearing to listen intently.

My mother turned toward me, eyebrows raised. "Honestly, Madeline, you really need to find out where that cat came from, and if you don't do it, I will."

She made it sound like a threat. I had no idea how she would manage it, but she was welcome to give it a go.

I grabbed my crossbow and nocked an arrow. "We're here to see the gnomes, Mother. If you can have your chat with them as fast as you can, that would be great." I scanned the hillside and the tree line. "We're sitting ducks out here."

My mother gave a martyred sigh and walked toward Beady. "Hello, old friend. Can we talk?"

A moment later, they disappeared inside the shed. Sam slipped through just before the door closed.

Ben's mouth opened. "They've never let *me* inside. How about that?"

"She's not called the 'entity whisperer' for nothing," I said with a sigh. "If he's making her tea, I hope he brings us a cup."

Ben grinned. "Who needs tea? Julia sent us off with a thermos of coffee." He reached inside the truck and emerged holding tin mugs.

Stu and Steve shook their heads, jogged about a hundred yards away, and began scanning the sky for any signs of the Megazotz.

My eyes rolled back in my head when I sipped the coffee. Julia had used Stu's stash of fancy dark roast, then added cream, sugar, and a dash of cinnamon. It was hot and delicious. I scanned the tree-lined ridge again. Since we had lost them on the heatmap, the Megazotz could appear from any direction.

We drained the rest of the thermos while I paced alongside the shed, wishing my mother would hurry. It was cold, and I had plenty to do, like try to sneak out of Chavez Ravine to steal some supplies from OA, maybe through Phantom's Pass. That would mean a lot of time outside, exposing myself to demon bats or perhaps even drawing them out of wherever they had gone. But it was beginning to look like my only viable option.

With any luck, I could find a resident with an ATV stashed in a garage. That could work if I had to go out through the woods.

I was so wrapped up in my thoughts that I was startled when the door banged open. Sam darted out, and a moment later, my mother emerged, followed by Beady and a half dozen gnomes.

"What did they say?" I asked.

My mother glanced down at the gnomes with a long sigh. "Quite a lot. They recognize the Megazotz. Those were the things that chased the gnomes out of their home world and into ours. The gnomes had never seen them before, and many were carried off. Their bodies would be discovered later, minus their little cabezas, if you can imagine such a thing." My mother shuddered.

"They said the Megazotz arrived in their world hungry and started to hunt them because they were small and easy pickings."

I could easily imagine it because Beady had sent some frightening imagery during our previous brief psychic connection. A big shadowy shape in the sky had been chasing him. It must have been the Megazotz.

"Do they know why the Megazotz showed up here?"

"No, but back in their world, a gnomish cunning woman said they were looking for something, or some*one*, and were systematically searching the realms for whatever it was." My mother seemed very pleased with herself for imparting so much information.

Ben raised his eyebrows in a silent expression of admiration.

A small smile played around the corners of my mother's mouth. "They call them 'flying devils,'" she said, with her usual dramatic timing.

There was a lot to unpack. If the so-called cunning woman was right, the Megazotz appearance in Chavez Ravine wasn't a random event. It was part of their systematic search. It also meant they were on the hunt.

"Maddy," Ben said, his voice urgent. He pointed toward the back fence covered in vines.

I heard it before I saw it. An insistent buzzing, like hundreds of bees. A slight vibration in the ground beneath my feet. My entire body thrummed.

"Madre mía de Dios, not again," my mother cried.

Ben crossed himself. Sam's fur puffed out, and he howled. The gnomes clapped their hands over their ears. One crumpled to the ground. Another scrambled under the truck.

Against a wall of ivy, fluttering pinpricks were gathering, forming a now familiar and terrifying shape. We had just seconds to take cover, and there were only two options. The rickety shed, which wouldn't withstand an aerial assault for long, and the truck.

The truck it was.

Ben threw open the passenger door, and I shouted, "Everyone inside." My heart pounded while I slotted an arrow into my crossbow.

Just when the shape solidified, I released the arrow. My right shoulder twinged from the effort. The arrow struck its target, right about where I had guessed the head would be, but it bounced away, as if it had hit a stone wall.

Before I could pull another arrow from the quiver, I was staring down a massive, winged creature. "Get back," I shouted.

With a deafening screech, it launched itself into the air and hovered as effortlessly as a hummingbird, wings flapping, creating a harsh wind that whipped my hair around my face.

I didn't know bats could do that, but then again, these weren't ordinary bats. We locked eyes. Something like recognition flashed in those terrible black orbs, and then it whipped its head toward a movement just off to my right.

A gnome, quaking like a leaf, too petrified to move.

Ben was holding the driver-side door open and gesturing wildly at the stranded gnomes.

My mother and Sam stared at me, wide-eyed, from inside the truck. Footsteps pounded somewhere behind me. I had forgotten about Stu and Steve.

"Stay back!" I yelled.

I readied myself to shoot again and let an arrow loose. Without a glance in my direction, the creature raised a wing, and again, the arrow bounced away. The wing's membrane was gray and semi-transparent, but it might as well have been made of steel.

The terror-stricken gnome snapped to life and bolted across the yard, his short legs pumping while he dashed toward an area covered by a canvas awning. Halfway there, the Megazotz was upon him, claws latching onto his shoulders.

Ben shouted. I whipped my head around and saw a flash of red fur darting away. It was Sam. My cat who couldn't resist winged things, no matter what their size. The Megazotz had lost some altitude and was careening around in the air, the gnome thrashing in its grasp.

"No, Sam!" I screamed.

Sam ignored me.

I watched in horror while he launched himself into the air, grabbed hold of the gnome's legs, and climbed his body like a ladder. When my crazy cat reached his destination, he chomped down on a skeletal hand.

The Megazotz let out a screech of pain and slammed its blunt snout into Sam's skull. Despite the blow, Sam's jaws remained locked until the gnome tumbled free.

A heartbeat later, Sam plummeted after him, landing in a motionless heap on the ground.

Chapter 10

The Megazotz, smarting from Sam's bite and with a whoosh of wind, flapped its enormous wings and disappeared over the trees.

I scooped Sam's limp body from the ground, fighting back tears. He was a big and brave Bengal, but the vicious Megazotz was so much bigger and stronger. I didn't know what I would do without him, and I fought back a sob.

When I approached Ben's truck, my mother climbed out, passed a hand over Sam's body, and shook her head. "He'll be fine, mija," she said gently. "It's just temporary."

My mother was no veterinarian, and Sam was no entity, so I wasn't sure how she could be so sure, but it was just the bit of hope I needed to keep from falling apart. I gently placed Sam on the truck's back seat.

Steve came running up, breathless. "Okay, that was awesome! So much observed data! The wing that deflected the arrow…What I suspect was a paralyzing venom…And I think it flew away because it hadn't fully formed yet. Interesting possible point of vulnerability."

I just stared at him, wondering if he had even noticed what happened to Sam.

Stu stepped in and gently asked, "Do you want me to see if I can find a vet?"

"No, but thank you. Entity injuries are a specialty, and nobody in Chavez Ravine has the training. I wish we could get

Sam to the clinic down in LA, though. An entity specialist might help...if we could get through the blockade." Despite my best efforts, my eyes were tearing up.

Stu nodded and put his hand on my arm. "Maddy, we can't leave the gnomes here. Now that those bats know where they are, the gnomes are vulnerable. We need to bring them to my house."

Stu and Ben rounded up the gnomes from the shed and wrangled them into the back of Ben's truck. I rode to Stu's house in silence, rubbing Sam's head the whole way.

The gnomes appeared happy to be in a safer location, but they refused to come inside. Ben and my mother did their best to make them comfortable in the garage until we could figure something else out.

I carried Sam into Stu's room and put him on the bed.

Julia followed, patting my shoulder. "You can do it. With your magic. You helped Sam before, yeah? When the vampire bird scratched him up?"

From outside the room, Dria asked, "She does magic?"

Steve whispered, "Yeah. She doesn't like talking about it, but everyone knows. It's an open secret."

The two OA researchers hovered in the doorway.

"Do you need any help?" Steve asked.

Dria pressed a hand against her mouth. "Poor thing. But he's coming around. That's a good sign."

She was right. Sam was beginning to move, and his green eyes flickered open. He licked a paw and raised it. Before he could rub it over his head, as I had seen him do thousands of times before, I stopped it.

"No, Sam," I said sternly. "You have a bite up there. I need to tend to it first."

He blinked a few times, the equivalent of rolling his eyes. Clare and Stu hurried in with a first aid kit, rubbing alcohol, and some clean rags.

Stu took Clare by the arm and said, "Let's let Maddy do her thing."

"But I want to watch," Clare protested. "I love Sam."

I turned to Clare and the others. "I think Stu's right. It's better when I work alone."

Julia exhaled loudly, her shoulder slumping. "I guess that means me too, yeah? But shout if you need anything. Clare, why don't you help me figure out what we're going to make for dinner? I told Malena she couldn't cook for all of us every night."

"I can help," Dria said.

A moment later, the door closed, and I was alone with Sam. I lifted him onto a soft, folded blanket, tugged on a pair of blue latex gloves, and began separating the damp, sticky fur on top of his head. And then I saw it.

A small sharp tooth protruded from a ragged hole. The Megazotz had left behind a present.

I rummaged around in the first aid kit, found a pair of tweezers, and freed it from its plastic sheath. "Stay still," I said, and for once, Sam obeyed.

I was nearly one hundred percent sure he understood me when I spoke to him, even though he pretended not to when it suited him.

"Good boy," I muttered.

He batted my hand with a paw. Until then, Sam had only allowed two people to baby him: Julia and my next-door neighbor Leo. Finally, we were making progress.

I plucked out the tooth. Sam hissed, and his ears flattened.

I held up the tooth and squinted at it. It was small and dagger-like, ending in a sharp point. The demon bat had a mouth full of them. Things could have been worse. It might have gone straight through.

I dropped the tooth into a little plastic bag, then poked around Sam's scalp, searching for more damage. Finding none, I squirted some warm water from a plastic bottle to irrigate the wound and patted it with an alcohol-soaked pad. Sam hissed again.

"I know that stings, buddy, but you're doing great. Next time, maybe consider the possible consequences before attacking like that."

Sam eyed me with disdain before glancing over at Little Lencha sitting on the nightstand. I was surprised to find her glowing faintly red.

"There!" I said triumphantly. "She agrees with me. She's warning you to make better choices the next time you see one of those things." I had no idea what Lencha actually intended, but I wasn't above co-opting her for my purposes.

Sam gave me a half-hearted swipe of the paw while I paged through one of my great-aunt's notebooks for inspiration. I wondered what the cunning woman from Beady's home world would have whipped up for such an injury. I liked that term. "Cunning woman" sounded more interesting than "healer." I wouldn't mind if people started referring to me that way.

Sam tucked his paws under his body and closed his eyes.

"You look like a loaf," I whispered.

He ignored me.

I had disinfected the wound, but I wanted to make sure there weren't any lingering effects from the toxin that had temporarily paralyzed Sam. If only I had the broad-spectrum anti-entity antibiotic Dr. Cheng had given me after my harpy bite. I thought about making an appeal to Jo. She was a cat person too, but if the chief was preventing her from sending supplies to help humans, there was little chance she would be able to come through for Sam.

It was time for a little brujería. Luckily, I had brought all the ingredients I needed.

After fetching my box of supplies from the mudroom, I selected several purple leaves known for their magical cleansing properties and left them to soak in a shallow bowl of water. When they had softened, I used a volcanic stone to grind them into a paste before adding crushed garlic for its antibiotic properties and a dash of rubbing alcohol I found in Stu's bathroom. The slurry was still too watery, so I crushed more of the purple leaves and incorporated them.

Much better.

Using a toothpick, I carved my intention into the thick paste, which was simple enough: rid Sam of the creature's supernatural venom. I lit a votive candle, sat cross-legged on the floor, and envisioned Sam expelling the venom from his body. When the candle was totally consumed, I dabbed the mixture onto the wound.

Hopefully, that would be enough to prevent Sam from contracting a nasty infection, but I was still worried he wouldn't be able to resist going after another Megazotz. No matter how special he was, Sam was still a cat, and the erratic movement of flying things triggered his hunting instincts. We needed a protection spell that would counter his prey drive and keep him safe from the monsters.

I dug out a small lodestone from the box, along with a piece of yellow silk, some beans and seeds, and a bay leaf. After I had gone through the steps, I cut a bit of the silk, laid the beans and seeds on the stone, and wrapped the silk around it to hold everything in place. I said a little prayer against evil and ill intent.

As usual, I didn't follow a script. The words were heartfelt but mostly improvised. I secured the silk with a bit of string and tied the little bundle to Sam's collar. To my surprise, he didn't protest, and moments later, he was snoring. I took that as a good sign and left him to sleep.

My thoughts turned to our predicament. We had no supplies, no prospect of supplies, no way to leave Chavez Ravine, and eighteen bloodthirsty Megazotz hiding somewhere inside.

The time for waiting was over. It was time to have a conversation with Steve.

Chapter 11

"No way," Steve said. "They'll fire me if they found out."

"They won't find out," I promised. "We'll be stealthy ninjas."

Dria giggled. Steve shot her a dark look.

In my opinion, he was overreacting. I was just proposing we sneak out of Chavez Ravine and pick up the supplies we needed from Occult Affairs, something Steve called "stealing" but I preferred to think of as "redeploying."

"Even if we got there," he said, "there's no way the guys at the warehouse are going to just hand it over because we show up begging—"

"Hey, women work there too," Dria said.

Steve ignored this and continued. "And you'd be surprised how many toadies there are in Occult Affairs. People angling for a promotion and willing to suck up to the chief. If anyone in the warehouse found out what we're up to, they'll call the chief, and it will be over. For me, at least. And you'd be arrested for trespassing."

Dria looked up from wiping down the kitchen counter. "That's true. The chief hates it when anyone disagrees with him. He calls them traitors, and it doesn't matter how much Occult Affairs needs their services. He pushes them out. Look at poor Augustina."

"That was personal," I said, sensing I was losing the argument.

"Everything is personal to the chief." Dria rinsed the sponge and set it in a small bowl at the edge of the sink.

"But what about the Megazotz's tooth I pulled from Sam's head? It needs to be analyzed. You don't have the right equipment here. We can stop by your lab so you can do your thing."

Steve scoffed. "I'm not the only researcher. Others can do it too."

"But OA has sealed us off. How are we supposed to get the tooth to them?"

Steve rolled his eyes. "Simple. I take it to a gate and hand it over. Or Dria and I just leave. Jo didn't say we couldn't. We're only staying because you might need us."

"I *do* need you. Chavez Ravine needs you. But come on…If you're not going to help me get the supplies and if you can't analyze the tooth, then what are you even doing here?"

That came out more harshly than I had intended, but I was so frustrated I could hear blood whooshing in my ears.

Steve bristled. "Wow. Well, actually, Dria and I have been coming up with ways to use the equipment we *do* have, the sonic probes, to see if we can track the Megazotz using echolocation."

"Because they're bats," Dria said hurriedly. "We're pretty sure it'll work. The probes weren't intended to be used that way, but we think we can modify them easily enough. But first, we need to get to Steve's car."

I had some nervous energy to burn off, so I grabbed a rag from the pantry, squirted it with Fabuloso, and began wiping the kitchen cabinets. "Steve's car is still in the parking lot at La Loma Plaza. We'll need to make another run for it. But even if you do whatever nerdy things you do and the echolocation works and you track down the Megazotz, what then? The Smoke Bombs didn't work, and the only stuff that might possibly sedate them is in a warehouse about two miles away."

I aimed the bottle at a stubborn spot of dried tomato sauce. There was another option, one that was less scientific and more magical. I hesitated because I would be in truly uncharted waters, but my magic was looking more like our last resort.

For what I had in mind, I required something from the Megazotz. Of course, I had its tooth, but I had to preserve that for OA. The Megazotz hadn't left anything else behind. It didn't have feathers or scales. It *did* have patchy bits of fur, but there was no way I was going to grab hold of some and yank it free.

Steve and Dria were silent while they watched me work. I finished with the cabinets and looked around for another chore. The sense of inertia was making me crazy.

I resisted the urge to clean the sink and pulled out my phone. It was time to ratchet up the urgency.

I opened my email inbox and held it out so Steve and Dria could see it. "Know what those are? Those are messages from residents who can't get to work or take their kids to school or get to doctors' appointments or go visit their elderly parents. There are hundreds of them, and more keep coming in. We can't keep asking people to put their lives on hold because the chief is a jerk and won't send help. It's our job to solve this, no matter what stands in our way."

Steve and Dria exchanged uneasy glances.

"I'll call Jo again," Steve finally said. "I think it's time she bumps this upstairs."

Dria's brown eyes widened. "But she's already gone to the city manager!"

"Not the city manager," Steve said. "The mayor."

I stopped mid-spray and turned to look at him. "Are you serious?"

Steve nodded grimly. "As a heart attack."

Predictably, the gnomes didn't like the garage. It was all concrete. They needed to be surrounded with greenery, their feet on the earth. At least, according to my mother.

"If we don't find someplace else for them to stay, I think they'll leave."

"If they do that, they'll be the Megazotz's next meal," I said.

Ben, Julia, my mother, and I were in the living room, having cafecitos. Hernan was taking another nap, and Stu was holed up in his office on a conference call. Chavez Ravine might have been in a lockdown, but Stu's security business was carrying on as normal. Clare was in her bedroom, reorganizing her closet, at my mother's urging probably.

Julia paled. "Do we know why the Megazotz are here?"

"I'm not sure," my mother said in a quiet voice. She looked away.

We sat in silence for a while. My mother had said the Megazotz were searching the realms for someone or something. It wasn't like her to downplay a situation so dramatic. In fact, it was far more likely she would talk it up while highlighting the important role she had played. Which was more suspicious than interesting.

"I have an idea about the gnomes." Ben shot a nervous glance in my direction. "What if we moved them to your other property, Maddy? Would you mind? It's got a tall fence, though I don't think the neighbors would mind since the gnomes are so popular."

"You mean, put them in Lencha's shed?" Ben had refurbished it, but it was a little small for that many gnomes.

He shook his head. "No. Me and a few of my guys can build something. Nothing fancy. Just a simple wooden structure. We could have it up in no time, but we'll need some of your people, just in case those things come back."

I drained the rest of my coffee and set down the mug on an end table, wishing everything wasn't so complicated and uncertain. The Megazotz were off doing whatever they did when they weren't scaring people and gnomes. Occult Affairs wasn't helping but had surrounded Chavez Ravine to keep people in, which didn't make sense. The OA brass was obviously nervous the Megazotz might be Entities 2.0, and they were eager to show the citizens of Los Angeles they were doing something while hardly doing anything at all.

Since my team wasn't actively battling creatures, I could spare a few guards to watch over Ben and his crew. "I can do that," I said slowly, "but anytime we're exposed, we're taking a risk. None of our weapons can take them out, as you saw with the one that showed up in the equipment yard."

Julia shook her head so hard her scrunchie flew off her hair. "No! It's too dangerous. What if they show up? You heard what Malena just said. They decapitate their victims! The gnomes will just have to tough it out here."

Which proved how scared Julia was because she wasn't the type of person to suggest anyone tough anything out.

With a sigh, Ben picked up the scrunchie from the floor and handed it to Julia. "I'm not crazy about it either, mi amor, but we owe it to the gnomes after all the work they've done for us. They can't continue to stay in the garage. It's not right."

A tear slid down Julia's smooth cheek. "I don't see why not."

Ben took her hand and kissed it. "It's not in their nature. But we are obligated to take care of them. It'll be fine. Don't worry."

Julia looked over at me with pleading brown eyes. "You'll go with him, yeah?"

"I think that's a good idea," my mother said, sitting at the edge of her chair. "And the sooner the better."

She sounded positively eager to get rid of me.

Chapter 12

The next morning, several people reported witnessing large unidentified flying objects circling above Phantom's Pass. Either it was the Megazotz or LA had an alien problem. The heatmap hadn't picked them up, but that wasn't a surprise. Airborne entities often didn't appear until they got close to the ground.

Ron and Justin went to investigate. It made me nervous, but someone had to go check it out. Augustina, in the command center, called to say the sighting was just outside the boundaries of Chavez Ravine. She asked how far I wanted the team to go into the wildland.

"Not far," I said. "We don't want OA to think we're overstepping our territory. I don't need to give the chief another excuse to hold up our supplies."

Augustina exhaled. "The chief is such an asshole."

I couldn't have agreed more. Had Augustina called him "chief" when they were married? I could wonder about it all I wanted. That was the kind of question that required splitting a bottle of wine to ask.

"Did the cameras pick them up?" I asked, referring to the creatures.

"No. They're just out of range, unfortunately. Oh, and I finally heard back from tech support about the heatmap. They ran a bunch of tests, and everything checked out fine. They couldn't explain why the new entities come and go like they do."

After we hung up, I went back to prowling around Lencha's backyard, crossbow at the ready, with my slingshot and ammo as backup. Ben and his crew of two nervous workers had nearly finished the low wooden structure that would serve as the gnome's temporary home. The sound of hammering echoed through the yard, and each strike jangled my nerves. With the lockdown in place, Chavez Ravine was unusually quiet, and I hoped the racket wouldn't attract the demon bats.

Ben walked past me after dropping some tools into the bed of his truck. "Almost done."

The gnome house wouldn't win any design awards, but it seemed solid enough.

One of the workers, a wiry man of about sixty with jet-black hair, stepped back and studied it with a frown. "I don't know, Ben. It sorta sticks out, you know, right in the middle of the yard like that. Maybe we should disguise it so those things can't see it so easy when they're flying around."

Ben raised his eyebrows. "What are you thinking, José?"

"Cover the roof with some greenery." He jerked his head at a stack of sod.

I didn't know whether camouflage would help much. If the bats used echolocation, they wouldn't see it anyway. On the other hand, a hard structure might stand out in a field of soft growing things. It was probably worth the extra time it would take to finish the project.

Ben hustled a ladder from his truck, and within half an hour, the three men had rolled out lengths of sod on the roof and lined the walls with bushes and succulents in green plastic tubs. Ben shimmied up a tree and gave a thumbs-up.

"Looks good!"

While Ben drove the men back home to lower Bishop and went to pick up the gnomes, I walked past the expanse of red clay to check out the newly refurbished shed. It was the remodeled version of the original that my great-aunt had used for her brujería work. The enclosure remained bare bones—I hadn't had time to fix it up the way I envisioned—but there was still something about the place. It had been empty for decades, but it felt like something important had once happened in that patch of dirt. And I belonged there.

A bit of fabric hanging above the door caught my eye. A pouch dangling from a nail. One I hadn't put there. I stood on a chair, took it down, and turned it over in my hand. The dull gray material was soft and worn. I guessed it had once been black but had faded over the years. The string that secured it broke as soon as I tried to untie it, and the pouch fell open in my hand.

I peered inside and found a little lump of red clay, along with some seeds and a battered tin medal of La Virgen de Guadalupe.

A protection amulet. I recognized it immediately because I had made a few for Clare and her friends to ward off chupacabras.

Footsteps sounded outside in the yard, so I stuck my head out of the doorway and held out the pouch. "Ben, did you put this up?"

Behind him, small figures with pointy hats filed into their new home.

Ben shook his head. "No. What is it?"

"An amuleto." The word came out in Spanish. Sometimes, that happened.

"What's it for?" Ben asked, coming closer.

"For protection. And to banish something."

Ben lifted his eyebrows. "That's handy. Considering. But if I didn't put it there and you didn't either, who did?"

The only person I could think of was Lencha Bantacorte, but my great-aunt was long dead, and while she had appeared to me once, that had been months before.

Yet there was no other explanation. Few people knew about the yard or the shed, and even fewer knew I had taken ownership of them. So why the shed? If Lencha wanted to keep us safe, why not put the amuleto on Stu's front door?

Knowing Lencha, she was trying to tell me something important. My heart jumped. Maybe she was urging me to use the red clay against the Megazotz. That had to be it.

Or was it? Lencha had been quite a bruja, but her communication skills needed work. When I got back to Stu's place, I would ask Little Lencha.

I put the pouch in my pocket and locked the shed. A group of gnomes emerged from their new home, peering around them with open curiosity.

"Don't go beyond the fence," I warned. "You're safer here." I wasn't super sure about that, but I didn't want them wandering around in the street, where they would be spotted by the neighbors.

Beady, the head gnome, nodded to show he understood. How about that? I had managed to communicate with him without my mother or my cat acting as translator.

The new residents explored their surroundings. I watched them from a distance. The gnomes came to an abrupt stop just in front of the expanse of red clay and let out a collective gasp. They bent their heads together, mumbling amongst themselves in their low, grumbly voices.

Ben joined me and crossed his arms over his chest. "What's up with them?"

Beady backed away from the red earth, his hands outstretched in front of him. He spun around. Our eyes locked, and I was far away.

I knew what was happening because it had happened once before. Beady was sending an image into my mind. A strong, clear one.

A small, stooped woman with long gray hair, wearing a shapeless brown dress. The cunning woman my mother had mentioned bent over a reddish mound of earth, scooping soil into a sack.

My skin went tingly all over. The gnomes recognized the red clay from their home world. The old woman seemed to revere it for its power, the memories it held, and the protection it offered.

That was how I felt about the clay in my new yard.

My phone went off like an angry hornet in my pocket. I stared into space for a moment, disoriented. The gnomes were pointing excitedly at the red clay.

I pulled out my phone. An emergency alert from Augustina, along with an address in Bishop. I recognized it immediately: the parking lot leading to Phantom's Pass.

My heart sank. It wasn't far from where the "flying objects" had been spotted earlier. Worst case, the flying objects had been the Megazotz, and someone had been attacked.

"You need to drive me to Bishop," I said to a startled Ben.

The gnomes must have sensed something was up because they disappeared inside their new home.

While we raced through the empty streets toward Phantom's Pass, my phone buzzed again. I answered the call from Augustina.

"I just got some new details, and it's bad news," she said breathlessly. "It's your mother. She's been hurt. One of those damn things got to her."

My stomach went into freefall. "My mother? She was at Stu's place. Did they get into the house?"

"No. She was with Steve when it happened. That's all I know."

I gripped the phone tighter. My face went numb. "Is she...okay?"

Augustina cleared her throat. "She's alive, but it sounds like it's serious."

Chapter 13

We found them in a clearing several yards from the Phantom's Pass parking lot. My mother stretched out on her back, completely still, an arm flung across her forehead. If it hadn't been for the nasty-looking wound on her hand, I might have thought she was posing for a dramatic photo promoting one of her entity whispering shows.

Steve, kneeling beside her, leapt up when he heard us running toward him. "I'm sorry, Maddy. I'm so sorry. This is all my fault. I should never have said yes. But she's very, very persuasive."

Guilt oozed from every pore on his face, but I didn't have time to deal with it. I crouched next to my mother and felt her pulse. It was there, but barely. Her skin was alarmingly cool, her body limp.

"I don't understand. What were you doing out here? What the hell happened?"

Ben tapped my shoulder. "We need to get your mom to the hospital."

My mother's face was the color of paper. And that wound…It looked like something had tried to chew her hand off.

"Yeah, you're right." I stood up and peered over at Steve, who lowered his gaze. "How did you get here?"

"We borrowed one of the trucks Ben left at Stu's." He scraped his hand over his face. "I don't think OA is going to let us out of here to take her to the hospital."

"They'll have to," I said, my voice rising. "She might not make it otherwise. And if they won't let us out, they can send an ambulance and pick her up. The Bishop gate is closest."

Ben shook his head. "It'll take longer that way in LA traffic. La Loma's closer to the hospital."

"Fine," I said, glancing up at the sky. "But let's get moving. Those things can come back anytime."

When we had finished carrying my mother to Ben's truck, all three of us were sweating. It hadn't yet broken fifty degrees, which was the Los Angeles equivalent of freezing.

I cradled my mother's head in my lap, and my fingers trembled while they brushed her forehead. "You're going to be fine." The words caught in my throat.

Her usually animated face was as still as marble. The sight of her, this woman who had survived everything life had thrown at her, made me feel like the earth had tilted and I was about to slide off into the unknown.

For all our battles and differences, she was the person who had made me everything I was. Without her, who was I really?

The truck rumbled to life, and we lurched forward. Through the high window, I watched trees whip by in a blur of green and brown. "Stay with me, Mom," I whispered. "Stay with me."

The truck came to an abrupt stop. Agitated voices drifted from the front. Ben was arguing with someone. I gently lifted my mother's head and placed it on a folded canvas tarp. Then I pushed open the door and scrambled out.

A guard peered out from the guardhouse, blinking rapidly. Peter was a new hire, a thickset man in his mid-fifties, who preferred the relative quiet of the gates leading in and out of Chavez Ravine to the mayhem of the command center.

"They said no one's allowed to go out." Peter jerked his head at the SUV stationed on the other side of the gate.

"We have a medical emergency. We need to get my mother to the hospital."

"I understand," the guard said in a low voice. "But I think they'll stop you."

I stepped around Peter and marched straight toward the SUV. The windows were tinted dark, but I could make out silhouettes of two figures in the front seat.

I knocked on the window. "Hey there. Matter of life and death. We need to get through."

The window rolled down. Two pairs of eyes stared back at me. I didn't recognize the agents, two young men who couldn't have been more than twenty-five. Probably straight out of the OA academy.

"Sorry, ma'am, but we're under orders," the blond one said politely. "No one is to leave the area."

"I think that's Maddy Madrigal," the other guy whispered. He had red hair and pimples around his mouth.

I shoved my hands in the pockets of my jacket and took a deep breath. *Don't lose your temper. Stay calm.* "Yeah, I'm Maddy Madrigal. Formerly with OA and now head of security here. I know all about your orders, but my mother's had an accident, and she needs medical attention. Immediately."

The two men exchanged uneasy glances. "We'll have to call it in. Check with the command center."

I shrugged. "Suit yourself. I'm going back to check on my mom."

The SUV was parked off to the side. Even if it moved, there would be plenty of space to dodge it. When I passed Peter, who was leaning on the half-door of the gatehouse, I said, "I'm going back to the truck. As soon as I get in, I want you to open the gate."

Peter grinned. "I can do that."

Ben nodded when I explained the plan.

Steve cringed, his shoulders curling forward. "They'll stop us." His voice was faint.

"It's not like they'll shoot at us," I said. There was a good chance they would use their SUV to ram us to a stop, but I didn't see any reason to mention that to Steve.

As soon as I pulled the doors shut behind me, the whir of the wrought iron gates opening sounded, and I held onto my mother when the truck shot forward. Moments later, we lurched to the right as Ben swerved around the SUV.

Seconds later, a siren blared.

"We're clear, but they're following us," Ben called over his shoulder. "They've got the lights going. They obviously want me to pull over. What do you want me to do?"

I obviously wanted my mother to live. The consequences could be dealt with later. "Keep going."

Steve groaned. I fumbled with my phone and texted Augustina, asking her to let the hospital know we were on our way with an entity victim.

Outside the window, I could see nothing but gray sky. My mother remained alarmingly motionless. The truck began to pick up speed while we headed down the hill. It was a long road out of La Loma, down into Los Angeles, and the bumpy ride seemed like it was lasting forever.

I began stroking my mother's forehead again. She was cold. I took off my jacket and tucked it around her neck and chest.

"Hang in there, Mom. We're almost there."

A shadow flickered in the corner of my eye, drawing my gaze to the high, rectangular window. Something was up there, darting through the gray murk. My heart beat faster, and I squinted at the object, straining to get a better view. It was a Megazotz, its leathery wings beating the air with sickening speed. The damn thing was pacing us, matching the truck's pace.

"Guys," I called, my voice sharp with alarm. "We've got company."

Steve gave a strangled cry. "Shit! Oh shit!"

"Keep going?" Ben shouted.

"Yes, keep going!" Steve replied. "We have the advantage of mass and momentum. If we stop, we'll become a stationary target. As long as we're moving, if it hits us, it'll do more damage to itself than it will to us."

Even through the closed windows, the creature's screeching was audible. Tiny hairs lifted on the back of my neck.

"Faster, Ben," Steve shouted.

"I'm going as fast as I can," Ben yelled.

The engine roared while we barreled down the hill. We hit a dip in the road, and the tires seemed to leave the pavement.

"Look!" Ben yelled.

A small black object was racing toward the Megazotz. For one moment, I thought it was a large bird. A raven, perhaps. But it was too fast. Too steady. Moving forward with a purpose that could only be mechanical.

A drone. Occult Affairs had dispatched a drone.

"I thought we were still testing those!" Steve sounded more than surprised, like he was offended he hadn't been consulted.

The drone climbed higher. It was gaining on the Megazotz. The demon bat was so fixated on the truck it seemed oblivious it had company. A puff of something blue shot out from the drone and hit the creature square in the chest.

In the front, Steve let out a whoop. "It worked! It actually worked!"

For a moment, I thought it had too. The Megazotz faltered, its wings spasming. It lost some height, dipping toward a row of impossibly tall cypress trees and nearly crashing into one before leveling out. The drone whizzed past it and banked sharply to avoid the trees.

The Megazotz let out an earsplitting screech. It wheeled around and flew back toward La Loma.

The truck made a sharp left. "What was that stuff the drone used?" Ben asked.

"An extra-strength liquid version of what we use in Smoke Bombs," Steve replied. "It's new. We've been using it with the larger, more problematic entities. We have a new pump-action water gun that has a reservoir of the stuff. I used it on the harpy that went after Maddy, and it completely dropped it. Looks like it's not as effective on the Megazotz, but hey. We'd never tried shooting it from a drone before. So cool."

Steve seemed to remember my ailing mother because he shifted in his seat and craned his neck.

"How you doing back there?" he asked.

"Anxious to get to the hospital."

Steve cleared his throat and turned to stare at the rearview mirror. "The SUV isn't following us anymore."

"No," Ben confirmed.

I wondered if the OA cadets in the SUV had deployed the drone.

"Was that the same Megazotz that attacked my mother?" I had to shout to be heard in the cab.

Steve swiveled around again, and his mouth fell open. He tilted his head and narrowed his eyes. "No, I don't think so. That one was brown. This one was darker, wasn't it?"

Ben made another turn. "I'd say it was almost black."

My mind was too busy spinning the possibilities to form words. Was it a coincidence that the black Megazotz had appeared out of nowhere and began following us? Or had its big brown bat buddy told it where to look?

Chapter 14

When we arrived at the emergency room's entryway, the hospital was in full Double E mode. Dr. Timothy Chen and several nurses were waiting for us out front.

"Was it the big Camazotz we've been hearing about?" Dr. Chen asked while they lifted my mother onto a stretcher.

"Yeah," I said. "Watch out for her hand. It bit her pretty good. We didn't have time to wrap it."

Steve hovered behind me, lips pursed.

The nurses guided the stretcher through the double doors.

"We'll take good care of her," Dr. Chen called over his shoulder before disappearing inside.

After the frenzy of our escape and the Megazotz attack, everything was weirdly calm. Ben went to park the truck. Steven followed me to the waiting room, his eyes downcast.

We found a quiet corner away from other people. A neatly dressed man who appeared to be in his mid-seventies was cradling his arm. He reminded me of Hernan, my mother's fiancé. Which reminded me...

I slumped into a hard plastic chair and turned to Steve. "You didn't call Hernan, did you?"

Steve shook his head. "No. That didn't even occur to me."

I thought for a moment. Calling Hernan would only panic him. He couldn't visit my mother, not with the OA guards at the gate, and I didn't know anything about her condition. I decided to wait until Dr. Chen could tell me how she was doing.

Steve was staring down at his phone. "Jo's sending someone to take our statements. They'll want to talk to all three of us. It's possible they'll arrest us."

I nodded absently. My mind was a whirlwind of thoughts. Sam had recovered from the Megazotz's venomous bite on his own after an hour or so, but he was a cat, and the injury hadn't been that bad. The giant bat had mangled my mother's hand and maybe injected more venom than Sam got. What if my mother didn't make it? How was she even still alive?

Steve sat beside me, his hands clasped tightly in his lap, eyes fixed on the speckled tile floor. Guilt practically radiated off him. Time to get some answers.

"Steve, let's chat, shall we? Let me know if I've got this right…My mom talked you into taking her to see if she could connect with the Megazotz in Phantom's Pass, no?"

Steve pinched the bridge of his nose and sighed. "Yes. And I'll be honest with you because you're bound to find out anyway. Jo thought it was a good idea too. She reminded me we have Malena on retainer, and there was no reason to believe she couldn't use her psychic abilities with the Megazotz. Your mother makes successful entity connections more than ninety-five percent of the time."

My eyes bulged. "Jo knew? She was in on it?" It felt like a betrayal. Jo might have run OA's command center, but she was also my friend.

"She was just doing her job." Steve sucked his cheeks in.

He was right, of course, but my stomach twisted at the thought of Jo approving such a dangerous mission for my mother without even giving me a heads-up.

"What were you doing out near Phantom's Pass?"

"It was your mother's idea. She said she'd been out there with you before, during the whole El Cucuy thing, and she thought that's where they might have gone because they used to live in a cave in Mexico, where they originally came from, and there are caves in Phantom's Pass. So, it made sense to me that's the kind of environment they'd search for. Plus, some of the entity holes were not that far away, just a bit east in the gully. We didn't get very far, though…" His voice drifted off.

"Because…" I leaned closer.

"Because a Megazotz showed up. Scared the hell out of us. We didn't hear it coming. One second we were alone, and the next, it was almost on top of us. Your mother didn't even have a chance to try and establish a connection. It went straight for her."

The mental image was enough to make my stomach flip.

"So how did she fight him off?"

Steve crossed his legs, then uncrossed them. "Well, here's the weird part. It all happened so fast, so I could have imagined it, but that thing had her hand in its mouth, and it was awful. She was screaming, and then she was saying stuff in Spanish, which I couldn't understand, and her other hand came up, and I could swear some red sparks came flying out."

My mouth fell open. "Sparks?"

"Yes. From her fingers. Don't ask me what they were because I don't know. Never seen anything like it." He wrapped his arms around himself, as if warding off a chill. "But whatever she did worked because it released her hand."

I stared at Steve, trying to process what he was saying. Red sparks? From my mother's fingers? That was new. And disturbing. I had seen my mother do a lot of strange things over the years, but sparking was *my* thing, not hers.

Steve rubbed his temples. "The Megazotz backed off, screeching, like it was surprised or in pain. Then it flew off. Your mom collapsed, and I grabbed her just before she hit the ground."

I could picture it all too clearly. "And she didn't say anything? About the sparks?"

"No. The venom kicked in, and she was completely out." He paused. "I hope she's okay. It's a good thing Dr. Chen was on shift. He's the best."

Ben walked in carrying a cardboard tray with three coffees. "I'm not sure how good it's going to be, but at least it's caffeine."

I sipped mine. It was hot and strong. Ben had added plenty of half-and-half and cinnamon, which helped disguise the faint bitterness.

"I hope you don't mind," Ben said, "but I called Julia to let her know what was going on, and then I talked to Stu too. He said he wouldn't say anything to Hernan until he heard from you."

When I glanced down at my phone, I saw several messages of support from Stu, with lots of heart emojis. Which was saying something because Stu wasn't an emoji kind of guy. I didn't have time to read them all, but his thoughtfulness brought a little warmth to my heart.

While we waited in silence, I thought about the sparks flying from my mother's hand. She had always been resentful that my great-aunt Lencha's magic had skipped over her and gone to me. My grandmother Liliana had learned some basic healing skills from Lencha and probably a bit of brujería too, but when the city had started its eviction process, she had taken the city's buyout for her home and moved with her new husband to Salinas, where my mother had been born.

She was hundreds of miles away when the city abruptly changed course and returned the properties to their owners, and for reasons we never completely understood, my grandmother never returned to reclaim her property. Liliana also allowed her skills to lapse and never passed them on to my mother. In midlife, my mother's latent psychic abilities awakened soon after the entities first appeared, but as far as I knew, she didn't have any magical powers. So, I couldn't explain the sparks.

The automatic doors to the waiting room whooshed open, and in walked two uniformed OA officers, a man and a woman, their boots clicking against the tile floor. They scanned the room, and their gazes landed on us huddled in the corner.

A jolt of tension shot through me when they approached, their faces set in stern lines.

"Maddy Madrigal?" the woman asked, her voice crisp. She was in her twenties, with short hair dyed magenta and piercing dark eyes. "I'm Officer Latorre."

I nodded, standing up. "That's me."

Her partner was another unfamiliar face. The tall man with a buzz cut looked at Steve and Ben. "We need to take your statements. All of you." His name tag read "Officer Roanhorse."

Steve sat up straighter and pushed his shoulders back. "Sure. I'm with Occult Affairs. In research."

"We know who you are," Officer Roanhorse said.

Ben shifted uncomfortably in his seat. "I was just the driver."

"The getaway vehicle," Officer Latorre said, correcting Ben without a trace of a smile.

I bristled at the officer's tone, but I reminded myself that they were just doing their jobs. "My mother is in there, fighting for her life. Can we make this quick?"

Officer Latorre's expression softened slightly. "We understand it's a difficult time, but the more information we have, the better we can protect the community."

That was a bit much. I rolled my eyes.

"OA has quarantined us, and they're not sending in the supplies I've requested, so if you really want to protect a community…" I could feel myself starting to lose it. "Oh, never mind. What do you need to know?"

Officer Roanhorse sat in a chair facing us and pulled a narrow notebook from his jacket pocket. "We'll need a timeline of events. When did the attack take place, where was it, and who was there?"

And so it went. When Steve was asked to recount the details of the Megazotz biting my mother, his eyes slid in my direction, but he made no mention of sparks flying from her good hand. A wise choice.

Officer Latorre raised her eyebrows. "Whose decision was it to drive out of Chavez Ravine, ignoring the order of OA officers at the La Loma gate not to proceed while they processed your request?"

"Mine," I said hurriedly. "I told Ben to drive out, and Peter, the guard, opened the gate at my request."

"And why did you ignore their order?" Officer Roanhorse's pen hovered above the notebook.

I met his gaze squarely. "Because whatever venom that thing injected into her was probably killing her, and I wasn't about to wait around for an answer. We needed to get her to the hospital. It was a life-or-death situation."

Officer Roanhorse scribbled something in his notebook, then turned to Steve. "And what about the drone? Whose decision was it to deploy that?"

Steve looked every bit as surprised by the question as I felt. "Beats me. Your OA officers presumably."

"It wasn't you?" It was Officer Roanhorse's turn to appear caught off guard.

Steve snorted. "You think I deployed and guided a drone from a fast-moving vehicle? I wish I had a drone to deploy! No. No way."

"Any idea where it came from then?" Officer Roanhorse tapped his pen against the notebook.

"No," Steve said. "But if you find out, you can thank them for me. For us."

Roanhorse flipped his notebook shut. The two officers exchanged uneasy glances.

"We'll need to follow up on this. I'll ask that you return to Chavez Ravine immediately," Latorre said. "In the meantime, if you think of anything else, don't hesitate to reach out."

He handed us each a card, which I dropped into my pocket. "Sure."

The officers nodded and walked away. When they were out of earshot, I turned to Steve.

"What the hell was that about? If it wasn't those guys at the gate, who was operating that drone?"

Steve gave a mystified shrug. "It had to be someone from OA research…" His voice faded.

His mouth opened and closed like a fish. He slapped the side of his head.

"Wait. *Dria.* Dria's on the drone team. That's what she was working on when I picked her up to go to dinner at Muertos Café. She must have had it in her backpack. She's always taking work stuff home, even though she's not supposed to."

Steve started tapping a message on his phone.

"But how did she know?" I asked.

Steve held up a finger while he waited for a response.

When it came, he smiled. "She knew your mother and I were in Phantom's Pass, so when she got the security alert, she knew we might be in trouble. I guess Augustina was watching the heatmap and guided her."

"I knew that Dria was smart," Ben said, "but operating a drone like that is a whole other level."

Whatever Steve was about to say was interrupted by Dr. Chen walking quickly toward us. He was wearing scrubs, his lips pressed tightly together. I stood up so fast I nearly lost my balance.

"How is she?" I asked, bracing myself for the answer.

Dr. Chen's expression was grave. "She's in critical condition. The venom spread, but we're doing everything we can to counteract it."

I sat back down in a daze, struggling to believe my mother might finally have met her entity match.

Chapter 15

Dr. Chen wouldn't let me see my mother, and I knew better than to argue. "We want to get her stable," he said. "Flush the venom out of her system so we can operate on her hand. We have a plastic surgeon coming in."

"How long do you think it will take her to stabilize?" I asked.

He pinched his lips together and furrowed his brow. "It's hard to say. This venom isn't like anything we've seen before. Your cat got some and recovered, so that's promising, but we suspect this entity did something called venom metering. Snakes do it. Spiders. Scorpions. They can regulate how much venom they inject, so we suspect the creature delivered a smaller dose to your cat and a larger dose to your mother, possibly because it considered her more of a threat."

"You're kidding?"

"I'm not, I'm afraid."

Steve snapped out of his funk and chimed in. "Some snakes can alter the potency of their venom. Do you think it's possible the Megazotz adjusted the biochemical mix of toxins specifically for a human Malena B?"

"That's an interesting question. I suppose it's possible. We're running some labs now, so I'll let you know what we discover. Maddy, from everything I've heard about your mother, she's a fighter. But I won't sugarcoat things. It's going to be touch and go for the next twenty-four hours. Go home. I'll call you if anything changes."

I experienced a strange and uncharacteristic surge of pride. My mother had managed to fend off a giant demon bat. One that might have been capable of adjusting its venom on the fly, and one that was known to decapitate its victims.

A lump formed in my throat. Steve and Ben turned toward me, their faces mirroring my concern.

"What do we do now?" Ben asked.

"Head back to Chavez Ravine. I need to tell Hernan about my mom, and I need to come up with a plan."

Steve raised his eyebrows. "Plan to do what?"

"To deal with those Megazotz. If they can communicate with each other, if they can meter their venom, we need to get ahead of things. I hate playing defense. We need to take the fight to the Megazotz."

"Okay, and just how are we going to do that?" Steve asked while we headed toward the exit.

Steve was right to be wary. A plan was beginning to form from the thoughts bouncing around in my mind, and he wasn't going to like it one bit.

When we got home, Stu enveloped me in a quick, warm hug, kissed my forehead, and then corralled everyone in the living room so I could update Hernan in private.

I had seen Hernan angry before. So furious he had actually tried to stab me after I thwarted one of his crazy plans. But I had never seen him distraught. His skin went a worrisome shade of gray, and he was trembling all over. Hernan had survived a heart attack *and* a stroke, and I was nervous about what the bad news might do to him.

I led Hernan to the bedroom he shared with my mother and settled him into a gray easy chair. The bed was neatly made. One of his signature black sweaters was carefully draped over the desk chair. There was no sign of my mother's stuff, which meant she had already unpacked. She wasn't the type to live out of a suitcase. Her things would be meticulously arranged in the walk-in closet.

Through the bathroom door's narrow opening, I caught sight of my mother's arsenal of anti-aging creams and serums lined up on the marble counter.

Hernan grabbed my hand and gave it a little shake. "How is she? What did the doctor say?"

I told him everything. Didn't hold anything back.

When I finished, he scraped a hand through his thick hair and groaned. "I was asleep when she left; otherwise, I would have stopped her. Or at least tried to. You know how your mother is."

I most certainly did. "It's not your fault, Hernan. Please don't start blaming yourself."

He shook his head, and tears welled in his eyes. "I should have guessed she was up to something."

The door opened, and a solemn-faced Julia came in. She silently placed two steaming mugs of tea on the low table between us. Julia blew me a kiss before leaving.

I picked up the mug, allowing it to warm my cold hands. The tea smelled of mint.

"I love Yerba Buena," Hernan murmured, sipping his tea. "Julia's a wonderful girl. So talented. She's been working on a figurine for Malena. It's of your grandmother Liliana. She'll be so happy to get it." He set down the mug on a gray flannel coaster. "I hope she lives to see it. She'll live, won't she? Tell me she's going to be all right."

I forced a reassuring smile to my face. "She'll be fine. She's Malena Bantacorte, from a long line of strong women. But, Hernan, there's something I need to ask you, and whatever you do, please tell me the truth. I need to know. Was my mother practicing magic?"

Hernan gave a little gasp and looked away. A long silence followed.

"She was trying," he finally said. "She was spending a lot of time in my shed. At first, she didn't want to tell me what she was up to. I think she was embarrassed, but eventually, she told me. She said she could never understand why Lencha had given you a magical boost and not her. She thought it was supremely unfair. I told her that this brujería might work differently. That it was inherited and that maybe it had skipped a generation, but she wasn't buying it. She thought if she worked at it, she might pick up a few skills. But she wasn't making any progress. At least, not that she told me about." He brightened. "But those sparks. Something must have clicked for her. Right?"

"Probably," I said. "It's the only thing that makes sense. Either she had practiced enough that it was starting to work or being in that kind of danger triggered it. We'll have to ask her when she comes around."

Hernan stared at me over the top of his mug. "I want to be at the hospital when that happens."

"I want you to be there too," I said, patting his knee. But I was careful not to make any promises. It was likely Occult Affairs would double down on its no-one-in-no-one-out policy. Which was going to make my plan a little harder.

———+··+·||||·+··+——

Stu drove us in the Hummer to the command center in Palo Verde, where I had called a meeting with my team. My crossbow sat in my lap while I monitored the sky for an incoming Megazotz.

"It's too bad Dria hadn't thought to bring more of that blue stuff in her backpack," Stu said. "That would have come in handy."

I sighed. "Yeah. It's a miracle there was enough in the drone to get the Megazotz to back off."

"That's what she was telling me. Usually, she drains the reservoir before she packs up the drone, but she was running late to meet Steve and forgot."

The streets were eerily quiet. Inside, the houses were filled with unhappy people dashing off angry emails to the HOA, demanding to know when the security team would get its act together and get rid of the things turning their lives upside down and wrecking their property values. The city's quarantine provided some cover: it made OA the bad guy, and I had no problem repeatedly reminding the residents that we thought it best to follow the agency's protocols, to have everyone remain indoors to keep them safe."

Movement somewhere off to my right made me go tense all over. Something large was hanging from a towering eucalyptus tree up ahead.

I touched Stu's arm. "Hey. Slow down. I think I see one."

Most people would have slammed on the brakes, but not Stu. He was too experienced in security for such a rookie move. The Hummer slowed. "Where're you looking?"

I pointed at the tree. It looked like a giant sheet dangling from the branches. "Over there." I nocked an arrow in the crossbow.

Stu craned his neck forward, squinting at the object now swaying slightly in the breeze. After a few tense moments, he chuckled. "It's not our Megazotz, but it fooled me for a second. The eucalyptus shed a lot of bark. It's just a big piece that got caught in the branches."

My body went limp with relief. "First good news I've had all day." I released the arrow and rested the crossbow on my lap. "Is Clare okay, with everything that's going on?" I asked. "I haven't seen much of her."

Stu reached over and rubbed the back of my neck. "You're a good person, Maddy. You've got plenty of worries of your own without fretting over Clare. She's fine. But she's freaking out that we might need to cancel the birthday party she was planning at her friend's beach club."

"Iris?" I asked.

"The one and only. Their birthdays are just a few days apart, and they were planning it together."

One more reason to solve our Megazotz problem. Clare deserved a creature-free eighteenth birthday.

Stu drove over the expanse of grass and parked as close to the entrance of the command center as he could. "So, what's the plan?"

I hesitated, wondering if I should tell him. If I did, he might try to talk me out of it. If I didn't, I might be missing a chance to get help from a fellow security professional. So, I told him.

When I was done, he sighed. "What's that Spanish word that means 'badass'?"

"Chingona?"

Stu smiled, and his blue eyes crinkled at the corners. In his faded black sweatshirt, he looked very sexy. When was the last time we had sex? If I had to wonder, the answer was too long. Long days plus monsters equaled sex drought.

"That's it," he said. "Chingona. That's a very chingona plan, Maddy. You just let me know how I can help."

Chapter 16

Augustina had made lunch for the entire crew. It wasn't fancy, but it was delicious, and I was impressed: roast beef and Swiss cheese sandwiches on bolillos—the Mexican version of soft French rolls—and Sriracha potato salad. For dessert, a fluffy pumpkin cake with cream cheese frosting.

"Where did you get the bolillos?" I asked.

"Palo Verde Market," she said with a shy smile. "I've heard so much about it. I signed up for one of the shopping runs yesterday after work, and Bailey took us. We picked up a few things for your neighbors too."

"That was really nice of you." I smeared some spicy mustard on the bread. "You didn't have to do this, but I'm glad you did."

Augustina made a no-big-deal clucking noise. "You didn't have to let me stay at your house, but you did. This is just my way of saying thank you. I really appreciate it, but I'm more of a baker than a cook. Hence the sandwiches."

Ron Mendez, wearing a camo sweatshirt, scooped up a forkful of potato salad and waved his hand in the air. "You can feed us anytime."

A round of hearty cheers went up. There was nothing like good food to fuel a meeting.

"I've been craving a Phillipe's French Dip, but since we can't get there, this is doing the trick," Steve said. He and Dria sat in the corner, a little away from the others. I had asked them to attend the meeting, and Justin picked them up on his way in.

I turned to Justin, who was starting his second sandwich. "How's the family doing with the lockdown?"

He paused, sandwich inches from his lips, and grimaced. "If the city didn't have us in lockdown, my wife would have gone to stay with her parents. They live near Griffith Park, and we all know what an entity hotspot that is, so that's how I know she's very upset."

"I'm sorry to hear that," I said. And I was. Not just because I hated the idea of Chavez Ravine residents living in fear, but when those people were the families of my staff, it compounded the stress they were already feeling at work.

Malik was there too. Not much seemed to faze the young man with swoopy bangs.

"You hearing anything back at OA?" I asked him.

"Just some noise about the drama in Dria's department. Someone figured out one of the test drones was missing and put two and two together. That person was trying to do her a solid by not ratting her out, but the chief sent in one of his goons, and he figured it out."

Dria lifted her chin. "The same goon who's always trying to touch my drone." Her almond eyes went wide. "Oh. That came out funny, didn't it?"

I set my plate aside and stood up. "All right, everyone. I have something I want to discuss with all of you, but first, let's hear from Augustina. Anything new to report?"

Augustina cleared her throat. She pushed a curly strand of hair behind her ear before speaking. "Yes. The heatmap picked up your Megazotz near the gully between Bishop and Palo Verde. I can't be positive it's the same one that attacked your mother, but it's highly likely. I tracked it all the way to La Loma, past the gatehouse, and then after the drone appeared, all the way back. And then the heatmap lost it. It disappeared. Just like that."

She snapped her fingers.

"I checked in with Jo. OA's heatmap showed the same thing, so at least we know our technology isn't on the fritz." Augustina cleared her throat. "Jo told me to send a crew to the area to look for the Megazotz. I did, of course. I would have done that anyway."

Liam slid a large square of cake onto a paper plate. "Sounds like Jo forgot you don't report to her anymore."

Probably true. Augustina had worked under Jo for a long time before the chief banished her to the far reaches of the San Fernando Valley.

"Maybe," Augustina said lightly. "I sent Bailey, Malik, and Justin." She nodded in their general direction.

Since Malik's and Justin's mouths were full of cake, Bailey said, "Yeah. So we went down into the gully because that's the most likely place where those suckers would hide. Well, Phantom's Pass makes sense too, but that's not where it was last seen. We looked and looked, and there was no sign of it. Anywhere. But we did see something interesting. The emergence holes looked different. Like something disturbed them. Some of the dirt at the edges had fallen in. We took some pictures and sent them to Steve."

Steve held up his phone. His brow was furrowed. "I had them take some measurements. The holes seemed to have expanded. Nothing too significant. Just a few inches."

"And you think that's because…" I made a rolling gesture with my hand.

"No idea." Steve shrugged. "We've had some wind and some early morning precipitation, so it could be natural erosion. Hard to say without going out there to check it out myself. It would be nice to have the proper tools."

"Agreed," I said. "That's why you're going with me to the warehouse to grab some of that nifty blue stuff and more of those spray guns. And while we're out there, if you want to make a pit stop for whatever tools you might need, we can certainly do that."

Steve's head reared back. "Me? I can't do that. I told you. If I'm caught, I'm fired."

"I think you should go," Dria said in a tight voice. "Considering what happened to Malena. You kind of owe Maddy, don't you think?"

I was starting to really like that girl.

Steve flinched. "I can't believe this. No. No, I don't owe Maddy. Malena has a contract with OA to do the thing she did."

"But Maddy is your friend." Dria nudged him in the ribs. "Yeah, sure, there's job stuff, but this was different." She crossed her arms in front of her chest. "You shouldn't have listened to Malena. I think you should help Maddy out."

Steve's face had turned an unflattering shade of red. His hand cupped the back of his neck. "Okay, sure...But it's a moot point because we can't leave Chavez Ravine."

"Sure, we can. We'll go through Phantom's Pass," I said. "We just need the right kind of vehicle. Like one of those all-terrain things. People around here have all kinds of recreational toys. Jet skis. Boats. Someone has to have an ATV."

Bailey snorted. Liam and Justin exchanged amused looks.

"What? Does one of you know where to get one?"

All three pointed at Ron Mendez, who puffed out his chest, eyes twinkling. "Well, well, well. Looks like I'm the man with the plan."

My face seemed to have developed a life of its own. My eyebrows shot up, and my mouth twitched. "You? *You* have an ATV? Since when?"

"Since I finished saving up for one," he said smugly.

It probably hadn't taken him long. Ron lived on his family's compound in Bishop and didn't pay rent. His mother and grandmother doted on him and cooked his meals, so he probably didn't have to pay for groceries either.

"Tell me it's in Chavez Ravine and not some storage place down in the city."

"It's in the garage at home. I've been waiting for some time off to take it out."

"Can I borrow it?"

Ron shook his head, jutting out his bottom lip. "No way. I'll drive." He sounded scandalized.

"But there won't be room," I said. "Steve has to come with me."

"I got a side-by-side Polaris." Ron rubbed his hands together. "It seats six people. And besides, I know Phantom's Pass. I can get us where we need to go and keep us under the radar."

Of course, he could. The guy didn't wear camo for nothing. Ron might not have been a traditional outdoorsman, but he was an enthusiastic one.

I clapped my hands and smiled. "Great! That means four others can ride shotgun. Or crossbow, in this case. If the Megazotz decides to join us, we're going to need as much firepower as we can get."

"I'm in," Liam declared, waving a large hand in the air.

Everyone except for Augustina wanted to go, so in the end, we drew straws. Liam, Bailey, and Malik would come along.

Chapter 17

The Polaris was bigger and fancier than I had expected, with an enclosed cab, hardtop, proper doors, and a cargo box for storage. It even came with AC and heat, which Ron turned on because the outside temperature was still hovering in the mid-forties, unusually chilly for Los Angeles.

I took shotgun next to Ron, with my crossbow in my lap. Steve sat behind me with Bailey at his side. Liam and Malik were in the back. The three guards had their crossbows ready to go, even though we all knew the best they could do was distract the giant bats.

Ron pressed a button on the dashboard.

"What's that for?" I asked.

"It activates the all-wheel drive." Steve gave a satisfied smile.

"How much did this thing cost anyway?" Bailey asked.

"I looked it up," Liam said. "You don't want to know. It'll just piss you off."

Malik laughed. "I think it's awesome. I want one."

"Over my dead body," Bailey said. A short silence followed, and then Bailey exhaled loudly. "Okay. Yeah. It's badass. Don't pay any attention to me. I'm just jealous."

The only one who hadn't said anything since we had started our bumpy journey through the winding trails of Phantom's Pass was our Occult Affairs researcher.

I pretended to check my face and glanced at Steve through the mirror. His shoulders were up around his ears while he scanned the sky. The man who had devoted his career to studying entities from the safety of his lab now found himself in the field with the biggest, baddest entities to have ever emerged. He hadn't signed up for this, and I felt a flicker of sympathy for the guy, but it passed quickly. We needed his brains, and we needed his knowledge of the warehouse.

"How you doing back there, Steve?" I asked.

"Oh, you know. Filled with resentment at getting coerced into something that will probably lead to my unemployment. The usual."

Liam chuckled. "Aw, come on, man. It's not that bad. It'll be fun."

"Yeah, right." Steve sounded as thrilled as a teenager forced to hang out with a parent on Friday night.

Despite the lighthearted mood inside the ATV, I couldn't shake off the unease settling in the pit of my stomach. The vehicle was sturdy, built to take whatever rugged terrain could throw at it, but it wouldn't withstand a direct hit from a Megazotz. Bailey had an open line on her phone with Augustina in the command center, so we would be alerted to any appearances on the heatmap, but we would probably lose the signal once we had gone far enough into the wilderness of Phantom's Pass.

Ron zigged and zagged along the endless stretch of serpentine trails. The surrounding trees closed in around us, blocking out the sky in some places.

Bailey groaned loudly. "God. It's like being in a tunnel. I'm going to have a panic attack."

"It's probably the after-effects of the Cucuy dragging you into a cave," said Liam.

"Deep breaths." Malik put a hand on her shoulder. "Close your eyes and imagine a peaceful place."

Ron made a hard left. "Like a forest. *Haha*."

"Not helping, Ron." Bailey kicked the back of his seat.

Eventually, the trees thinned out, and Ron navigated the Polaris through a dense patch of undergrowth. Every time I was convinced we had veered off the trail, the dirt path would reappear. Ron's confidence never wavered, and I was glad he had insisted on driving.

And then we were out in the open air, which was more unsettling than being under the dark canopy of trees. The back of my neck prickled, and I had the sensation of being watched.

When I glanced over at Ron, he was leaning slightly forward, biting his lip. "We're wide open. I don't like this."

Neither did anyone else, judging from the tension wafting from the backseat.

"Guys, look!" Liam shouted.

A massive shadow soared above the treetops far off to our right. The Megazotz. The soot-colored one with frosted fur.

It moved with a sinister grace, its leathery wingspan allowing the demon bat to keep pace with us effortlessly. Like a hawk tracking a field mouse.

My stomach went tight. I gripped the edge of my seat while the Megazotz continued to shadow us. The creature let out a bone-chilling screech, causing a flock of startled birds to burst out of the bushes.

"How fast can this thing go?" I asked.

"Seventy on a paved road, but I can't go any faster here. We'll flip over."

"We're never going to make it," Steve cried.

The Megazotz swooped lower, heading directly toward us.

Ron's hand came up to smack the ceiling. "Oh yes, we will." The Polaris lurched to the left and shot into a thicket.

Bailey let out a yelp from the backseat. "This is insane!"

The Polaris hit a pothole, and the jolt rattled every bone in my body. The vehicle continued barreling through the dense undergrowth. The branches clawed at the sides and windows, wood scratching against glass and metal. When the Polaris burst out of the brush and back onto the trail, the Megazotz was ahead of us, hovering in the air, blocking the path.

"Shit!" Ron yanked the wheel to the right, and then we were bouncing down an embankment. Somehow, he managed to avoid several boulders. The ground straightened out, and we careened back into a thicket toward a rock- and debris-covered gully. Ron slammed on the brakes.

"I don't think it can get to us through all the trees," Liam said. "It's too big."

Bailey leaned forward and patted Ron's shoulder. "You did good, stuntman."

"Thanks." Ron sighed. "But now what? That thing will be waiting for us the second we're back out in the open."

A long silence followed. Steve was the first to break it. "I have an idea."

I unbuckled my seatbelt and turned to stare at him. "We're all ears." It came off more sarcastic than I had intended, but Steve didn't seem to notice.

"I brought Dria's drone." He grimaced. "Except I didn't tell her…But I thought we'd need it if a Megazotz showed up."

"But we don't have any more of the new elixir," I reminded him. "The drone won't do much without it."

Steve lowered his eyebrows and shook his head. "It doesn't know that. Even if it's not the same Megazotz that went after you guys in La Loma, we're pretty sure they communicate. It'll know what the drone did. It might back off to avoid getting blasted again and give us a chance to get away." He shrugged. "It's worth a try."

"Sounds like a plan to me," Liam said.

It was a plan. Whether or not it was a good plan remained to be seen.

Ron was right. The Megazotz would bide its time and be waiting with all the determination of a red-vested greeter at a big box store.

It was too bad the drone couldn't do more than frighten the Megazotz. Then again, with luck, maybe it could.

I turned to Ron. "Any chance you have some rope with you?"

He cocked his head to the side and narrowed his eyes. "Uh, yeah. I do, actually. It's in the back. What do you want it for?"

I quickly explained. My plan was met with skepticism but no objections. "It's worth a try," Steve said.

We clambered out of the vehicle. Liam, Bailey, and Malik stood watch, crossbows in hand, while Ron rummaged around in a black cargo box and Steve unpacked the drone from its hard case.

Ron held up the length of white rope. It was sturdy enough but too long for what I had in mind. I borrowed Liam's pocketknife and cut off a section about five feet in length.

"If this works, Dria is going to be very, very mad at me," Steve said.

I patted his arm. "If it works, you'll get her another drone from the warehouse." I tried to sound confident. If anything went wrong, someone could end up with a nasty, venomous bite.

The five of us left Ron to maneuver the ATV back up toward the path. We were counting on the noise to provide us cover while we hiked up the slope, through the tangle of trees and brush, and toward a clearing.

Our group stopped behind an enormous boulder and scanned the area for the Megazotz. Eventually, we spotted it hanging upside down, hidden among the long and drooping branches of a eucalyptus tree.

"Sneaky fucker," Liam whispered.

"I wish we had a blowtorch." Bailey readjusted her beanie. "I'd love to roast that thing."

I eyed Steve, who was clutching the drone to his chest as if someone was threatening to take it away. "You sure you know how to work it?"

He gave a dismissive sniff. "Yes. Of course I do."

"What now?" Liam asked, keeping his voice low. "Do you want to send the drone out first, or should we make some noise and get its attention?"

Bailey shook her head. "We only get one shot at this. We need to give the drone enough space to get airborne so the Megazotz doesn't try to swat it down. We need to distract it."

"Good idea," Malik said. "What about running out together and then splitting up? If we head back for the trees, it can't follow all of us."

No, but it could follow one of us, with dire consequences. Since I couldn't come up with a better idea, I agreed.

Steve set the drone on the ground and powered up the controller. "I'll move the drone into the open once you get a running start."

I glanced at my crew of four, standing shoulder to shoulder. Sometimes, I wished I could swaddle them in bubble wrap to keep them safe, but they were trained officers, not children. "Be careful," I said, and then we were off.

Liam, being Liam, did his best to draw attention to himself by shouting obscenities at the Megazotz and waving his arms in the air. The Megazotz pulled its head up, and then it was peeling itself away from the trees and flapping toward him.

The giant bat was almost upon him when Liam threw himself on the ground and rolled into a space beneath a fallen log. Then it was Malik's turn to yell at the Megazotz, which wheeled in the air and hovered there, as if confused. It wasn't looking at Malik, but at something behind him.

And then I heard it. The unmistakable mechanical whirring of the drone's propellers.

When I turned, Steve was standing at the edge of the clearing, feet planted wide apart, the remote control in his hands. The white length of rope dangled from a clip attached to the bottom of the drone. It swung back and forth while the machine picked up speed.

The Megazotz faltered mid-flap. Steve hadn't been wrong. The creature remembered the blue blast from the previous encounter. It veered away, giving Liam enough time to scramble out from under the log and make a run for the trees.

Before I could stop her, Bailey had snatched off her beanie. She waved it over her head, her copper hair the brightest thing in the dreary woodland.

"Over here, you ugly bastard," Bailey yelled. Within seconds, she was directly underneath the drone.

The Megazotz couldn't get to her without encountering the drone.

I held my breath while the drone ascended higher, the rope swinging like a pendulum. "Come on, come on," I muttered.

The Megazotz tracked the movement and let out another screech. One of frustration.

Bailey whipped her head around like she was dancing at a heavy metal concert. The movement proved too much for the Megazotz. It dipped toward her, and the drone shot across the bat's flight path. The trailing rope snagged on a passing claw.

The Megazotz flapped its wings to free itself, but the desperate movement only pulled the rope across its body, and with it, the madly buzzing drone, throwing off its balance. The harder it flapped, the more erratically it flew. The drone's propellers beat against its body and wings. Within seconds, the creature was in a corkscrew downward spiral.

Bailey sprinted away with a victorious whoop.

The Megazotz crashed to the ground. It thrashed on the forest floor, its leathery wings beating against the dirt and debris, kicking up a cloud of dust. The creature screeched while the drone's propellers continued to assault it. I wasn't sure how much more of the racket I could stand, but I didn't have long to wait.

"Watch out," Liam shouted. "There's another one."

We retreated deeper into the thicket. My heart hammered in my chest. A smaller Megazotz, this one rust-brown, swooped down beside its fallen comrade.

With surgical precision, it severed the rope using razor-sharp teeth, then flung the drone away with a contemptuous flick of its clawed hand. It crouched low. The fleshy skin flaps around its nostrils quivered, and those black glittering eyes swept the clearing.

We shrank further into the shadows. Steve was nowhere in sight. Hopefully, he had found a good hiding spot.

The newcomer maintained its vigil until the larger bat recovered. Minutes later, both creatures took to the air and vanished over the tree line.

Chapter 18

Dria's dead and mangled drone plunged Steve into a worried silence for the rest of the uneventful ride through Phantom's Pass. I half expected Occult Affairs officers to be waiting for us in the parking lot, but there was no one. Yellow cones and tape blocked off the park's entrance.

A pathetically weak effort to keep us inside Chavez Ravine, in my humble opinion. I guessed OA hadn't anticipated anyone using an all-terrain vehicle to get through the notoriously rugged woods.

As we expected, an SUV with darkened windows waited just down the street. Stu's idea. He had said we couldn't very well drive the Polaris through LA, so he arranged for someone on his security team to ferry us around. Louis was a taciturn man about my age, with a square head, deep-set eyes, and a buzz cut.

With a curt nod toward the group and a brief flick of interest at the Polaris, he opened the cargo area and pointed to a cooler. "There's some water if anyone's thirsty."

We took him up on the offer. The bottles were one of those fancy brands I refused to buy because they were so expensive. I was surprised and a little annoyed by how good it tasted when the water slid down my dry throat.

My phone buzzed. I pulled it out and checked my messages. It was from Dr. Chen.

Your mom's starting to improve. She's regaining consciousness so we're going to start working on the hand wound now.

Thank you, that's a huge relief!

Before I put my phone back in my pocket, I checked the time. Nearly four o'clock. We had made good time, but it was still too early to start pillaging OA's research lab. Luckily, the nerds worked from 8:00 to 5:30, so we wouldn't have to wait long. Malik had a buddy working in the warehouse whom he called a "Chavez Ravine sympathizer." They had agreed to smuggle out the supplies we had requested. It was reassuring to know someone in Occult Affairs recognized the injustice of our situation.

We would need fuel to keep us going. Once we completed our mission, we still had a long and bumpy return journey through Phantom's Pass. In the dark. At least we would have some proper ammo should the Megazotz show up. That was assuming everything went according to plan and we weren't caught. At a minimum, we would be charged with trespassing. I hated to think of what the maximum penalty might be. The chief was a vindictive jerk.

Once we settled into the SUV, I turned to Louis. "Any chance we can stop someplace to eat? We need to kill some time."

"Oh, thank God," Bailey said from the backseat. "I'm starving."

"Me too," Liam and Malik echoed.

Steve cleared his throat. "I could eat."

Louis shrugged. "Up to you. I'm supposed to drive you wherever you want to go and stay out of your way unless you ask for my help. Where to?"

"Phillipe's," I said.

Louis must have flicked on the seat heaters when I wasn't looking because my butt was feeling nice and toasty.

His eyebrows lowered. "Where?"

"Phillipe's," I repeated. "You know, the home of the French dip…on North Alameda."

"Is that how it's pronounced?" Louis sounded positively taken aback. "I always thought it was Fuh-leeps, not Fe-lee-pays. My grandparents came over from France, and the place was started by a French immigrant, so I've been eating there since I was a kid. My family always called it Fuh-leeps."

I turned in my seat, my surprise mirroring his own. "How have I not heard that before?"

Liam's plate-sized hand appeared and thumped the side of my seat. "Because you're pronouncing it like a Spanish word."

"I call it Fuh-leeps," Malik said.

The discussion continued for the rest of the drive, which was mercifully short. Louis parked in the lot across the street, next to a Chinese restaurant.

"Mind if I come in with you?" he asked.

"Course not," I said. "You can't sit in a car within yards of world-class French dips and not come in. That's practically…illegal."

Louis didn't exactly smile, but his expression softened, and he followed us down the steps into the restaurant.

From the outside, it wasn't much to look at. A corner building painted beige and brown, with striped blue and gray awnings. Inside, it had a vintage charm all its own, with sawdust on the floors and communal high-top tables in the cavernous main room. It also had lots of nooks and alcoves filled with tables and an entire second level.

I turned to Bailey. "Why don't you give me your order and go upstairs and snag us a table?"

It wasn't likely we would run into someone we knew at this hour, but better safe than sorry. Someone connected to OA or the LAPD spotting us free-ranging outside of Chavez Ravine might raise uncomfortable questions.

Everyone placed their orders with the women behind the counter wearing old-school blue uniforms and triangular hats. I always got the same thing: a lamb sandwich with Swiss cheese, macaroni salad, and a kosher pickle. Instead of my usual iced tea, I ordered a hot tea. In addition to sandwiches and sides, everyone else ordered pie. Apple. Banana cream. Key lime.

We carried our trays loaded with food up the stairs and down a hallway lined with rooms. A middle-aged man was talking loudly on his cell phone in one of them, his half-finished meal on the table, a bottle of beer at his elbow.

"She won't go for it," he said hotly. "No way. The terms are unacceptable. Not for that part. And may I remind you, you *need* Becca. Without her, the series doesn't work."

That got my attention. Just past the door, I slowed down. I had an actor friend named Becca Tey, and I wondered if the man was talking about her.

"Fuck you," he continued. "Yeah, she had a bit of a health setback, but it's all cleared up now. She's fine. More than fine. Now listen…Quit being an ageist, sexist asshole and do her legions of fans a favor and give her the part. And quit trying to lowball her."

Yep. That was exactly who they were talking about, all right. The man had to be Becca's agent, fighting the good fight on her behalf. I made a mental note to check in with her when things calmed down. Whenever that was.

Bailey had found a quiet brick-lined room at the end of the hallway. We had it all to ourselves.

Our group dipped the edges of our sandwiches into the little bowls of extra jus and began eating. Mine was delicious, as always, and even better after I smeared the top of the roll with Phillipe's famous spicy mustard. Each bite sent fire up my nostrils. In a good way.

Louis daintily dabbed his mouth with a napkin. "So, Madeline. Stu told me your mom was attacked by one of those bat monsters and she's in the hospital. I'm real sorry to hear that. How she doing?"

I looked over at him, my sandwich frozen in the air. "You know my mom?"

He dipped his head. "Yeah. Had the pleasure of meeting her during her last tour. I was on her security detail. Great lady. We had a lot of fun."

I had heard that sort of thing a lot over the years. My mother was fantastic. A hoot. How lucky I was to be her daughter. The truth was, I saw her differently. Or she wasn't the same around me. But after years of keeping my self-centered mother at arm's length to preserve my sanity and self-esteem, I was finally ready to begin building a new relationship. It was time for me to move beyond my past grievances.

And the truth was, she *did* seem to have mellowed slightly. Maybe because she had finally met a man who adored her and treated her nicely, unlike my dirtbag of a father. Or maybe it was because she was feeling her age.

"She's doing better, thank you," I said. "The doctor thinks she's over the worst of it."

"I'm not surprised," Louis replied solemnly. "She's a tough lady."

Bailey rapped the table with her knuckles. "So, are we all going in with Steve, or just you, Maddy?"

It was a good question. We hadn't had the time to discuss the details, and it was now or never. "Just me, I think. If we're caught, I see no reason to drag you into this."

Bailey nodded and glanced over at Steve. "What about security cameras? Do you need to worry about those?"

Steve shook his head. "Not really, no. I was there when they installed them. No surprise, they cheaped it up. Didn't think we were doing anything so special that required anything beyond the bare minimum. I know where all the blind spots are, so all we have to do is stick to those, and we should be fine."

"How about your card key?" I asked. "Don't you use those?"

"Yes, but it doesn't send anyone an alert. It just records comings and goings, and no one ever checks it unless there's a problem."

I sipped my hot tea and stared at him. "We're making off with a bunch of stuff. Won't that be a problem? Won't that make someone check?"

Steve snorted. "You haven't visited the lab, have you? The place is a mess. I can hardly find anything, and the new guy in charge won't do anything about it because he's too busy sucking up to the chief."

———→·⇀·▥·◂·◃·←———

Steve hadn't been exaggerating. After creeping down a hallway, sticking to the cameras' blind spots, we entered the lab— a large room crammed with tables and lined with small glass-enclosed offices. The sea of clutter was overwhelming. Steve did his best to explain it all: fume hoods, centrifuges, autoclaves, and cold storage.

"That's the pharm room," Steve said, pointing to an adjoining, smaller space.

I poked my head in. Rows of glassware filled with faintly glowing liquids. Flasks. Vials. Several things that resembled old-fashioned stills. It was tidier in there. And spotless.

Steve crossed the lab and threw open another door. "And this is the delivery system room. Dria spends most of her time here. She does her best to keep it all organized, but it's a losing battle."

I scanned the chaos, taking in the Smoke Bomb pouches, dart guns, mist sprayers, aerosol cannons, and drones. Most of the stuff I recognized as part of OA's standard-issue anti-entity arsenal, but some of it was new to me.

Steve headed straight for a wall of steel lockers, opened one, and slid a black case from a middle shelf. "This is another drone. It's new, and the guy who's in charge of them hasn't logged them in yet, so with any luck, no one will notice."

It seemed like an awfully casual attitude to have about such expensive equipment. "I thought those things cost a fortune."

Steve slung the case onto a table and began rummaging around in another locker. "Procurement got a bulk deal from China. We've lost a few while testing and messed up some experimenting with payloads. There's no way around that, unfortunately."

"What else are we taking?" I asked, looking around. "Do you have more of that blue stuff in here?"

"Not here. At least, not enough that'll do us good. We'll get that from the warehouse. But I've got some early models of the sprayer around. We made some minor tweaks before we released the final version, but they work fine." Steve looked around helplessly. "If we can find them. I cannot stand working in such a chaotic environment."

Something of the right shape in a hideous shade of purple sat atop a tall bank of lockers. "Is that them over there?"

Steve glanced over and smacked his forehead. "Yes, thank you. They're supposed to be locked up, not just lying around like that." He marched across the room, pulled the pump-action sprayer off the shelf, and set it on a table.

After an extensive search, we found two more: one under a desk and another in an office belonging to the new lab manager.

It, too, was a mess, with a cheaply framed sign hanging on the wall behind the desk.

I stared at it, my toes curling.

DO NOT DISTURB THE BOSS—HE IS VERY BUSY AND ALSO ARMED.

Poor Steve. Losing the promotion to such a jerk.

"This guy can't last," I said, snatching the pump-action sprayer from a credenza cluttered with plastic dragon figurines, sticky notes, and specimen jars filled with murky liquid.

Steve stood in the doorway, his lips pinched together. "One can only hope. He and Edwina Wong went to the same college, and they've known each other forever," he said gloomily. "I'm hoping she sees the error of her ways."

We shoved everything into two black duffel bags, and within minutes, we had made it out of the building without being noticed. So far, so good.

We doubled back to the SUV and headed toward the warehouse district that ran parallel to Alameda Street and the Los Angeles River, adjacent to Chinatown. Lofts, galleries, and event spaces dotted the area, but Occult Affair's warehouse was located in a section that had remained stubbornly industrial and gritty.

The dimly lit parking lot was empty except for two white Transit vans and several smaller vehicles, all bearing OA's logo.

Louis slowed down when we approached the gate. It was closed.

"Want me to park out here?"

"We can go in," Malik said from the backseat. "I brought the remote." He clicked it, and the gates began to open.

The guy never failed to astonish me. Most people would have forgotten it in their car or another jacket pocket or lost it in Phantom's Pass while we were running around, but not Malik.

"Are you sure your buddy is okay with this?" I asked. The consequences would be severe if they were caught going against the chief's direct orders.

Malik didn't hesitate. "Positive. One hundred percent."

"All right, then." My voice betrayed my anxiety.

"It'll be fine," Bailey said.

Liam gave a nervous laugh. "Let's hope so."

The warehouse was a long one-story building made of faded red brick and punctuated by steel roll-up doors. Louis drove the SUV through the gate and followed Malik's instructions to pull into the last cargo bay.

The moment we stopped, I asked, "Now what?"

"Now I text my buddy," Malik said. "Tell them we're here."

Several tense, agonizing minutes passed.

"This is weird," Bailey said. "What's taking them so long?"

Liam groaned. "I've got a bad feeling about this."

"Me too." Steve's voice was barely above a whisper.

My stomach had tied itself into a pretzel. Even Louis was beginning to show signs of unease, drumming the steering wheel with his fingers while he scanned the parking lot.

The roll-up door shrieked, causing all of us to jump. It opened slowly, revealing a pair of jeans-clad legs, a maroon turtleneck sweater, and finally, a pair of red glasses I would have recognized anywhere.

Jo, head of Occult Affair's command center.

My heart sank. We were caught. And in all kinds of trouble.

Chapter 19

I told everyone to stay inside the SUV and got out to face the music. Jo watched my approach with one foot resting on an overturned crate, her arms crossed over her chest. Her expression didn't tell me much because it was blank. Like her face had forgotten how to move its muscles.

"Desperate situations call for desperate measures," I said, walking toward her. "Just don't blame them. I roped them into it."

She gave an I-couldn't-care-less shrug. "You know what the chief will do if he finds out?"

"I can guess." I looked past her into the shadowy warehouse loaded with supplies. None of which I would be putting in the SUV like I had planned. It was a major setback, and it made me feel like I was wearing a weighted vest.

Jo made a sound between a sniff and a snort. "Well, he's not going to find out. Not if I can help it."

"What do you mean?"

"It means I've been Malik's inside source all along." She came over and took my hand. "Malik asked me to help. Pleaded with me, actually. Even had the nerve to lecture me about my responsibility to the greater good of Los Angeles and to you as a friend."

I stared at her while my confused brain tried to make sense of what she had just said. After a few moments, it finally clicked.

"Wait. *You're* Malik's buddy? I thought he said his friend worked in logistics or something?"

Jo grinned. "Or something. It doesn't really matter, does it? I have access to the warehouse and can order supplies. I can even find a way to hide said orders if it suits me."

"Now you're just bragging," I said, a smile coming to my face. And then, because I couldn't stand it a moment longer, I threw my arms around her. "I can't believe it! I was really freaking out. Thank you, Jo. Thank you. You have no idea how grateful I am. You're the best!"

She hugged me back, then pushed me away. "Let's not be dramatic," she said, adjusting her glasses. "Malik was right about one thing. We can't afford to let those things out of Chavez Ravine and into Los Angeles, and you guys can't do that without our help. And even the mayor knows it. He's not willing to publicly oppose the chief—he made that much clear—but he did let me know, in his own political way, that he'd back me behind closed doors if the chief found out."

"The *mayor* wants you to help us?" I gasped. "You're kidding?"

Jo glanced over her shoulder and beckoned at two men carrying boxes. "He's no dummy. He wants this problem solved too. He told me to give you whatever I thought you needed."

This wasn't just *good* news. It was the *best* news. Tears began to swim in my eyes.

"And this all started with Malik?"

Jo's dark eyes grew wide behind her glasses. "Oh my God…You're not crying, are you? You never cry."

I hastily wiped my eyes with the back of my hand and sniffed. "I guess I've been more upset than I thought. It wasn't like you to refuse to help us, so I thought maybe I'd become a giant pain in your ass or something."

"That's ridiculous!" Jo scoffed. "And no, it didn't start with Malik. I contacted him first, and he agreed to help out."

I wasn't going to let Jo off that easily. "So why all the secrecy? Why didn't you just tell me what you were up to?"

Jo flapped a dismissive hand in my direction. "Lots of reasons. I didn't want the chief's suck-ups to find out and screw things up. I also didn't want to raise your expectations. Things were looking iffy for a while. So enough of the chitchat and let's get moving, shall we?"

I nodded happily. My team piled out of the SUV and began loading the boxes Jo had stacked at the edge of the dock.

Under her breath, Bailey scolded Malik for keeping his secret from her.

Steve put himself in charge of the inventory and made notes on his phone. "I brought along some of the early pump-action sprayers," he said to Jo. "But I think we can do with a few more of the updated models. One for Stu. He's an excellent shot. Plus one for me and Dria. Just in case. Oh, and one for the landscaper. He's been helping out a lot. Driving people around and stuff."

"The landscaper?" Jo's hand came up to her hip. "Why would the landscaper need one of those?"

Steve finished tapping on his phone and glanced up. "He's the guy who was driving the truck when the Megazotz showed up. Plus he's staying with us at Stu's. Those sprayers aren't complicated, and he's a capable guy. I thought it might be a good idea if he had one too."

"They don't grow on trees, you know," Jo snapped. "Whatever. Fine. But that's it. Any more and someone will notice."

I stood next to Jo, watching my team load plastic canisters of the newly formulated extra-strength anti-entity mixture into the back of the SUV, thinking about the long, dark trail through Phantom's Pass that awaited us.

"Any chance we can use the La Loma entrance to get home?" I asked Jo. "It's less than three miles away."

She slung an arm around my shoulder and sighed. "Sorry. I don't trust the officers up there. They're too young. Too ambitious. They see you coming, and they'll blow the whistle. I'm sorry, Maddy. Phantom's Pass doesn't sound like fun."

I patted her hand and held it against my face. Her skin was dry and warm. "I get it. No problem. And when all this is over, I'm going to have you and Holly over for chilaquiles."

Jo jabbed me in the ribs. "I love your chilaquiles, but isn't it almost time for tamales?"

That gave me something to think about on the bumpy ride through Phantom's Pass. The return trip was slightly less tense than the journey out had been, thanks to our loaded pump-action sprayers.

The beginning of tamale season would mark my ninth month living and working in Chavez Ravine. It felt like both forever ago and just yesterday. The passage of time was funny like that, especially because so many things had happened. Entities and monsters. My first pet. My first serious romance. And a thawing relationship with my difficult mother, who, according to Dr. Chen, was being released from the hospital the next day.

Chapter 20

I slept until nearly nine o'clock, and when I finally woke up, I was gripped with dread. For no particular reason. The Megazotz still hadn't reappeared, so it wasn't that. We had all the supplies we needed from Occult Affairs, so it wasn't that either. Halfway through a long, hot shower, my thoughts kept drifting toward my magic—or the lack thereof.

The Megazotz might be Entities 2.0, but they were also supernatural creatures that might need more than a blast of Occult Affairs's elixir to get the message that they weren't welcome.

While I dried off and dressed in jeans and a thin black cotton sweater, my mind raced with possibilities. They all started with the magic-infused red clay I had been ignoring for too long. And then I remembered the Megazotz's tooth I had pulled from Sam's head. It was still sitting in a glass jar in the mudroom. Though I needed to preserve it for research, maybe its essence would come in handy.

I was eager to get started, so I hurried downstairs.

Everyone had already had breakfast and was in the living room, watching a documentary about the history of Chavez Ravine. Everyone except for Stu, who was probably holed up in his office, working.

"Come and watch, Maddy!" Clare called. "It's really good!" She was sitting on the couch, sandwiched between Julia and Hernan, a throw draped over her legs.

Julia blew me a kiss and waved me over. "I can't believe I haven't seen this one before. Grab a cafecito and join us."

"They've got an interesting segment on Chinatown," Steve said.

Dria looked up from her phone. "We should rewind it so Maddy can see it from the start."

The doorbell rang, and I hurried to open it, wondering if it was some sort of emergency or if one of Stu's neighbors wanted to complain about the lockdown. It was neither.

It was my mother, cradling her bandaged hand, with Stu at her side.

"I'm back!" she cried, brushing past me. "I wanted to surprise you, so I called Stu, and he came to meet me at the hospital. Didn't you, Stu?"

Stu blinked slowly. He locked eyes with me, like a hostage signaling an S.O.S. with their eyelids. "Yes, I did." He flashed a brief smile at my mother, took my elbow, and pulled me closer. "You were still asleep, and I didn't want to wake you. I didn't know what to do."

I pecked his cheek and patted his arm. "It's fine," I whispered, even though she had already made it into the living room, where Hernan was making a big fuss. "She was coming home anyway. You were just the delivery guy."

Stu shoved his hands in his pockets and rocked back on his heels. "She's made a remarkable recovery. I'm not sure if *I* would bounce back from something like that so fast."

Stu escaped to his office before my mother could ask him for any more favors, and I went into the living room, where everyone was gathered around my mother, bombarding her with questions. She was eating it up like Norma Desmond in the final scene of *Sunset Boulevard.*

My mother brought her bandaged hand to her chest when she saw me. "We don't have any time, Madeline. I need to get straight to work."

Something tightened in my chest. "To work? Doing what?"

"Brujería," she hissed into my ear. "We need to get rid of those things."

We. My mother had just said "we."

I took a giant step back, trying to distance myself and figure out what she was telling me at the same time. After steering her out of the room, I said over my shoulder, "My mom and I are going to catch up. Why don't you finish that documentary without me, and Stu and I can watch it later?"

We went into the kitchen, where I pulled out a chair for my mother and settled her into it. I poured two mugs of coffee from Stu's fancy machine and added a splash of cream and a half teaspoon of sugar to each.

"So." I put down the mugs. "What's with you sneaking off to Phantom's Pass without telling me?"

My mother slowly sipped her coffee and pursed her lips together, as though it was the best thing she had ever tasted. I hated it when she played coy.

I cleared my throat. "And what's this about brujería?"

My mother regarded me over her mug with dark, penetrating eyes. It was the look she gave people who dared to challenge her. "Well, you know how they say things happen for a reason?"

"Mmhmm?" I said, trying to keep my face neutral.

My mother gave a little shudder. "Well, that horrible bat bit me, and I believe it was for a very good reason. Because when it did, it activated something deep within me. Something…mystical. Something I didn't know I had. Something I thought skipped right over me and passed straight on to you. But that's not what happened at all. It turns out I had it all along."

My throat had gone completely dry. I went to the sink, poured a glass of water, and drank it down. When I was done, I leaned against the counter. My heart was beating uncomfortably fast.

"The sparks. Steve thought he saw sparks fly from your fingers when the Megazotz was attacking you."

My mother folded her hands on the table. "So, he noticed?"

"Hard not to notice something like that. What are you saying exactly? That the Megazotz flipped some sort of bruja switch?"

"Oh, that may have been an important moment," she said self-importantly. "But in this case, *my* case, it's part of a bigger story. In other words, you're not the only bruja in Chavez Ravine."

My mother's words were like a sucker punch to the stomach. They left me reeling.

She, on the other hand, was perfectly calm. "I, for one, am delighted. And relieved. How could I not be? It seemed the height of unfairness that my great-aunt's brujería should skip a generation—skip *me*, of all people. A psychic famous for her ability to communicate with entities!"

My mother put her mug on the table and looked me in the eye.

"There may not be much I can do about you inheriting *two* Bantacorte properties, properties that should rightfully have been mine, but this does help to make up for what I've always considered a terrible injustice." She made the tiny-bit gesture with a thumb and finger.

I pressed my hands to my temples to keep my head from exploding. All this time, I hadn't realized how competitive she had felt. Competitive with her daughter. It did explain a lot.

I had hoped we could have a conversation about fighting the Megazotz—well, after I scolded her for her little field trip to

Phantom's Pass—but it had turned into a gripe session. And though I tried to fight it, I could feel myself taking her bait.

"Real talk, Mom. I've had some sparks come out of my fingers too, but that's a far cry from being the real deal and practicing brujería that actually works. It's been…hard. *Really* hard."

"That's because you refused to accept the gifts your grandmother tried to pass on to you." My mother bit her lip and looked away.

It *was* a touchy subject. After leaving Chavez Ravine, my grandmother Liliana had distanced herself from the healing arts and immersed herself in her farming and the raising of my mother. It was only after I was born that she rekindled her interest in brujería.

I scraped my hands through my hair. "I've told you, Mom. I was just a kid. I didn't understand!"

"If you say so." My mother shrugged.

We were close to reaching an impasse that would result in one of us stomping out of the room. This was too important to let that happen. I needed to find out what she had learned from her contact with the Megazotz and determine whether she had skills we could use to get rid of them.

There was no better way to do that besides using my words. Like an adult. I took a deep breath and counted to ten.

"Okay. So, you think you're a bruja and—"

"No. No," she said, a hand shooting into the air. "I don't *think* it. I *am* a bruja. Now, please, continue."

I cleared my throat. My fingernails bit into my palms. "You said you want us to get rid of the Megazotz. That's what you said, right? Us, as in you and me." After she nodded, I continued. "How do you propose we do that? Exactly? Spell? Amulet? What?"

She gave a little shrug, as if those minor details didn't much matter. "I'm sure we'll figure it out. The important thing is that we work together. Mother and daughter. Brujas unidas."

I almost choked on my lukewarm coffee. We had barely reached the point of cooking together without arguing over how to make Mexican rice, and now she wanted to be bruja besties?

"We need to do this, Madeline," she said firmly. "There's something I haven't told you. I *did* connect with the Megazotz. Briefly, but long enough to learn why they're here in Chavez Ravine…" Her words drifted off. Her chin came up, and the muscles tightened around her dark eyes.

The room tilted. My mother had made a psychic connection with a demon bat. An Entity 2.0. I should have felt pride and admiration that she had succeeded. But instead, it was like I was standing on a runway when an Airbus was about to land.

"And they're here because…?"

"Because it's *us* they've been looking for. You and me. The ancestors of Lencha Bantacorte."

The woman sure knew how to bury the lead.

Chapter 21

I was abruptly aware my mother and I had company. Hernan had entered the kitchen at some point, and he stood in the doorway, eyes wide.

"What's going on?" he asked warily, lowering himself into a chair next to my mother.

She explained while I listened, holding the sides of my own chair like it was about to take off.

"It was flying above us, me and Steve, and I was trying to make a connection. Those things are smart. It sensed my powers and tried to block me, but I pushed back. I've always been able to break through, as you know, Hernie. And I did. Just for a moment. Long enough to learn they were looking for us. Then it must have realized how strong I am, so it attacked me and broke our connection before I could find out more."

When she was finally done, Hernan nodded. "I see. But I have some questions, corazón. Why? Why are they after your bloodline? What do they want?"

My mother shook her head. "I don't know. It all happened so fast."

Hernan reached for her hand and held it in his. "Of course, of course." The retired professor shifted in his chair to look at me. "And you, Maddy? What do you think?"

"I think we need to find out how to get rid of the things, and it will help to know why they want us Bantacorte ladies so badly."

I poured myself another coffee, topped off my mom's mug, and poured one for Hernan too. "Any ideas how we can do that?"

"Santa Muerte," they replied in unison.

My heart sank. I wished there was another way. Santa Muerte was more than a little intimidating. For all the help she had given me when El Cucuy showed up, I always felt I was one step away from pissing her off. I didn't want to press my luck, but I didn't have any better ideas.

"Okay, Santa Muerte it is," I conceded. "So, how are we going about this?"

Before they could reply, Sam sashayed straight toward me with a loud purr, bumped his head against my calf, and stared up at me with large, pleading green eyes.

"Do you want a treat?" I asked him, pushing back from the table.

Instead of the usual meow that meant "yes, I deserve a treat," my huge cat rammed into my leg, then darted through the door. It was strange behavior, even for Sam. I got to my feet and followed him out of the kitchen. He stopped in the hallway leading to the back of the house, tail swishing back and forth against the hardwood floor.

"What's going on, Sam?" My heart started to beat faster. I hoped there wasn't a Megazotz hanging upside down from a tree in the backyard. Surely, Sam would have been howling and throwing himself at the windows if that were the case.

The cat sprinted away. I hurried after him into the mudroom.

At the doorway, I stopped. A yelp of surprise escaped my mouth. A small brown woman sat on the counter, ankles crossed.

"Lencha!" I gasped, stepping toward her.

She raised a hand and pointed at the door behind her. I took her meaning and pulled it shut, then leaned against it for support while I returned her piercing gaze. My great-aunt had appeared to me briefly once before. But this time, everything was different. In a flash that sent an electric jolt through my entire body, I understood why. It was almost laughable.

Who better to consult with than the original Bantacorte bruja, Lencha herself? The woman who had learned brujería in Mexico, who came from a long line of brujas. Why hadn't it occurred to me to ask for her help? Some bruja I was.

Lencha's disdainful expression seemed to say the same thing.

There was nothing warm and fuzzy about the woman. The men I had brought back from the dead to help me defeat the vampire birds had known Lencha. They told funny stories about the quiet, serious bruja who had doled out cures and spells to help the people of Chavez Ravine. They were fond of her and respected her, but no one messed with her.

I dipped my head. "Aunt. You've come."

Sam jumped up on the counter and pressed against her. She patted his head.

"He's a good gato, but I didn't come all this way to talk about your loco cat. I felt, from my resting place, that you needed me."

I watched her stroke Sam's head. Lencha was not completely solid, as if she had only partially materialized, but her voice was clear enough. She spoke with a slight accent, something Hernan would have called the old East Los Angeles way of speaking. Her voice was stern but pleasant, with a slight musical quality to it.

I was so happy to see her I wanted to throw my arms around her and give her a big hug, but she didn't look like the hugging type. And given her flimsy appearance, I wasn't even sure it was possible.

"You're right," I said. "I *do* need you. We have a problem. Not just me. All of Chavez Ravine. We're dealing with some creatures we call Megazotz."

When Lencha stared at me blankly, I rushed to explain.

"Sorry. 'Mega' means *big*. Really big. I'm sorry. I'm doing a bad job of explaining things. You probably know them as Camazotz. Demon bats from Mexico. The Megazotz are giant Camazotz."

The lines in Lencha's face deepened. Her features came into better focus. "I know them. The pinche bastards."

I barked out a laugh. "I think I've called them that too." A good insult took a little power away from them, reducing their threat to a common annoyance.

"They're bad," Lencha said. "Real bad. What are they doing here? I thought I got rid of them once and for all."

Dozens of questions rolled around in my head, fighting to get out. But I couldn't risk overwhelming this woman who had just hauled herself from her world into mine. Plus, it was slightly unnerving to be in her presence. In death as in life, I supposed.

I asked the easiest and most obvious question first. "Can you tell me what you mean when you say you got rid of them?"

Lencha shrugged, and her ghostly shoulders shimmered. "I thought I killed them. Or at least sent them back to el infierno...or wherever those pinche diablos came from. But I might have been wrong. Things didn't end so well for me."

Sam meowed and pressed into Lencha's side, then kept going and toppled over. He righted himself with an expression that said, "Oh, silly me." But it hardly registered because I was too busy trying to process the bombshell my great-aunt had lobbed.

I grabbed a chair and sank into it. "Are you saying you fought them and they...killed you?"

"Ay, yes." Lencha flapped a hand at me, a gesture that seemed solid enough. "Don't make it sound so dramatic. I always knew something like that might happen. Our home was at the base of the mountain, where those fiends lived. I can remember my grandmother using the red clay in our yard to cast a spell. She had lots of jobs on the rancho, but the hardest one was making sure those things never got out because if they did, they'd make life hell for the people who lived nearby. And life was hard enough back then.

"The clay was good for all kinds of things, just like it is today. My grandmother used it, just as generations of brujas before her had, to cast a spell banishing those bats back to their cave, where they belonged. It worked…because the clay trapped them in there for a long, long time. I guess her spell wore off, or maybe the clay washed away…Or the demons got more powerful as time went on. I don't know.

"What I do know is our bloodlines are connected, the Camazotz and the Bantacortes. They hate the way our ancestor banished them, and they've been hungering for revenge ever since. And now it's your job to send those things back to the mountain, where they belong."

Chapter 22

I flopped back in my chair, stunned. My great-aunt had appeared from the dead to confirm something that was nearly impossible to believe.

The Megazotz were in Chavez Ravine, looking for us, the only living Bantacorte brujas.

My head spun. Sam must have sensed how unsettled I was because he jumped onto my lap and began kneading my knees. His warm bulk and rumbling purr slowed my pulse rate, and I relaxed a little. My great-aunt had delivered some difficult news, but she had also come to offer assistance.

I couldn't forget the image of a Megazotz tapping the windshield of Steve's car when I was trapped inside. "I came close to one," I said. "It pointed at me, but I thought I was imagining things. Do you think it sensed who I was?"

Lencha shrugged again. "Maybe. Not all of them are as smart as the leader. They're not like bees. That's what my grandmother used to say. They don't have…What do you call it? A hive mind. A long, long time ago, in the time of our ancestors, there used to be just one. Then there were more. How many are here now?"

"Eighteen," I said automatically.

Lencha's core glowed faintly red. "Ay, eighteen. There were only two when they came to find me in Palo Verde."

Two of those creatures against a small, defenseless woman was enough.

"But your house was in La Loma."

"I was staying with my friend Bertita. She was an old woman by that time, and she needed help. One day, just as it was getting dark, I went out into the backyard. She had a shed back there where I liked to do my work. Those things appeared out of nowhere and came after me. I knew what they were right away, of course. I locked myself inside the shed, and I could hear them out there, flying around in the air, making terrible noises. I was worried Bertita would come out to shoo them away with her broom. She was brave like that. But I made a big mistake."

Lencha paused and closed her eyes, and for a moment, I thought she was nodding off. But her eyes opened again, and she continued.

"My mother had a dried gourd filled with our ancestors' teeth. She said if I ever saw one of those things, I should shake it hard, like a rattle. They didn't like the noise, and they would go away. I don't know how it worked, and my mother didn't either."

Lencha gazed at me expectantly, and I thought for a moment.

"The Camazotz are basically big bats, and they have sensitive hearing, from what I know. Maybe the gourd made a noise that hurt their ears."

"Maybe," Lencha said, looking around the counter, taking in all the stuff I used in my own brujería. "It didn't matter because I didn't have it with me. That was my big mistake. If I had my red clay and my most powerful stones, I might have been able to make something strong enough to send them away. I'd done it before, but my supplies were a long way away."

"How did they…" I stammered but couldn't bring myself to finish. It was probably horribly rude to ask a spirit how their life had ended.

Lencha mimed cutting her throat. "They broke down the shed and got me. They wanted the last of the Bantacorte brujas dead. I should have known they'd come for me. My mother had died just months before."

I gently moved Sam to the floor and began pacing the length of the mudroom. So many questions were forming at the edges of the swirling mass of thoughts in my head, and I wasn't sure how long I had with Lencha. "I'm sorry, Aunt. I'm sorry life ended for you that way."

"It's all right, mija," Lencha said, her voice softening. "It was…quick."

I stopped pacing and turned to face her, my eyes stinging, my chest tight. The thought of her dying alone, in such a violent way, squeezed my heart until it ached. Sam brushed against my ankles, and his purrs filled the room.

Lencha watched me. "It's all right, mija," she said gently. "It was a long time ago."

I took a deep breath, trying to compose myself. There was no time for tears, not now. Not when there were still so many questions that needed answers.

I had to focus on the present, on the fact that she was there, offering help. But there was a bit of important history I needed to clear up. "You said the Camazotz wanted to kill the last of the Bantacortes, but what about my grandmother? Why didn't they go after her?"

Lencha's brown face faded to a pale, silvery gray. "Ay, Liliana. Such a beautiful girl. So kind. Did you know she came to live with me when La Llorona haunted Chavez Ravine? I taught her what I could, but she was more interested in learning the healing ways than she was in brujería. Then when the city tried to evict us, she took the buyout. By that time, she had met a nice man working for the railroad, and he wanted to go back to his home in Salinas, so she went with him. Liliana never became a true bruja. I don't think she had the gift, so she posed no threat to those monsters."

It made sense, the way Lencha explained it, but not totally. "But the Camazotz are here now, looking for me and my mother. As far as they know, we don't pose a threat either."

Lencha's form flickered, and her expression turned thoughtful. "Ay, yes. I always thought brujería in our family was something you learned. Knowledge passed down from mother to daughter. So, I thought I was the last of the brujas. But I was wrong. My mother and grandmother never said anything about our magic being passed down through blood, and it never occurred to them either." She paused. "And then you came along. There was nobody to teach you, but you had the power anyway. It was in your blood."

I swallowed a few times to get rid of the lump in my throat. "In my blood. So, this means my mother inherited brujería too?"

Lencha took a long time to answer. "I guess she's part of it," she said ruefully. "You'll need to watch her, though, mija. She has ganas. Plenty of ganas. But she's not like you."

It took a moment to remember the meaning of the word. I hadn't heard it in a long time. Ganas. Desire. My mother had faults, but lack of motivation wasn't one of them. Once she decided to do something, she was an unstoppable force hurtling toward her goal.

I wanted Lencha's advice on how to deal with my difficult mother, who had more confidence than competence as a bruja, a potentially dangerous combo, but my great-aunt hadn't come all this way to help me with my mommy problems.

"You mentioned your red clay. I'm not sure if you know this, but I have your property now. The house is gone, but your shed is still there, and so is the clay. I know it's powerful magic. I can feel it. But I'm not sure how I can use it against the Megazotz."

Lencha's form stabilized into a more solid and reassuring appearance. "The red clay, mija, is very powerful. I brought some of it in a jar from our rancho in Mexico. My grandmother said it held the spirits of our ancestors, and I believed it. Our family had lived on that land, lost it, took it back, bled on it, and died on it. They're in that clay. When I had enough money, I bought my little house in La Loma, and one day, I poured the clay out in the backyard. Suddenly, it started raining and storming something fierce, and I thought that's it…It's gone forever. In the morning when I went outside, I couldn't believe my eyes. The back half of the yard was filled with red clay. It wanted to be free. Back in the earth and not stuck in a jar."

I leaned against the counter, as close to her as I dared. "So, how can I use it? What do I need to do?"

Lencha's gaze drifted to the counter. Her eyes scanned the herbs, stones, and trinkets scattered about. She shrugged. "I don't know. Brujería is personal. You have your own connection to the clay. There's no recipe for this. It's something you'll have to do on your own."

Her words struck like tiny pebbles hitting my face. I flinched. It was not the answer I wanted to hear. There were no shortcuts, no instructions to make the Megazotz disappear. Just me, my intuition, and whatever bond I might have with the red clay. Somehow, I had to save everyone in Chavez Ravine from the demon bats while keeping my Bantacorte head connected to my neck.

The door banged open, rattling the herb jars on the counter. My mother filled the doorway. Her heavily mascaraed eyes widened, and her mouth fell open in a perfect O of shock.

Lencha's form shimmered and began to fade. Her edges blurred. She vanished with a sigh that sounded a lot like, "Ay, ay, ay."

Chapter 23

There was no consoling her. My mother locked herself in the bedroom, and sobs were coming from inside. Hernan was completely and utterly mystified.

"One minute she's making a very successful connection with Santa Muerte, and she's running down to tell you about it, and the next moment, she's in tears. I don't understand. What in tarnation happened?"

The retired professor of mystical studies wore his winter outfit of gray flannel pants and a black sweater vest over a crisp white shirt. Not the type of man to lounge around in a robe all day.

Julia and Clare pressed in around us, full of concern. "Is your mom all right?" Julia asked. "Is it her hand? Is she in pain? Should we call the doctor?"

"She's just a little upset." I patted Julia's arm. "She'll be fine."

"I'll make her some tea." Clare disappeared into the kitchen.

Julia shook her head. "This calls for champurrado," she said, following Clare through the swinging doors.

Ben Tomas had driven Steve and Dria to the command center in Palo Verde to sort out all the supplies Jo had...deployed...for us.

When I was sure we were alone in the hallway, I said, "My great-aunt Lencha appeared in the mudroom. We were having a conversation about the Megazotz when my mother came in, saw her, and got upset. She's a little sensitive about things. Family things. You know."

Hernan lowered his bushy eyebrows. The things looked like baby squirrels. They badly needed a trim. My mother was stumbling on her duties as a fiancé.

"Ah. Lencha appeared to you and not her. Is that it?"

"Yeah. That's it. And for the record, I didn't summon Lencha. At least, not intentionally. She just…showed up."

Hernan nodded slowly. If his eyebrows got any lower, they would have slid down his nose. "It's too bad the woman couldn't wait around to meet your mother. She would have loved that. She's never understood why her aunt ignores her and gives you all the attention." He took my hand and gave it a squeeze. His skin was dry, warm, and surprisingly reassuring. "It's not your fault, hija. She'll get over it. Eventually."

I was too stunned to move. Hernan had just called me "hija," daughter. That was a first. After he and my mother married, I would officially be his stepdaughter, but "hija" felt like an unexpected promotion. And the biggest surprise was that I didn't mind. It actually felt nice, although I wasn't about to start calling him "Daddy."

My mother refused to open the bedroom door to me but finally unlocked it after Hernan resorted to pleading. Her face was red and puffy, and my hard little heart softened around the edges a bit at the sight of her. She appeared genuinely upset, not like she was performing to get her way. But still, I was wary.

The scent of vanilla was overpowering, and the moment I crossed the threshold into my mother's inner sanctum, I saw why. Flickering votive candles surrounded the Santa Muerte statue. Saint Death regarded me with cool detachment from her place on the dresser. My mother's well-worn tarot cards were spread out on the bed.

"Any luck?" I asked.

My mother collapsed into an upholstered chair, and Hernan hurried to cover her lap with a throw. She was recovering from a serious Megazotz bite, and it was nice to watch Hernan attending to her.

"Yes. Absolutely, one hundred percent, yes. Santa Muerte has shown me the way, but before I tell you about it, I'd like to know why you denied me the opportunity to meet my aunt!"

Shown me the way. Not *us*. *Me*. That didn't bode well. "I did not *deny* you anything. She just…showed up."

My mother sniffed. "You summoned her. You must have."

"I did not," I said firmly. "It was a total surprise. It's not like I went into my room, closed the door, and had a private séance."

My mother acted as though she hadn't heard a word. "What did she want? What did she say?"

There was no harm in telling her. My mother was a Bantacorte, maybe even a Bantacorte bruja, so she deserved to know. I repeated everything about our ancestors' role in containing the Camazotz.

Hernan listened, wide-eyed. "Your bruja lineage must date all the way back to the time of the Maya!"

My mother gave him a tight knowing smile, then turned her attention back to me. "Did Lencha say anything specifically about me?"

I crossed the room and blew out the votives, buying myself some time to think about how best to answer. My mother would be furious if she knew her aunt had advised me to keep an eye on her.

"Not really, no," I finally said.

Hernan cleared his throat, obviously trying to head off a tantrum. "Well, between Lencha appearing and Santa Muerte gracing us with her presence and guidance, I'd say the Bantacorte brujas have had a very, very good day!" His eyes slid from my mother to me, pleading with me to play along.

Which reminded me. "So, what did Santa Muerte have to say?"

My mother wrinkled her forehead. "A lot, actually. I was quite surprised by the clarity of my vision." She snatched a card from the bed and held it in the air. The five of swords.

I stared at it, my heart sinking. "Interesting."

"Isn't it, though?" my mother said coolly.

"You do remember that's the same card I pulled when I asked for Santa Muerte's help with El Cucuy, right?"

My mother shrugged. "I can't help that. It's the card Santa Muerte helped me choose."

"It's not surprising," Hernan said hurriedly. "You're engaged in a conflict with an ancient demon, and the only way to win is through battle. Hence the swords."

Maybe, but the whole thing felt a little suspicious. Stu would probably have called it derivative.

"So, what's *your* take on that?" I asked my mother, unable to keep the suspicion out of my voice. "Are you saying we need to fight those things with swords? Because that's going to be a little complicated, what with the Megazotz being flyers and all. They aren't going to just stand around and wait for us to stab them."

My mother flicked the card back onto the bed. "Can you please try not to be so negative, Madeline? They won't just be regular swords. They will be coated in a little extra something." She actually winked.

My legs were getting tired, standing around doing nothing, so I sank onto the bed. "A little extra something," I echoed. "That also sounds awfully familiar, Mom. I came up with a magical boost for the swords we used against the Cucuy. Are you saying I need to come up with the same sort of thing? And then what?

Stand on a roof and hope one comes flying into the blade? I honestly do not think that's going to work."

I was just making things worse. Yes, I should have let her finish and kept my skepticism to myself. I should have been supportive, even if I didn't feel it. But it was Malena B, and I just couldn't help myself.

"We have something better than your magical boost," my mother said airily. "It's ready to go."

After that little tidbit registered, I gasped. "Wait. You're not talking about OA's new extra-strength anti-entity blue stuff, are you?"

"Yes, and why not? It's actually quite clever, I think. A mix of the old ways and the new ways. And I'm not the only one who believes it will work." She inhaled so deeply her nostrils flared. "Your friend Steve thinks it's a fantastic idea."

Steve did not use words like "fantastic," but whatever. He had nothing to lose by humoring her. But I did.

"Steve does not—and I repeat, *not*—direct my staff," I said hotly. "He works for OA, not Chavez Ravine. He has no authority here. I'm in charge. Me." My face felt like it was on fire.

"Oh, calm down, Madeline," my mother snapped. "He knows that perfectly well, and so do I. We all know you're the queen bee around here, and we have no intention of using any of your people without your permission."

"Then how—"

Before I could finish my sentence, the doorbell rang, and my mother pushed herself to her feet with her one good hand. She cocked her head and smiled.

"How about that? Malik got here so quickly."

Chapter 24

In each of the British mysteries I loved to read, some long-suffering character was sure to get a harsh scolding, something described as a "bollocking." I wasn't exactly sure what that meant, but it sounded pretty unpleasant.

Steve didn't deserve anything as severe as that, but I did need to clear the air.

"I just can't understand why, after everything, you still thought it was a good idea to keep my mother's ridiculous plans a secret. From me!"

Steve turned a light shade of red. "I'm so sorry, Maddy," he stammered. "I thought you'd be okay with it. I mean, you seemed fine with her talking to that scary statue. And I didn't want to bother you while you were doing your magic or whatever. She seemed so confident. She said she had it all worked out."

Of course, she had. Steve didn't know my mother like I did, and she did specialize in bowling people over with her charm. Or, if that didn't work, pestering them until she got her way.

I took a deep breath. "Next time—if there *is* a next time—please come to me first. We can't just go rogue, especially not with something this dangerous."

Dria, who had been silently watching the exchange, finally spoke up. "Steve didn't mean any harm. He was just trying to help. This stuff with your mom is kind of confusing to us outsiders, and her plan doesn't sound bad. If you think about it, it's sort of like alchemy, a mixture of science and something a little…magical? It could work. It would be really nice if it did. Don't you think we have a responsibility to try?"

I sighed. It only sounded like a good plan if you didn't understand brujería. My mother had always accused me of taking shortcuts, but she was trying to take an extremely dangerous one herself. Combining two random things that had worked in the past under completely different, less dangerous circumstances and hoping they would frighten the Megazotz…I couldn't believe how dumb her plan was.

Also, I had to be honest. I didn't like my mother inserting herself into my neatly ordered world with a process and a chain of command. And me in charge.

"Okay. But going forward, let's all work together. She takes the slightest encouragement as permission."

Dria walked over to Steve and placed a hand on his shoulder. "Sometimes, it's better to ask forgiveness than permission, right? What if you had said no just to spite your mom and we wouldn't be able to try it? At least rule it out as an option?"

Ouch. I hadn't realized I was flying my mommy issues flag quite so high.

"Fair points," I conceded, taking another deep breath. This wasn't going to go away. "All right. I hear you both. Let's give it a try."

What else was I going to say? Malik was downstairs, getting a lesson in basic sword fighting techniques from Hernan, while my mother, Julia, and Clare sat watching and sipping champurrado.

I turned to leave, but when I reached the door, there was a thundering boom that shook the house. A chorus of screams erupted from below.

I rushed down the hall, with Dria and Steve on my heels. We raced down the stairs to the sound of shattering glass and splintering wood. I rounded the corner into the living room and skidded to a halt.

A massive black form was stuck halfway through the front window, its body writhing and leathery wings beating against the remaining shards of glass. A Megazotz, its eyes gleaming with malice, snapped its jaws mere feet from where Hernan stood frozen, a sword clutched in his hands.

Sam was beside Hernan, hissing, his fur puffed out. I knew what that meant.

"Don't you dare, Sam!"

My mother was huddled between a horrified Clare and Julia. Stu stood between them and the enormous demon bat.

"Steve, get a squirt gun loaded up with elixir!" We probably didn't have time for him to get it ready, but we had to give it a shot.

Malik was already moving, lunging forward to grab the sword from Hernan. Nothing seemed to faze that kid.

In all the chaos, my hands grew hot. When I glanced down at them, they were glowing red. Not slightly red; they were the color of a Santa hat. Everyone was busy watching the Megazotz try to wriggle into the living room, so nobody noticed what was happening to my hands.

Red hands meant my unpredictable magic had decided to wake up, and I wasn't about to miss the opportunity to use it.

I didn't dare risk getting too close to Malik just as he was about to take a swing, so I yelled, "Malik, stop!"

He whirled around in surprise, just missing Hernan, who yelped and then shouted something in Spanish.

Malik's floppy dark hair covered his eyes, and I understood the advantages of a boring, regular haircut. He was momentarily blinded, and one hand left the sword long enough to brush the strands out of his face. His expression said, "Why are you interrupting me?" even if his mouth didn't.

I held up my hands and wriggled my fingers in the air. The Megazotz let loose with a series of sharp clicks.

Malik's eyes widened. "Oh, shit."

"The sword. Now!" I grabbed the blade from Malik's hand.

"Be careful, Maddy!" Julia cried.

At that moment, Hernan said the same thing but in Spanish. "Cuidate, Maddy!"

This was *not* going to be a careful maneuver. I had to get within striking range of the Megazotz and its snapping jaws, even if it meant risking a venomous bite. The sword wasn't long enough to give me the distance I would have liked.

From the heated discussion going on behind me, Steve and Dria were dealing with an unexpected problem and couldn't get the elixir into the gun.

Clare shouted, "We have a funnel in the kitchen!"

Sam headbutted my calf, a reminder to keep moving.

I moved forward, gripping the sword tightly. My glowing red hands cast an eerie light on the creature's grotesque, writhing form. My hands trembled more than I would have liked when I brought the blade down on the Megazotz's neck.

The sword sliced through the leathery skin, but the bone beneath was like steel. The blade bounced upward, jarring my arms, and the monster let out a deafening screech. Black blood spurted from the wound, splattering across the floor and walls.

With an undignified yelp, I jumped back to avoid the splash.

The giant bat thrashed wildly, its wings beating against the broken window frame, sending shards of glass flying in all directions.

And then someone was standing next to me. Malik, holding the spray gun like he knew how to use it.

A blast of blue liquid hit the Megazotz square in the face. Its nose leaves fluttered madly, and it slammed its body against the window, finally dislodging itself from the opening and retreating outside.

It flew away unsteadily, its erratic flight leaving a trail of black blood in its wake.

Chapter 25

Ben Tomas rushed, dripping wet, into the living room, with a bath towel wrapped around his waist. He looked around open-mouthed, taking in the damage.

"What the hell?" he muttered before running back upstairs.

Minutes later, he and Stu began boarding up the window while Steve and Dria scraped the Megazotz's blood into glass containers. A very useful nerd activity.

Hernan was stretched out on the couch, eyes closed, hands folded across his chest, trying to recover from what my mother called a bad case of susto.

She had said it like it was a real thing, but I wasn't so sure. Susto was more than just a fright. It was a reaction to something so traumatic it caused the soul to leave the body. As if we didn't have enough to worry about. Fortunately, Hernan's soul appeared to be intact.

"Mom, he's a brujo and a professor of mystical studies," I reminded her while she continued to fuss over him, trying to get him to drink a bit of warm water with sugar. "And he's conjured up a few monsters of his own. I seriously doubt the Megazotz would scare him that badly."

Clare was next to my mother, kneeling in front of Hernan. "He's breathing funny."

I peered down at him, and my neck muscles tensed. Clare was right. Hernan's breaths were coming fast and shallow.

My mother glanced up at me. Her dark eyes glittered with worry. "Of course," she murmured. "It must be his heart." She waved a hand at me. "Can you look in our room? There's a bottle of pills on the nightstand."

"I'll do it," Julia said. "He takes a lot of medication, yeah? What am I looking for?"

"The one called Lasix," my mother replied, adjusting the pillow under Hernan's head.

I patted my mother's shoulder. "If he's not better in a bit, we'll take him to an emergency room."

My mother clutched his hands in hers, as if I had just threatened to separate them. "We can't go out there. Not after what just happened. There could be more of those things out there, just waiting for us!"

Malik joined us and brushed his wayward hair from his face. "I just checked in with Augustina. The heatmap recorded the Megazotz, and she's got people headed our way, but it's the only incident. The only one. Don't you think that's weird?"

His tone said he thought it was *totally* weird, but he didn't want to say it. Honest opinions weren't always welcomed in Occult Affairs, especially by insecure weenie bosses.

I sighed. "It's definitely weird."

The Megazotz didn't attack random people. They seemed focused on us. The way the Megazotz came and went from the heatmap was a total mystery. And I couldn't figure out why they hadn't appeared as a group, all at the same time. It would have been impossible for us to fight them all.

Just the idea sent a chill tingling up my spine.

The pounding of hammers was loud and sharp and made me flinch. Hernan didn't even stir. Julia came rushing back with his bottle of pills, and after some brief drama over the childproof lid,

Julia and my mother elevated Hernan's head and got him to swallow one of them.

Malik pulled me aside, studying me from under his swoopy bangs. "Right? This is the first time an entity has tried to break into a building. So why *this* building? Why not one of the restaurants or another home?"

My mother obviously overheard him because she hurried toward us. "It must have sensed our power." She sounded positively triumphant.

Before she could say any more in front of Malik, I hustled her into her bedroom, where we could chat in private.

"Lencha said our bloodlines are connected, so they can probably sense us," she said excitedly the moment the door closed. "When she appeared, there were three Bantacortes in this house, so our power must have been…amplified." She gave my arm a little shake.

I took a deep breath. "Mom. Listen. You can't go around telling people about what Lencha said, about the Bantacorte brujas and the Camazotz."

"Why in heaven's name not?" she asked, pressing a hand against her chest.

With the suddenness of a sneaker wave, I understood we were coming from two very different places. I wanted to make sure everyone in Chavez Ravine was safe, and I didn't want them to think I had somehow drawn the demon bats to the neighborhood.

But my mother needed a career boost, and she saw a way to use the Megazotz to prove she was not only psychic, but also had magical powers and could summon Entities 2.0 creatures. The crowds would go wild.

As usual, we were in direct opposition.

I booped her nose. "I'll tell you why not. Because, Mom, if the HOA board finds out I'm the reason those things are here, they'll fire me and kick me out of my house. And if the board finds out *you* are also the reason they are here, they'll kick you out too. And then where will we be?"

"Stu and Hernan would never allow that to happen!" she hissed, booping my nose back, but her boop was much harder than mine had been.

However, she didn't sound so sure of herself anymore.

"They wouldn't have much of a say, would they? Not with something so big. Has Hernan ever told you about Eileen Simpson? She's never been happy that we live here, and she'll go door to door if that's what it takes. And the moment people start thinking getting rid of us would solve the Megazotz problem, we'll be out on our nalgas."

My mother gasped, and not because I had mentioned our favorite Spanish word for *butt*.

"But your team needs to know, don't they?" she asked, wide-eyed.

I grimaced. "I hate keeping things from them, but no, they don't need to know. Malik, Steve, and Dria don't work for me, and I can't expect them to keep my secrets. If I tell my team, someone in OA is bound to find out. Malik is going out with Bailey, and you know how it is. She'll tell him, and there's no telling who he'll share it with. Magic is pretty juicy stuff, you know?"

I had learned the hard way that keeping secrets from my team—even for the best of reasons—didn't always go well, but I couldn't think of another way around it. At least for now.

My mother nodded absently. "I suppose it is. So, we'll keep it a secret."

"For now," I agreed. "But that doesn't keep you and I from doing what we need to do, whatever that is. And it won't stop me and my team from trying to get rid of the Megazotz. We have its blood now. Steve and Dria can run some tests and see what they can learn."

My mother's forehead wrinkled, something I hadn't seen for quite some time. The Botox must have been wearing off. "What are you going to do?"

"Make a plan," I said with confidence.

We returned to the living room. Hernan had managed to sit up, looking dazed. I was still holding the sword. Dria sidled up and, with her blue-gloved hand, pried it from my grip.

The Megazotz's black blood on my wrist had dried to a hard crust. The sight of it was enough to make me feel itchy all over. I excused myself and went to wash it off.

My mother's voice came from the other room. "Brujas unidas!"

I messaged my team and asked them to meet at the command center in two hours, which gave me time to work on a formula I hoped would be effective against the Megazotz.

In the mudroom—with the door locked and Sam at my side—I dumped the creature's nasty tooth from the glass storage jar into a stone mortar and gave it a good whack with the pestle. It broke into several pieces with a satisfying crack. Sam's tail swished back and forth against the counter while I ground the bits into a fine powder. Lencha glowed a comforting shade of orange but remained a clay figurine.

I had wrung about a teaspoon of thick Megazotz blood from my shirtsleeve. Steve and Dria might not want to give me more from their stash, so I didn't want to use all of what little I had. I measured out exactly half into a bowl. The blood was disgusting:

thick and tar-like, with an oily purple sheen. To that I added about a quarter cup of red clay from Lencha's yard and mixed it up with a wooden spoon and some water.

Yuck. The resulting mixture was an unpleasant black-red slurry with tiny bone-white flecks that caught the light. I added the same herbs I had used before—pungent epazote, rue, sage, and basil—and ended with a heartfelt incantation, which made my hands tingle and glow faintly red. Hopefully, that meant my brujería was in good working order.

I had to use a spoon to scrape the stuff into a clean glass jar, which wasn't easy because it had thickened into a viscous substance. When I was finally done, I stood back and stared at it.

There was no way I could do what I had in mind without Steve's help.

Dria was in the living room, crawling around on her hands and knees, wearing a headlamp, and examining the floor under the window where the Megazotz had come through. I found Steve in the kitchen, hunched over the table covered with a sheet of plastic. He was peering into a microscope.

"Where did you get that?"

"From the OA warehouse," Steve replied without looking up. "They stock mobile kits. It's coming in quite handy." He held up a dropper and pinched the bulb. A single black bead fell onto a waiting slide. "I'm not sure if the blood will tell us anything helpful, but it's part of our standard analysis. In a perfect world, we can modify the elixir so it targets the Megazotz more specifically."

"Speaking of that," I began cautiously. "I hope you don't mind, but I came up with something I'd like to try in the squirt gun."

Steve's head snapped up. "What?"

"Yeah…I put a few things together from my workshop. You know…with my magic. I came up with something I'd like to add to the blue elixir to give it a little boost. Trouble is, it's a little too thick. I'm afraid it might gunk up the nozzle, and I don't think I should add any more water."

Steve's eyebrows lowered. "All right," he said slowly. "Sure, we might as well try it. As Dria said, this stuff is a bit like alchemy. Why don't I take a look?"

I moved the jar from around my back, where I had been hiding it, and set it on the table in front of Steve.

He leaned forward, elbows on the table, and squinted at the substance. "What's in it? Exactly?"

After I told him, he sat back, rubbing the side of his face.

"Huh. I was hoping to use that tooth myself. But if this works, it'll be worth it." Steve picked up the jar and held it up to the light. "I'm thinking vinegar will thin the slurry and prevent the blood from coagulating and clogging up the nozzle. Plus, vinegar has antimicrobial properties, so it will have a preservative effect and may help stabilize the organic components."

I liked vinegar too, but for other reasons. Lencha called for it in several purification rituals to drive away evil spirits.

"Great. Vinegar it is." I went into the pantry and found a large bottle of white vinegar on a shelf, next to its fancier cousins.

Steve unscrewed the lid and poured some into the jar, releasing a rotting stench into the air. We coughed and waved our hands in front of our noses.

"That's disgusting. It didn't smell like that a few minutes ago," I said between my fingers.

"It's the blood." Steve squinted at the mixture. "It's beginning to clot. These things are ancient, so it may be decaying at a fast rate now that it's been exposed to the air, but who knows? Maybe the blood doesn't like that red clay."

I stood next to Steve while he transferred the concoction into a large glass bowl. He poured a thin stream of vinegar into the thick, sluggish mess. The mixture hissed, clots dissolved, and it thinned into a uniform reddish-black liquid.

"That worked." Steve sounded pleased. "Now what?"

My mind raced ahead, coming up with a way to conduct two experiments at once. It would be a little complicated, and I would need my mother's cooperation, but it was worth doing.

"Now you let me have one of your pump-action squirt guns, and we'll see if this stuff works."

Chapter 26

I explained to my team how I had prepared the blood-based elixir for the pump-action sprayers. They knew about my brujería. My team also knew I didn't like making a big deal of it, so I trusted they would keep the conversation to themselves. Mostly.

We were all gathered in the command center, with the windows boarded up as a precaution against another Megazotz attack. The last thing we needed was for one to bust through and take out the heatmap. That thing had cost a fortune.

Liam leaned forward in his chair, forearms resting on his thighs. "Did you make enough for all of us?" he asked eagerly.

"That would be really awesome," Bailey added. She had just come in from the cold and was still wearing a puffer jacket that almost matched the color of her copper hair.

I shook my head. "No. I had just enough blood to make one batch. If it works, I can talk Steve into giving me more of the blood he and Dria collected at Stu's house."

Liam's wide shoulders dropped. "But we'll be there when you put it to the test, right? As backup? With OA's blue stuff locked and loaded?"

"That's the idea." I glanced around the room.

Augustina was there, and so were Malik, Justin, and Ron. The pump-action guns were laid out on a table in the storage room, their reservoirs filled.

"Where are we going to do this?" Malik asked, frowning. "The Megazotz are pretty unpredictable. How do we make sure they'll show up where we want them to?"

I had an idea about that, but it was going to be tricky explaining it without revealing more than I wanted to. My plan was to get my mother and me together, hopefully with the spirit of my great-aunt Lencha. If my mother's theory was right—and I suspected it was—we would draw the Megazotz out of wherever they were hiding. Then I would get close enough to get off a few blasts from the squirt gun. Without losing my head, ideally.

"I'm working on that. I'm thinking about an open area with places to hide nearby, just in case it doesn't work. Like the open space where we dodged the Megazotz on our way to the OA warehouse, only closer."

A long silence followed.

Finally, Augustina cleared her throat. "I've been looking at maps of Chavez Ravine. There's an old water pumping station in La Loma that might work. It sits alone on a greenbelt, away from houses." She pulled her keyboard toward her and tapped away. A moment later, a color photo of a field with a small structure appeared on the large wall screen. "Here it is. The building's a pump house made of stone, so it's sturdy enough. No windows, and the door is steel. Would that work?"

I smiled. "Like a charm. Oh, and by the way, I'm going to bring my mother. She wants another crack at making a psychic connection with the Megazotz."

The last bit was a lie, but it seemed to work.

"That's brave," Bailey muttered, "considering what happened to her the last time."

Ron grinned. "She's a total chingona," he declared, then had to explain to the non-Latinos in the room that in today's parlance, it meant "badass."

For once, I had to agree. My mother hadn't hesitated, even for the briefest moment, when I asked her to tag along for my experiment with the pump-action gun. She had even agreed not to say anything to my team about the real reason she was there: to put our theory to the test, to prove that together, the Bantacorte brujas could summon the Megazotz.

A few hours later, we piled into two borrowed landscaping trucks, picked up my mother at Stu's house, and made our way through the empty streets to the old water pump in La Loma. The stone structure loomed ahead, sturdy and isolated and surrounded by open fields. Augustina had done well finding the location.

When we approached, a shiver snaked down my spine.

My mother walked beside me in a black tracksuit and sensible white sneakers, clutching the clay figurine of Little Lencha wrapped in newspaper. The others fanned out, finding places to hide.

I punched the code into the keypad, and the door clicked open. Inside was a small room filled with pipes and motors. It had a bare concrete floor and gray walls. The air smelled of chemicals and damp.

My mother looked around as if she expected something to jump out at us.

"Mom, are you okay?"

She sighed and held up her bandaged hand. "I won't lie. I'm a little nervous. But we'll get through it." She lifted her chin. "We Bantacorte women aren't going to let some pinche demon bats get the better of us."

My heart softened like a pat of butter hitting a saucepan, and I pecked her on the cheek. "Your darn tootin' right." I winked.

My mother gave a wan smile. "Hernan is a good man. I'm glad you two have made up. It means the world to me, actually."

For once, I didn't doubt her sincerity. I took the bundle from her good hand and peeled the layers of newspaper away, revealing the figurine of my great-aunt.

"Now what?" my mother asked.

I set Lencha down on the cement floor and thought for a moment. "We form a triangle. We need to focus our energy."

Without argument, my mother took her place, forming a perfect triangle with me and the clay figurine of Little Lencha. "Shall we hold hands?" she asked.

"Good idea." I put my squirt gun on the ground and took her good hand in mine. Her skin was as cool and damp as our surroundings.

"So…We should start getting their attention. Do you want to do the honors, or shall I?"

"Oh, Maddy…I'd like to flex my brujería, if it's all the same to you. I'll start."

My mother began saying something in Spanish. I wasn't as fluent as she was, but I understood enough. She started right in by saying we, the Bantacorte brujas, wanted to bind the Megazotz to our will.

A flutter of panic rose like tiny birds behind my ribcage. That would surely piss them off. Then again, if anything would get them to show up, it would be a direct challenge like the one she kept repeating.

I began to chant with her. The words grew more familiar on my tongue with each repetition. The minutes stretched on. I had no idea how much time had passed, but I didn't dare check my phone and break the flow of energy we were channeling.

The air in the pump station seemed to shift, growing colder and heavier, like the atmosphere itself was being compressed. The hum of the machinery faded into the background when a new sound emerged: a distant, high-pitched screech that made the hairs on the back of my neck stand on end.

Someone pounded on the door.

"They're coming," Ron shouted through the steel. "There are two of them."

My mother's eyes popped open. "It worked! I knew it would, didn't I, Maddy?"

It *had* worked, but there was no time to think about what it all meant. "You stay here," I said firmly. "Seriously, Mom…Stay inside."

I grabbed my squirt gun and sprinted outside. The steel door clanged shut behind me. Two massive Megazotz swooped down from the steel gray sky, heading straight for me.

I held off as long as I could before raising the sprayer. When their rat-like heads were nearly upon me, I raised the gun and worked the pump, releasing a burst of blood-enhanced elixir. It hit both Megazotz in their chests. I jumped out of the way.

The giant bats shot past me with a sizzling sound.

I let out a whoop.

When they wheeled around, facing me again, their skin was smoking. They let out cries of rage and pain, but their eyes glittered with fury. I glanced down at the spray gun's reservoir, and my heart sank. Nearly empty. Not enough for a second blast.

"Backup, please," I shouted.

Liam and Bailey emerged from their hiding spots, their guns loaded with OA's blue stuff. They flanked me, taking up positions on either side.

"Steady," Liam murmured. His voice was barely audible over the shrieking Megazotz.

Bailey's grip tightened on her gun. "We've got you covered."

The creatures closed in, their wings flapping erratically.

166

Streams of blue liquid came from somewhere overhead. It took a moment to register what was happening.

Justin had positioned himself in a nearby tree, and Ron and Malik had climbed to the roof of the pump house. Liam and Bailey joined them from below and emptied their reservoirs at the Megazotz, which were struggling to stay airborne. The blue stuff hadn't burned them like my blood-based concoction, but it did seem to irritate their eyes.

"Damn...These things are tough," Liam grunted.

The pump-action guns had one major flaw. They were hard to refill and required a funnel. Not easy to do when one was facing down a pissed-off demon bat.

"Reloading," Malik called from above.

But the Megazotz had apparently decided to take their smoldering hides back to wherever they hung out. They veered off, their wings once again cutting through the air with powerful strokes.

I watched them retreat, with a mix of relief and frustration churning in my stomach. We had hurt them, but not enough to take them out. Not enough to end this once and for all.

Chapter 27

When Steve walked solemnly into the kitchen, I knew he had bad news.

"Sorry, Maddy, but our analysis protocols used up almost all the Megazotz blood. You might get a little by scraping the sides of the storage jar, but that's about it."

I took a sip of the Yerba Buena tea Julia had made and put my head down on the kitchen table.

Stu slid his chair close to mine and rubbed my shoulders. "You'll figure something out. You always do."

"How much blood do you think there is?" I lifted my head and held my breath, waiting for the answer.

Steve and Dria exchanged an uneasy glance.

"Less than an eighth of a cup?" Dria said.

I gave a strangled laugh. "I'll take it, but I sure wish we had more." I put my head back on the table.

My anti-Megazotz concoction had promise. It had burned the giant bats on contact, but it hadn't been strong enough to kill them. To do that, I was certain my potion needed more Megazotz blood. But that wasn't going to happen unless I walked up to one and stabbed it.

My mother came into the crowded kitchen, took one look, and rolled her eyes, like I was a teenager sulking because my boyfriend dumped me right before prom—true story. She pulled me down the hall and into her bedroom for a talking-to.

"Now listen, Madeline," she began. "You have no idea whether the blood caused the Megazotz to burn. None whatsoever. It could have been something else. Like the red clay. Maybe it's the clay from Lencha's yard that's the real magic. Maybe you just need more of that. And maybe there's another ingredient or two that you can add. I know you think I'm not much of a bruja, but I do know you. You're impatient. Do you know how many experiments Thomas Edison tried before he invented the lightbulb? Thousands! You tried one. One! and now you're moping around, feeling sorry for yourself."

I slumped a little lower in an upholstered chair, one leg slung over the arm. "I don't have time to conduct a thousand experiments, Mother," I said through gritted teeth. "We're in lockdown limbo with no end in sight. And those things are still out there."

My mother flicked a piece of lint from her sporty black jacket. "Well, you're not going to solve it sitting around here. That's for darn sure."

"I'm processing my disappointment," I replied stiffly. But she had a point. Plus, she might have been onto something. Maybe I didn't need more blood. Perhaps I just needed more clay, and I had plenty of that.

I swung my legs around and looked up at my mother, who was still frowning down at me.

"I'm going to say something else you might not like," she said.

My mother wasn't the type to preface her lectures with a warning, so my muscles went all stiff.

"Oh?"

"Hernan and I need to move back to his place. You and I shouldn't stay together in the same house. We don't want our brujas unidas powers to attract the Megazotz again and put the others at risk."

My mother was full of surprises. She was very good at some things, like self-promotion and self-care. Not so great at thinking of others. Moving back home, without Stu and me to protect them from the Megazotz, wasn't exactly in her best interest. While I could see how it made sense, I wasn't comfortable with them being completely on their own.

I thought for a moment. Hernan's house was spacious. He must have had at least three extra rooms.

"I understand your point. And I agree, but only if I can find out if someone would be willing to stay with you. Maybe in exchange for some homemade food."

Ron Mendez came to mind, although he already had a mother and grandmother who coddled him.

My mother smirked. "I'm way ahead of you, hija. I've already asked Malik, so he and Bailey will be staying with us. I promised them pozole tonight."

Of course she did. My mother never met a boundary she didn't cross.

I could have pointed out that she shouldn't have spoken directly to a member of my team without my okay. That probably would not have gone over well. Or I could just let it go. My toes curled so hard my right foot cramped up. I really didn't have time for a fight. And I needed to figure out a new potion that didn't rely on Megazotz blood.

So, I decided to let it go. Then I congratulated myself for behaving like a full-fledged adult. One in control of her mommy issues.

———❖·◦❖·||||||·❖◦·❖———

Stu insisted on joining me for my clay-gathering and potion-mixing expedition. Ben drove the landscaping truck, with Ron

Mendez and Justin as lookouts. All of us had loaded pump-action squirt guns in case the Megazotz showed up.

On the short drive to Lencha's former property in La Loma, I called Augustina and let her know where I would be. I planned to spend as much time in Lencha's shed as possible, working up an anti-Megazotz solution.

"And please let me know if any of those things show up."

"Of course. I would do that anyway," she said.

"I know. I'm sorry," I replied. "I'm just a little on edge. Everything okay on your end? How's the house working out?"

"Everything is fine here," she said, her voice smoothing out. "And the house is wonderful. It's such a treat to have a place all to myself. It's enough to make me wish the lockdown would just go on and on. When I get home, I take a long hot bath and eat whatever I want, and I just started another mystery from your bookshelf."

"Good!" Every woman deserved a few simple pleasures in life, and it sounded like Augustina, who had more than earned them, hadn't been able to enjoy any for some time.

"Oh, one thing before we go." Her tone became businesslike and brisk. "I used the surveillance cameras to track the two Megazotz that showed up at the pump station. Usually, they fly too high to show up on the cameras, but I was able to remotely change the position of several of the newer models so they pointed higher, and it worked. Guess where they went?"

I rubbed Sam's head while staring fixedly out the window. "Phantom's Pass?"

"Nope! They headed straight for the gully between Palo Verde and Bishop."

Strobe lights went off in my brain. "The same place as the emergence holes?"

"I think so. I've sent Malik to pick up Steve and Dria, and Liam and Bailey are on their way to meet them there. There's no activity registering on the heatmap, so they should be fine for now."

My head spun, and my mouth went dry. "Do you think it's possible the Megazotz are going back *into* the emergence holes?"

I didn't have to explain the significance of that to Augustina. She had been one of the first LAPD officers to join Occult Affairs and knew the history of the entities backwards and forwards. Once the entities emerged, they had never ever tried to go back. Not once. It never seemed to occur to them.

The Megazotz traveling between our world and other realms strongly suggested they were entirely new. The case for Entities 2.0 was theoretical: no one had ever proved it. But the Megazotz were so different from the first wave of entities that they might not be Entities 2.0 at all. They might be something entirely different. Something on the hunt for the Bantacorte brujas, who happened to live in Chavez Ravine.

Sam batted my cheek with a paw, jolting me out of my thought spiral.

"Maddy?" Augustina was saying. "Are you there?"

"Sorry, yeah. Excellent work, by the way. Thank you. Can you ask Steve to message me when he's back from the gully?"

"Will do," Augustina promised.

———→·→·▥·◄·◄———

Stu hadn't visited my new property since the gnomes moved in, and he whistled when he saw their new home. "Wow, fancy! Looks like something out of *Lord of the Rings.*" He clapped Ben Tomas on the back.

Ben shrugged. "It's the grass on the roof, which I can take no credit for. That goes to one of my crew. But yeah. They seem to like it. No complaints so far."

"I'm sure Sam would let you know if they had any," Stu said dryly, watching the cat slip through the door.

I took a hand shovel and a small bucket from Ben's truck, dug up some of Lencha's magical red clay, walked to the back of the yard, and opened the shed door.

"I'll be working in the shed, but please come get me if anything weird happens out here."

Stu gave a little salute. "You'll be the first to know, babe."

My heart did a little bumpity-bump at the endearment. I wasn't used to smart, hunky guys like Stu talking to me like that.

Ben and Stu each grabbed a loaded squirt gun and paced around the yard, eyes on the sky.

I put the bucket down on the workbench and started to assemble my ingredients. A glint of light in the far corner caught my eye. It was coming from a large gold frame. I went over for a closer look and discovered it was a mirror. Vintage, with curling leaves decorating the edges. The silver backing was cracked and worn in places, and the whole thing was speckled with tiny dark spots.

My reflection stared back at me. Somehow, my eyeliner hadn't smudged, but I appeared pale, and the skin under my eyes looked faintly purple. Apparently, worrying about ancient Mayan demon bats had a way of undermining even the most careful skincare routine. Which mine was not, but still. I couldn't remember looking so washed out. Like I was one studded choker away from being the HOA's first goth head of security.

The mirror had a dreamy quality to it, as if the past still lingered there.

I went to the door and poked my head out. "Ben, there's a mirror here that wasn't here before. Is it from Julia?"

Julia was big into vintage shopping—and thoughtful too. I could easily imagine her picking it up somewhere on a whim and having Ben install it.

Ben turned to look at me. "No. Wasn't me." He glanced over at Stu. "A little surprise from you, maybe?"

Stu barked out a laugh. "With my taste? Only if it's made of plaid and has cup holders."

"You want me to get rid of it?" Ben asked.

"No, just curious." The mirror wasn't ugly or offensive, but I did wonder where it had come from.

I forgot about it as soon as I began mixing up a new anti-Megazotz potion. While I didn't have another bat tooth, I did need an animal ingredient, so I rummaged in my crate of goodies and pulled out a box of small, bleached bones I had picked up on my last visit to the botanica. The owner swore the bones came from Mexico and called them "oddities." They had intrigued me enough to buy them, but I had stashed them away and forgotten about them until now.

I pulled one out and set to work grinding it into a coarse powder in my molcajete, then transferred it to a steel bowl with a teaspoon of Megazotz blood, not daring to use more. There was no telling how many more batches I would need to make before finding one that worked.

I made notes on my phone so I could remember what I had done: two cups of clay, a tablespoon of ashes to represent fire— because I hoped to burn them back to hell—the blood, and a few other ingredients known to have a sinister side.

For the final step, I poured in white vinegar and let it fizz. The stuff didn't reek like the last batch had, and the color was different too. More terra cotta and less creepy dark shine. Because I used so much clay, the concoction was too thick, so I added some distilled water.

174

When I was finally done, I went outside. Stu and Ben both paused their patrols. I had never seen Stu in a flannel shirt before, and he was looking like one of those hot guys on the cover of a small-town romance novel.

"You done in there?"

"I haven't decided yet," I admitted. "I'm not sure how much of this stuff I should make. We can test what I have—it's enough for about three pump-action guns. But that means hoping the Megazotz come out to play when we want them to. And if more than a couple of them show up and the stuff works, we won't have enough to take them out. Or I can make a lot, and we give them all we've got, but if it doesn't work, we're screwed because all our weapons will be filled with my dud mixture and we won't be able to chase them off. So, you can see my dilemma."

Stu gave a low whistle. "This is why I'm glad I'm not you. That's a tough call. But I'd say, 'Go for broke.'"

I nodded, then began retracing my steps back to the shed. He was right, of course. I had already known that on some level, but once in a while, it was nice to consult with my hot colleague.

"And, Maddy…" he said. "One more thing."

I turned around, raising my eyebrows. "What's that?"

Stu grinned, and his blue eyes twinkled. "You've got to do something about these monster episodes once and for all." He lowered his voice. "They're killing our sex life."

To show just how much I agreed, I sprinted back to the shed.

Chapter 28

Something tapped on the roof above my head, and for one terrible moment, I thought a Megazotz was up there, trying to get my attention. The reality was less scary. Just a few raindrops.

The door to the shed banged open, and Stu and Ben crowded in.

"We've got some bad news." Stu looked glum.

Ben frowned. "I checked the weather first thing this morning, like I always do. It was supposed to be another cool and cloudy day, but the forecast has changed." He pulled his phone from the pocket of his jeans and tapped the screen with a dismissive sniff. "*Light showers will gradually intensify into periods of heavy rain by late afternoon as the storm system moves in.* Hah! There was no mention of a storm system a few hours ago."

My heart sank. "Storm system? How bad is it supposed to get?" We didn't often receive heavy rain in Los Angeles.

Ben grimaced. "The weather guy is calling it a 'deluge.'"

"A *deluge*?" I echoed. "How long do we have before that happens?"

Ben stared at his phone, swiping a few times. "According to the radar map, it'll hit around three, three thirty."

"Well, okay." Stu touched my elbow. "What do you want to do, Maddy? Maybe we should let the storm pass and try the new formula then."

I thought for a moment before shaking my head. "No. We can't afford to wait, and I want to use the stuff I made while it's fresh. There's no telling how long the shelf life is. The vinegar could break down, the Megazotz blood could start re-coagulating, and God knows what else."

My phone rang. It was Steve.

"What's up?"

"Augustina told you where she sent us, right?" he asked.

"Yes. The gully between Palo Verde and Bishop. You seeing anything?"

"Plenty," he said, his voice rising with excitement. "The holes show signs of disturbance. It's not erosion like we thought. We think the Megazotz are re-entering their emergence holes. There's no sign of them, but we're getting some interesting readings from our equipment that suggest recent activity."

"Tell her about the echolocation," Dria shouted from a distance.

"Oh yeah. We're using the probes we modified to poke around the holes, and they've detected a tunnel or a void or something. There's some really interesting resonance."

It was all too easy to imagine Steve kneeling at the edge of the hole and a Megazotz tearing his head off.

"Is that really such a good idea, Steve? Poking emergence holes now that we know what those things are? I can't believe Dria let you do that."

Steve chuckled. "Oh, she's the one who did it, not me. Once she saw our initial readings, there was no stopping her."

So Dria was every bit as nerdy and loony as the other OA researchers. I shouldn't have been surprised. Of course, there were tunnels or voids or whatever beneath the emergence holes. What else would there be?

"Well, at least now we know where they're going. But, Steve, what goes down those holes will eventually come up again. You both need to leave. As in immediately."

A short silence followed.

"Yeah, you're right. I think we got a little carried away. We'll pack up and get out of here."

Stu and Ben, leaning against my workbench, stared at me expectantly. That was the thing about my job: everyone who lived in the community looked to me for answers, including my boyfriend. I needed to think. The weather forecast gave us about three hours to put my magic-boosted concoction to the test before the rain arrived. Did bats fly in the rain?

I held up a finger to Stu and Ben and did a quick search on my phone.

No, bats did not fly in heavy rain unless they were starving and couldn't avoid it. Rain interfered with their echolocation, which made hunting difficult. Of course, the Megazotz weren't ordinary bats, but they certainly resembled bats and acted like them, for the most part. I figured the Megazotz wouldn't come out of their holes while it was pouring rain, which basically made them honorary Angelenos. We all freaked out at wet weather.

"Ben, do your radar maps tell you how long the so-called deluge will last?"

Ben checked his phone and grimaced. "Well, the system is expected to settle over the region and persist for the next twenty-four hours, bringing continuous rain bands into tomorrow. It looks like it's going to be a big storm."

Stu's snort was even louder than my own. "Are you moonlighting as a meteorologist?"

Ben scoffed. "No. I'm just reading what the caption says."

"Then we gotta move fast," I said. "We need to set up a trap zone to lure them out and then do what we did at the pump house. Hide and surprise. That was a good location, but I don't think they'll fall for the same trick at the same place. You know

Chavez Ravine better than anyone, Ben. Any ideas for an alternative location? An open area with shelter nearby?"

Ben's mouth twitched from side to side. "How about the area in back of the equipment yard in Palo Verde? It's away from any houses, and there's a long stretch of open space between the fence and the hill. It's narrow. You've been back there before, when we had the situation with the dead goat. Do you think it'll be too tight for what you have in mind?"

I remembered it well. The goat had been one of the first clues that we had some particularly nasty new visitors in Chavez Ravine. Those were flyers too. What a coincidence.

"A little tight maybe, but it's got other advantages. There are plenty of trees for my team to hide out in."

Stu nodded. "Narrow spaces have their advantages. They create natural kill zones. If you can funnel those things into a confined corridor, they're forced into a predictable flight path rather than being able to swoop in from any direction. And once they're in the corridor, they can't veer away. At least, not easily. Plus, you might be able to put some of your team at the top of the hillside and have them shoot downward. The higher vantage point will give them increased accuracy."

All that tactical talk coming from Stu was enough to turn my insides to molten lava, but since ripping his clothes off right there wasn't an option, I knocked my hip into his instead. "Wow. Mind if I steal that so I can show off in front of Liam? He went to military school, and he's tough to impress, but I think those sexy words will do the trick."

Stu flushed. "Come on. It's pretty basic stuff."

It was my turn to scoff. "For you, maybe." I clapped my hands. "Okay. I'll get to work making more of my stuff. Can you two round up my cat and let him know about the storm?"

"If someone ever told me I'd be talking to a cat and it would understand me, I wouldn't have believed it," Ben said on his way out.

Stu muttered, "It's not a normal cat," and pulled the door shut.

Chapter 29

Dark clouds rolled in from the southwest while all my available guards, plus Malik, Stu, and Ben, assembled behind the Palo Verde equipment yard. Maybe it was the increasing gloom, but I had a bad feeling, and no matter how much I tried to ignore it, I couldn't shake it off.

Little Lencha was with me, and as soon as everyone was in their assigned hiding spot, the two of us went for a stroll up and down the area we were calling the trap zone. There were only two of us Bantacorte brujas this time, and one of them was a figurine, but I hoped that was enough to summon the Megazotz.

I kept the Little Lencha in my jacket pocket because I didn't want to call too much attention to my reliance on the figurine. Stu didn't even know I was using her as bait. Well, technically, she and I were both bait.

Not that I was trying to hide anything from him, like I had earlier in our relationship. I trusted him fully and completely. He didn't have a problem with my brujería, although he might have been understandably concerned about the whole bait situation, given the long and weird history of the Bantacortes and the demon bats.

The weight of the figurine in my pocket was a reminder of the dangerous game we were playing. When I turned to make another loop, I glanced up in the direction of Bailey, Malik, Liam, and Stu hidden high on the hill and got a thumbs-up in return. I took a deep breath, trying to steady my nerves.

Nearly an hour had gone by, and the Megazotz hadn't shown up.

The roads of Chavez Ravine were empty. Members of my team were either indoors or hiding a few yards from me, so there was nothing to distract the Megazotz from the double bruja temptation. The only human activity was me taking a nonchalant stroll. I had assumed the Megazotz would find me irresistible, but they were resisting just fine.

Maybe they were too smart to be taken in by my ploy. Or perhaps they could sense the storm coming and wanted to stay where it was dry and cozy.

An hour passed, and then another. The nearly black clouds hovered above us with a promise of wind and water.

But still, the Megazotz stayed away.

When the wind began to pick up and large raindrops pelted the forest floor, I waved my arms over my head, signaling to the team it was time to give up. By the time we reached our vehicles, the rain was coming down in sheets, soaking through our clothes in seconds.

"We'll try this again when the weather calms down," I shouted over the stormy wall of white noise.

I hopped into the truck with Ben and Stu. We could barely see through the windshield while we drove out of the equipment yard. The wipers worked at top speed to clear the sheets of water. We had just made a left onto the main road when my phone buzzed in my pocket.

It was Hernan. "Maddy! You need to come over. Now, please."

My heart squeezed into my throat. "What? What's wrong?"

"Okay, well...You're not going to like this, but Malena tried her hand at brujería, and something went wrong."

Stu turned in his seat with eyebrows raised. I covered the phone's microphone.

"Sorry, guys, but we need to head over to Hernan's house. There's some kind of trouble." I took my hand off the microphone. "What went wrong, Hernan?"

"She was only trying to help," he said. "Please don't be mad."

I took a deep breath and counted to five. Even though ten was better, it would have taken too long. "Hernan. Just. Tell. Me."

"Would you just come already, Madeline?" my mother shouted in the background.

And that was how I knew it was really bad. My proud mother never asked for my help unless she was desperate.

"Hernan," I said sternly. "I need to know what we're dealing with. I'm with Stu and Ben. Are the three of us enough to handle whatever my mother did? Do I need to call for backup? Do we need elixir? What did she do?"

Hernan coughed. "Yes, okay. I understand." There was a long pause. "She made a golem. From the clay in my shed. The idea was for the golem to kill the Megazotz."

It took a moment for my brain to register what my mother had done.

A golem. Large enough to take on giant demon bats.

My stomach went as hard as a day-old Bolillo roll.

Stu gripped my arm, and his eyes snapped open. "Oh, shit."

Oh shit was right. Ben looked equally alarmed. He made a U-turn and punched it, speeding toward Bishop.

Another deep breath, and I tapped on my phone. "Hernan, I've put you on speaker so Stu and Ben can hear you since they'll be part of the cleanup crew. So, my mother created a golem to kill the Megazotz. Hernan, what kind of golem, and where is it now?"

"It's...well..." Hernan stammered. "La Lechuza."

"La Lechuza!" I nearly shouted. "Are you kidding me? My mother's not powerful enough to do that! Wait, wait. You helped her, didn't you?"

La Lechuza was a legendary Mexican monster, a witch owl with an old woman's face. There was no way my mother had created it all by herself. Hernan was just enough of a brujo to get himself into trouble, so the two of them must have combined their questionable forces.

"Maybe..." Hernan said. "All right. Yes, I did. She's my fiancé, mija. I can't tell her no when she asks for my help. Are you almost here?"

"Did you use the same clay you used to make Dog Face Bride?"

"Yes, yes. We did."

That was good news. I had dealt with Hernan's clay creatures before, so I should be able to do it again.

"Hernan, where's La Lechuza now?"

I squeezed my eyes shut while I waited for the answer, which was long in coming because my future stepfather had a coughing fit.

"We're not exactly sure where she is," he finally said. "We were trying to explain what we wanted from her, and she just sort of...stormed off."

I pressed a finger against an eyelid to keep it from twitching. "You mean *flew* off?" La Lechuza was famous for terrifying people from the air.

"Sort of," Hernan said. "She wasn't too good at it, you know? She hit the side of the house, and then she kind of rolled over the roof. She could be anywhere by now."

"Okay, Hernan, sit tight. We'll be there soon. And no more magic!" I ended the call.

Ben groaned. "My Texas grandmother used to scare the crap out of me with her stories about La Lechuza."

"It's a good thing everyone's already on lockdown," Stu muttered. "What do you want to do?"

Wring my mother's neck.

"First, we need to find La Lechuza. In the meantime, I'll call Augustina and tell her what we need to neutralize the golem. Ben, do you happen to have any fertilizer sprayers in the truck?"

He nodded. "I do. There's a box of six in the back."

I called Augustina and informed her what was going on.

"And I thought I had it bad with *my* mother," she said. "I'll send Justin and Ron with your stuff. Where do you want them to meet you? At Professor Frias's house?"

Hernan would have been thrilled to hear someone refer to him as "professor."

"Yes, please. I'll call them if anything changes."

When we turned onto Hernan's street, the rain began to ease up, but the sky remained a dark, churning mess. The truck's headlights cut through the gloom, illuminating the slick pavement and the familiar houses lining the road. I scanned the swaying trees, searching for any sign of the creature my mother and her fiancé had unleashed.

And then I saw it.

Perched on the rooftop of the house belonging to none other than Cora Bernal was the grotesque figure of La Lechuza.

She was even more hideous than I imagined. Her body was misshapen, as if twisted from a disease that afflicted her bones. Her feathers were matted and dripping from the rain. And that face. Eyes as deep and black as holes. Long, flowing hair the color of dirt and ash. Skin brown and wrinkled like a walnut.

"Yuck," Stu said.

Ben slammed on the brakes and rested his head on the steering wheel. "I think I'm going to have a panic attack."

I had never seen Ben so nervous. Not that I blamed him. La Lechuza was a ten on the freaky scale.

I was a bit anxious myself. Not about the owl lady, but about what I had to do next. I dug out my phone and called Cora. She picked up immediately. In the background, a baby was screaming its head off.

"Maddy! I was just going to call you. I think there's something on the roof of my house. I hope it's not one of those horrible bats. It's scratching around up there and woke up my grandson, and I had just put him down for a nap. All the windows are locked, but I brought him downstairs with me."

Beside me, Stu gasped. The witch-owl creature flung herself skyward with an awkward flap of matted wings, only to plummet almost immediately. She ricocheted off the rain gutter before vanishing into the side yard of Cora's house.

"That's gotta hurt," Ben muttered.

"Cora," I said into my phone, "I'm going to keep you on the line, just in case anything changes." I locked my phone, slipped it into the deep pocket of my trench coat, and pulled out my slingshot. "Why don't you guys wait here until Ron and Justin get here?"

Stu shook his head. "No way. I'm coming with you. I can bring the squirt gun. What do you think?"

"No. That elixir is meant for the Megazotz, so it's not going to work on our golem. I can probably corner her with my slingshot ammo and buy us some time until the guys get here." I turned to Ben. "Can you unpack those fertilizer sprayers so they're ready to go? I'll text Ron and Justin and have them mix up a batch of Dog Face Bride Special and bring it our way."

Ben gave a thumbs-up, recovering a bit from having seen his childhood nightmare.

Stu and I hurried toward the side of Cora's house. The rain had stopped, but judging by the phalanx of dark clouds blowing in from the southwest, the lull in the storm wouldn't last. Our boots sank into the sodden grass while we made our way across the lawn. We rounded the corner and immediately came upon an obstacle.

A very tall, carved wooden gate had been installed since the last time I had visited Cora, and it was locked.

"Can you help me over?" I asked.

Stu exhaled loudly. "I'll go first."

I rolled my eyes. "That's a brand-new gate. It must have cost a fortune. You'll scratch it up with your manly size twelve boots."

"Fair point." Stu laced his fingers together and offered me a boost.

The gate was so tall I couldn't see what was waiting for me on the other side. I put a foot on Stu's hands, reached up, and pulled myself over. My feet landed hard enough to jar my bones.

The side yard was narrow and lined with foliage and flowers. Through large windows I could make out the formal living room and the more casual great room that opened onto a small patio area. The air was thick with the scent of wet earth.

I crept forward, with the slingshot gripped tightly in my hand, hoping La Lechuza wasn't waiting to pounce and scratch my face off with her talons.

When I peered around the corner, my breath caught in my throat.

There, sitting at the patio table, was La Lechuza. She was hunched over a plate of tamales. Her gnarled fingers peeled back the corn husks and shoved the food into her mouth. The sight was so utterly bizarre that all I could do was stare.

Tap, tap, tap.

Cora was standing on the other side of the sliding glass door. She gave a little wave.

I mouthed, *Tamales, really?*

She raised her arms, palms upward, and shrugged.

I rolled my eyes, retraced my steps, and unlatched the gate.

"The guys are here," Stu whispered. "What's going on?"

"Cora decided La Lechuza needed some tamales, that's what. And the owl lady is eating them up."

Stu's mouth opened and closed. "I gotta see this for myself."

We peered around the corner.

"That was brave of Cora," he said into my ear.

"That was risky," I whispered. I pulled out my phone and unlocked it. "Cora, what were you thinking? You could have been hurt!"

Cora sniffed. "Don't be silly. La Lechuza only goes after drunks on the road and people wandering alone at night."

"And children!" Why did Mexican baddies always go after children?

Cora continued. "And look at her! Pobrecita is starving!"

Pobrecita. Cora felt sorry for the hideous creature in her backyard. She looked at La Lechuza and saw a pitiful creature. All I saw was a monster. A monster of my irresponsible mother's making.

"My guys are coming to take care of her," I whispered into the phone. "Do not open the door and give La Lechuza any more tamales."

Cora sighed. "All right. I'll save them for your crew."

Ron and Justin were walking toward us, their fertilizer sprayers filled and ready.

"We're locked and loaded," Ron said, wearing head-to-toe camo.

Justin grinned. "This should be easy."

There was no point in sticking around. That poor creature was too busy finishing off the last tamale to put up a fight. I signed off with Cora and began heading toward the truck with Stu.

Moments later, the hiss of the sprayers was followed by a short, sharp screech, and I cursed my mother under my breath.

Chapter 30

Cora Bernal took the news in stride. I was furious at my mother for her ridiculous plan, but the HOA president didn't seem upset in the least. Probably because she had met my mother and sensed how difficult she could be.

Cora pressed a foil-wrapped bundle into my hands when Stu and I headed for the door.

"A little tamale snack for later. And Maddy…" She leaned in so I wouldn't miss a word. "You must get rid of those awful bats. They're going to destroy our community."

If it had been anyone else, I would have fired off a sarcastic remark, but she didn't deserve that. She was under a lot of pressure too.

"Cora, that is my top priority. It's just a matter of time."

Which was technically true, except I had no idea how much time I would need.

At Hernan's house, I sat the aging lovebirds down in the living room while Stu faded into a corner and sipped some very fancy Reposado. I didn't have to say a word. My mother took a defensive and unrepentant tone.

"We just wanted to help. It's not my fault the ridiculous creature could barely fly."

I rolled my eyes. "Well, whose fault is it? You created a monster! A crappy one!" I turned to Hernan. "And *you*! You should have known better. Especially after the Dog Face Bride fiasco. You lost control of La Lechuza too!"

"Was the owl lady ever *in* their control?" Stu sounded like he was trying hard not to laugh.

I rolled my shoulders. "Good point. It didn't look like it to me."

My mother and Hernan sat pressed together on the couch, both wearing identical, defiant expressions.

"She got away from us for a little bit," my mother snapped. "That's all."

Hernan's head bobbed up and down in agreement.

I stopped pacing long enough to wag a finger at him. "That's not all. You asked for my help, remember? You didn't know where she was. And why in the world did you decide on La Lechuza? She's a total nut job. Why did you think she would be the solution to our great big Megazotz problem?"

My mother recrossed her legs and sniffed. "That should be obvious. She's part owl, isn't she? And a witch? Owls eat bats. We looked it up on the internet, didn't we, Hernan? Logical! It's in their nature. And when we did our spell, we were very clear about what we wanted her to do."

"Really? You made La Lechuza because owls eat bats? Mother, there's a big difference between logic and magic! You should know that!"

I walked over to Stu, took the glass from his hand, drained the last of his tequila, and then went to the liquor cabinet and topped him off.

"Plus, the version of La Lechuza you conjured up was pitiful. She wasn't capable of taking on a bunch of demon bats. She couldn't even fly!"

Neither my mother nor Hernan was contrite. I had run out of things to say, which didn't really matter because they weren't listening anyway.

I stomped upstairs to take a hot shower.

After I dried my hair, I stood at the bedroom window and watched the rain create a blurry world beyond the glass. It was an unusually heavy storm. The raindrops crashed onto a stretch of dirt beyond the hot tub. The ground had turned into a swirling mess of brown slush, forming a little stream rushing toward the back fence.

Every nerve in my body jangled with alarm.

If the pelting rain can do that, what must it be doing to the magical red clay in my backyard?

With my heart beating in my chest, I ran downstairs to look for Stu and found him in his office, still in his damp clothes, sitting in front of his computer and talking to someone on speakerphone.

He gave a little smile of apology and mouthed, *Sorr-ee.*

I went to look for Ben. He was in the kitchen, leaning against the counter, opening a beer, and talking to Julia and Clare.

"There you are!" Julia came over to give me a hug. "It sounds like you deserve a cerveza too!"

I shook my head. "I do, but I can't. I'm sorry. I hate to do this, but I need to borrow Ben again."

He turned toward me, his brown eyes wide. "Anything wrong?"

"We need to go to Lencha's place. I'm worried about the clay."

Ben set the bottle down on the counter and swallowed. "That clay has survived rain before." He paused and checked his weather app again. "Wow, this is a big storm. Very unusual. Yeah. Let's go."

Less than ten minutes later, we were standing in the pouring rain, and I was numb all over. The once-solid clay patch had turned into a quagmire. I fell to my knees, feeling the slippery mud beneath my fingertips, watching rivulets of muddy, red water run down the yard and under the fence.

My worst fears were coming true. The clay that was the source of the Bantacorte power was washing away in the relentless downpour.

"Is there anything we can do?" I asked.

Ben didn't bother to answer, but ran over to the gnomes' long, low house and pounded on the door. "I need your help!" he shouted, pulling the squares of grass from the roof.

The door opened, and Beady stuck his head out. He glanced from Ben to where I was standing next to the terra cotta stream, nodded, and then went back inside. A moment later, Beady and a half dozen gnomes were helping to transfer the sod mats from the roof onto the soggy stretch of clay.

I understood what they were trying to do. Attempting to cover the clay, to stop it from washing away. But the rain found the gaps between the slabs of sod and continued to erode the magical clay.

Maybe it was the cold and damp, but I could feel no fire within me. No spark of magic. No spell that could save the clay. The storm was winning. If I needed more of the magical earth to use against the Megazotz—and I surely would because they were on a mission to destroy the last of the Bantacortes and wouldn't give up easily—then I was out of luck.

It was like watching my plan to save Chavez Ravine literally dissolve beneath my feet. Like Mother Nature herself was against me.

Who was I kidding when I decided to become a bruja at the advanced age of forty? Sure, I'd had some successes, but I had never done it alone. I had always had help.

"It's not working!" Ben's voice sounded a long way away.

I was vaguely aware of gnomes rushing around the yard, working furiously to save what was left of the red clay. But I couldn't bear to continue standing there, doing nothing, feeling useless. I stumbled toward Lencha's shed. My hands shook while I dug into my pockets for the key.

Once inside, I kicked the door closed and gripped the edge of my workbench, light-headed. Waves of cold and heat washed over me. Was I having a panic attack? My chest tightened, and my ears began to ring. What was happening to me?

I lurched to the mirror that had appeared out of nowhere and caught sight of myself. My skin had gone ghostly pale, and the cords of my neck strained against my skin, as if they might snap.

A flicker of movement behind me sent my heart racing, and I whirled around. There was nothing there, but when I turned back to the old mirror, a shadow wavered and twisted. It wasn't a reflection of something in the shed with me; it was something in the *glass*.

The edges of the shadow solidified, and a figure emerged. A woman with the perfect oval face of a brown-skinned Madonna. A strip of red cloth tied around her forehead gave her the appearance of a warrior. She didn't speak, but I instantly knew who she was.

The first Bantacorte bruja.

Her presence filled the shed with an energy that made the air crackle around me. A weightless hand rested on my shoulders, and I shivered.

Her eyes bored into mine, and a vision unfolded before me, like an old foreign movie that I didn't need subtitles to understand. Her name was Chimalma. I saw her, centuries ago, hiding in her home while the Spanish conquistadors brought death and destruction to her village. She escaped into the hills and, at the mouth of a cave, had summoned the Camazotz, commanding them to rise against the invaders. Not just one appeared, but many, flying out and sending the Spanish running. Those they caught lost their heads.

But the victory was short-lived. The Camazotz were fierce wild things, and they refused to be enslaved by the bruja's magic. They turned on the village. Chimalma, desperate to save her people, cast a powerful spell to banish them back to the caves.

The vision faded, leaving me breathless and disoriented. Chimalma's dark eyes remained locked onto mine. She had shown me the past for a reason. Those things were back. They were larger and more powerful than in Chimalma's time, and it was my turn to face them. But how could I hope to control them when Chimalma, with all her power, had ultimately failed?

Chimalma faded away, and in her place, Lencha appeared, as solid and real as she had been in life. I reached out to touch her, but my finger encountered only the speckled glass.

"Tell me what to do, Lencha," I pleaded. "I don't know what to do."

Lencha sighed. The puff of air brushed my face.

"The answer, mija, is in yourself. Just recuerda. You are a chingona. All of us Bantacorte brujas are."

And then the old mirror was just a mirror, and I was alone again, my head filled with distant memories and Lencha's words of encouragement. But I was no closer to knowing what I had to do.

An action plan was what I needed, not an ancient newsreel.

I paced in front of my workbench, fists clenched, trying to turn Lencha's cryptic advice into a practical solution. Outside, Ben was shouting frantic instructions to the gnomes to help him pull tarps over the clay. But the wind was tearing at the canvas.

Not even Chimalma herself would have been powerful enough to control the forces of nature.

My gut was a cauldron of bubbling anger fueled by helplessness. I wanted to scream. Wanted to pick up the molcajete stone and throw it against the wall.

Bits of red clay clung to the crevices of the molcajete. Nice, dry clay. A wheel began to turn inside my head. I couldn't stop the storm—I was sure of that. But maybe that was the wrong way to approach the problem. Maybe I could do something to the clay. Perhaps I could harden it to prevent it from washing away.

I would need something to activate that level of magic. The blood from the Megazotz had been one of the key ingredients in my concoction. Would *my* blood work? The blood of a chingona bruja?

Lencha had said the answer was in myself. An electric tingle ran from the tips of my fingers, across my hands, and up my arms.

That was it.

I grabbed my iron scissors from a hook on the wall and ran outside.

When they saw me, Ben and the gnomes froze, as if I had hit a remote and paused them mid-action. The sight of those startled, wizened faces underneath their soggy hats was enough to make me laugh. When I did, I sounded unhinged.

Ben's eyes dropped to my hand holding the scissors, and his eyebrows came crashing down. "What are you doing?"

Instead of answering, I yanked aside a slab of sod, revealing the muddy red mess below. I pushed up my sleeve and put the tip of the scissors against my forearm.

"Maddy!" Ben shouted.

The gnomes clapped their little hands over their mouths in a parody of horror.

I pressed the tip against my skin. A line of fire blossomed when it broke through the surface. The hand holding the scissors trembled slightly, but the fiery orange glow that surrounded the wound kept me going, and I lengthened the cut until the pain sharpened. The blood began to drip onto the ground.

Ben cried out again and came rushing toward me.

"Stop!" I yelled. "You'll ruin it."

My tone was enough to bring Ben skidding to a halt. His eyes were wide with fear and confusion. The gnomes huddled together and whispered in their grumbly voices.

The world around me seemed to slow, and the pounding rain faded into the background. The magic within me responded to the ancient power of the clay and the sacrifice of my blood. The ground trembled, and the muddy mess began to churn and shift.

I closed my eyes and reached out with my senses, trying to connect with the essence of the clay, once the earth of Mexico and now the magical soul of Chavez Ravine. And it was whispering back to me. Or maybe it was the generations of Bantacorte brujas before me, urging me on.

After a few moments, Ben's voice broke through, as if from a great distance. "Look!" he shouted. "Look!"

My eyes snapped open.

The rain had slowed to a drizzle, and the clay was hardening, becoming firm and resilient. Ben called out to the gnomes, and then they were lifting the sod mats and throwing them aside, revealing the expanse of red clay below. More of the clay was turning to hard earth, still red, but no longer muddy. There seemed to be even more clay than before the rain had started.

If I could do that, maybe I was ready to face the Megazotz.

Feet pounded toward me, and when I snapped out of my reverie, Stu was running toward us, yelling about the blood. My phone blasted to life in my pocket with a command center alert.

The reddish-orange glow of my hands began to fade when I held up the screen to read the message. Warm blood continued to drip from my throbbing arm.

Alert: Megazotz registering on the heatmap. All 18 of them.

Chapter 31

The screeches of the Megazotz echoed through the hills while they circled in the stormy gray skies of Chavez Ravine.

I worked in Lencha's shed to make a fresh batch of magic-infused elixir, but I could hear them in the distance. They seemed to be avoiding the yard and its bed of red clay.

The elixir I had made with the clay and a touch of Megazotz blood had damaged the demon bats, not stopped them. But since then, the clay had been transformed. My blood, the blood of my ancestors, had strengthened the red earth and infused it with a power I believed could turn the tide in our favor.

I needed to work fast. Residents were jamming the emergency hotline with reports of sightings. The damn things were everywhere. Bailey had gone to help Augustina field the calls and assure the anxious residents a plan was in place "to exterminate" the demon bats. Credit to Augustina, who had chosen "exterminate" to make it sound like the Megazotz were no more dangerous than ants or aphids.

But magic took time, and I needed to speed things up. With a sigh of resignation, I asked Stu to fetch the only other witches in Chavez Ravine.

He rubbed the side of his face and grimaced. "Are you sure? You want your mother involved?"

"I definitely don't *want* her involved, but I'm afraid I *need* her involved. Those things are spooking our residents, and I need to get rid of them before they get violent again."

Forty-five minutes later, my mother swept into the shed, eyed the workbench, and wrinkled her nose. "Honestly, Maddy, I have no idea how you can possibly work in such a mess." A hand fluttered to her heart, and she gasped. "And madre mia de Dios, what happened to your arm?"

"A little cut. Nothing to worry about."

A little lie, but I figured it saved me at least twenty minutes of questions I didn't want to answer.

The workbench *was* a mess. Red clay splattered the walls. Dried herbs covered the workbench. I had knocked over a jug of vinegar, and the place reeked of it.

With her mouth pursed, my mother bustled around, straightening things up. "Something happened," she said. "I can sense it."

Hernan was in the far corner, inspecting the mirror, arms crossed in front of his chest. "Stu was pretty tight-lipped on the way over." He gave the mirror a tentative tap. "Where did you get this?" His voice was laced with suspicion.

I took a deep breath and fought a wave of irritation. The questions were going to keep coming, so I decided to provide a brief explanation of everything that had happened so we could move on.

My mother and Hernan listened, eyes wide with disbelief, while I wrapped up my story. My arm throbbed where I had cut it. Stu had rustled up a first aid kit, but the antibiotic cream hadn't done much to alleviate the pain.

"So, once again, one of our ancestors appeared to you and not to me," my mother said through clenched teeth.

Hernan dropped into the only chair in the shed. "Maddy's our warrior, Malena. It's not personal."

My future stepfather couldn't have chosen worse words if he had tried.

My mother's neck turned the shade of a pomegranate. "Oh, Hernan, listen to you." She passed a bejeweled hand across her forehead. "Honestly. She's head of HOA security. That's all. She's not some kind of high priestess."

Hernan shot me a furtive, apologetic glance. "What do you want us to do, Madeline?"

I went over the instructions, and we got to work. My mother muttered about the unfairness of Chimalma's snub.

As unpleasant as my mother made things, I was glad for the help. When we were finally done, I called Augustina and asked her to send over my team with their weapons.

"And please have them empty their storage containers before they leave. I have a new formulation we'll all be using."

Next, I asked my mother to help me have a little chat with the gnomes. The request seemed to mollify her. When I explained what I needed the gnomes to do, she gave a little gasp of surprise.

"I'm not sure if they'll go for that," she said. "They're terrified of the Megazotz. Absolutely terrified."

"I know," I said. "But it's the best shot we have at getting this to work."

The rain had picked up again, pelting us while we walked across the yard. My mother knocked on the door of the gnome shelter, and a moment later, it creaked open. As usual, she was invited inside while I was left to stand out in the cold, imagining my mother and the gnomes sitting around a cozy table, snacking on oat cakes or whatever gnomes ate, and sipping hot tea. Perhaps it was payback for Lencha and Chimalma's choosing to speak with me.

I hurried back into the shed to stay warm and found Hernan straightening up the workbench.

"You are a very messy bruja, Maddy," he said disapprovingly. "But a talented one, I've got to admit."

"Thank you." It was a little weird getting a compliment from the brujo who had once been my nemesis.

We spent the next several minutes in companionable silence, tidying up and stacking the plastic canisters filled with the red clay concoction I hoped would exterminate the Megazotz.

When my mother finally reappeared, she didn't mince words. "They'll do it, but only on one condition…" She let her words trail off for dramatic effect.

My mother was going to make me ask. I stifled a sigh.

"And that would be?"

"A guarantee that they will be allowed to remain in Chavez Ravine, doing what they're doing now and living in the house that Ben made for them." She paused. "They like it here."

I could sell that to the HOA board, no problem. They liked the gnomes and the free labor, and the residents, surprisingly, were enamored by them too. But allowing them to stay indefinitely on my property might present problems. Which would require me to explain it to my mother, who would then have yet another injustice to complain about. But there was no other way around it.

"Deal," I said. "But tell them we may need to move their house to the back of the property if I decide to build here myself."

My mother's mouth opened and closed. "Is that something you're planning?"

I shrugged. "Maybe. Stu might sell his place, and if he does, we were thinking about building a new home here."

"Mmm. That's not a bad idea," she said and left.

Hernan chuckled. "I bet you weren't expecting that."

I was saved from replying by the arrival of my team.

Bailey hoisted her weapon over one shoulder and practically snatched a canister of magically boosted red clay liquid from

Hernan's hands. "This is going to be awesome," she declared in a sing-song voice.

Ron, dressed in waterproof camo pants and a hoodie, helped my mother and Hernan into a massive SUV to drive them home before Operation Exterminate Megazotz got started. "I hope it doesn't rain again." He glanced up at the darkened sky.

"It's not supposed to rain until late tonight," Stu said, carrying my squirt gun and steering me toward the gate.

"If the meteorologists aren't wrong again," Ben added gloomily. He opened the back of the truck for the gnomes, who clambered in.

Liam scanned the sky to the west. We couldn't hear the Megazotz, but they were out there somewhere, according to the latest update from Augustina.

"I hate these fuckers even more than those vampire birds."

That made two of us. The ancient demon bats weren't just another annoying security threat. They had a longstanding grudge against the Bantacorte brujas, and my mother and I had big targets on our backs.

Stu was quiet while he drove us in his neighbor's Hummer.

He steered with one hand and squeezed my knee with the other. "I still can't believe you used your own blood." He glanced over at me. Lines creased his forehead. "Your witchy ways take some getting used to."

I leaned over and booped his nose. "Brujería," I corrected. "One of these days, you'll learn to pronounce it."

Stu grimaced. "You're on. I can't wait until the most important thing you have to do is teach me Spanish."

I smiled. I felt the same way. But the knot in my gut told me that might not happen for a long time.

Chapter 32

The gnomes were nervous. They had agreed to my plan, but it had been a lot to ask.

I was anxious too. The gnomes had become a part of the Chavez Ravine family, and I was asking them to be the bait in my plan to lure the Megazotz into the trap zone behind Ben's equipment yard. If my elixir failed, if my team was unable to get clear shots, or if the wind turned against us, the gnomes could pay the price.

But in the end, the gnomes did their jobs.

It was only a few minutes after the gnomes lined up at one end of the path that the Megazotz appeared. Beady was the first to sense their arrival, and he led his group up the path at top speed. The Megazotz followed, swooping down on the gnomes while they ran for their lives.

Just as Stu had predicted, the narrow trail forced the flying demons into a confined space, where we unloaded our pump-action guns.

From behind a tree, I heard a screech somewhere to my left, then a whoop when my new concoction made contact with their skin. Smoke trailed two of the creatures, who flapped erratically away. One even burst into flames and went crashing into the ground. For one joyous moment, I thought we could take them all out the same way.

But the scene was chaos, with blasts of red-tinged elixir coming from all directions and the frantic beating of giant bat wings. The Megazotz were screeching, squealing, and chirping. It was impossible to tell where the fallen Megazotz had been hit, so it was impossible to direct my crew to find that vulnerable spot on the others.

The gnomes made it to the end of the barren path and disappeared through a hole Ben had cut in the fence.

The Megazotz tried to follow. Some of them landed on the ground but appeared confused by the gnomes' disappearance.

We had emptied our weapons and needed to refill them, an awkward business. It seemed to take forever. Sometimes, the most ridiculous things got in the way of monster hunting.

Ron and Bailey were the first to finish reloading. They dropped out of the trees onto the path, waving and yelling at the biggest Megazotz, the huge one from the patio of Olga's Cantina. It wheeled around in the air and began to dive, resembling a jumbo jet making a trembling descent.

The big Megazotz let out an earsplitting screech, and its wings shuddered when it corrected to avoid the treetops.

The creature faltered mid-flight, and its massive form shimmered like a mirage. I rubbed my eyes, thinking it was a trick of the gloomy light, but when I looked again, its wings were folding in on themselves. Its body compressed like a deflating balloon. It seemed to be disintegrating before our eyes, and I thought we had done it.

But I was wrong.

Wrong. Wrong. Wrong.

We hadn't eliminated the monster. It was transforming its big, ugly self into a swarm of tiny creatures the size of sandflies.

My heart pounded. That was about the last thing I had expected.

I jumped out from behind the tree and yelled, "Run!"

Several things happened at once. The swarm surrounded Bailey, and she began to scream. Another Megazotz also began to change. Its enormous form grew smaller at an astonishing rate. Their loud screeches became squeaks, then a high-pitched buzz. It was hard to make out their tiny dark forms against the grayness surrounding us.

Liam and Malik charged past me, headed for Bailey. She had curled into a ball on the ground, trying to make herself as small as possible while the swarm converged around her.

"Form an outward-facing circle!" Liam thundered.

Instead of the Megazotz fanning out to attack the rest of us, all of them converged around Bailey. I was no tactical expert like Liam, but even I could understand their mistake.

Stu scrambled down from a tree and quickly caught up with me.

Liam tossed his weapon to Malik, snatched up a massive palm frond from the ground, and began waving it around. The swarm scattered, and we rushed in to form a protective circle around Bailey.

Liam scooped up Bailey, and we shuffled backward as a unit, our weapons pointed outward. The swarm had regrouped at the far end of the unused tract, buzzing angrily, a dark cloud ready to descend on us again.

"Make it last, people!" I shouted. The loud buzzing made it impossible to be more specific.

When the cloud dove at us again, we sprayed the elixir in short bursts, trying to keep the creatures at bay. All except for Ron, who either had blown through his reservoir tank or hadn't had time to refill it. He darted out of formation, grabbed the palm frond, and used it to swat at the tiny demons.

"Keep moving!" Liam barked.

Stu was on my right, his breath coming in short, ragged bursts. He squinted at the encroaching horde. The tiny creatures sizzled and popped each time the elixir connected.

"Dammit," Justin muttered to my left. He must have emptied his weapon because he whipped off his jacket and began snapping it in front of him.

The parking lot seemed miles away. Time slowed while we inched our way toward the vehicles.

The buzzing cloud was thinning, but so were our reserves. The weight of my weapon grew lighter with each pump. The swarm was relentless. Retreating, then advancing.

Bailey was dead weight in Liam's arms. I couldn't tell if she was conscious.

"Keep together," Liam called.

We edged closer to our vehicles. And then, finally, we made it. There was a wild scramble to get inside the SUVs. I was pulling the door shut when something stung my cheek, and I yelped.

Moments later, we were racing away. Our convoy was followed by the swarm of black dots.

"Where to?" Stu asked.

"The command center," I replied. I tapped a message on my phone to my team, then called Augustina and told her what to do.

"Yeah, okay. I have an idea," she said before hanging up.

When we rolled to a stop in front of the command center, Augustina ran out wearing a long rain jacket with the hood up. She had a large fertilizer sprayer attached to her back, and she doused the swarm surrounding our vehicles. I watched in amazement while the little creatures scattered.

Without waiting to see if the swarm reformed, I jumped out of the Hummer. My heart roared like an ocean in my ears. The others did the same. The air smelled of something strong and repulsive, as if some crazy person had mixed sulfur and garlic.

Liam charged through the door of the command center, with Bailey in his arms.

The door slammed behind us, and someone locked it.

Augustina shrugged out of the harness holding the sprayer and peeled off her jacket.

"Where the hell did you get that?" I gasped.

She patted her chest, trying to catch her breath. "It's been outside the back door forever. One of the gardeners must have put it down and forgot about it."

I glanced over at Liam, who was carefully laying Bailey down on the floor. Augustina snatched a sweater hanging from the back of a chair and gently slid it under Bailey's head.

"Augustina, what was in that spray that got them to back off like that?" I asked.

She smiled. "Just some neem oil. It's the stuff gardeners use to get rid of insects and plant mold because it's non-toxic to humans. But it definitely reeks."

The stench had followed us into the command center. Ron was waving his hands in front of his face and gagging.

"Good move. The Megazotz sure seem to hate it." I knelt beside Bailey.

She was pale, her breath coming in shallow gasps. Her face and hands were covered in red welts.

"At least they didn't bite her head off," Ron said.

Liam's eyes rolled upward. "*Dude.*"

"Sorry."

"Bailey, can you hear me?" I asked, trying to keep the panic out of my voice.

Malik nudged Liam aside and began untying the chin strap on her hood. "Bailey, baby, can you hear me? Can you talk?"

Bailey's eyes fluttered open. A moment later, they came into focus. "The fuckers stung me," she croaked. "It hurts."

Everything I needed to make a salve to ease the pain was in my shed, but there was a first aid kit somewhere in the command center. Augustina was a step ahead of me, pulling one out of a cabinet.

Malik snapped on a pair of blue gloves from the kit and began wiping down the red spots with antiseptic.

"Ow!" Bailey yelped, her eyes snapping wide open. "That shit stings."

Malik kissed her forehead, squirted hydrocortisone from a tube, and smeared it around. "I know, I know. But this is gonna help, I swear."

"It better," Bailey whimpered. She turned her head away so we wouldn't notice the tears welling in her eyes.

Augustina handed Malik a bottle of water from the mini fridge and two pain pills. We watched while Malik propped up Bailey's head and gave her the medicine.

I rooted around in the first aid kit, searching for something else to help alleviate the pain. "Here's some lidocaine." I held up a small pink bottle. "Does anyone know if we can mix it with the cortisone cream?"

There were several computers in the room, but phones came out, and seconds later, we had our answer. "Safe to use," Justin announced.

Malik dabbed the anesthetic on Bailey's wounds. She closed her eyes and sighed.

"Oh, thank God...That's better. Thank you."

The marks were red and painful-looking, but they didn't seem to be getting any worse.

"We may have got lucky when the Megazotz changed shape," I said. "The Megazotz venom that incapacitated my mother and Sam seems to have been diluted in the miniature version. It just looks like an allergic reaction."

"Allergic reactions can be fatal," Ron said in a low voice. "That's how my grandfather died."

My cheek exploded in pain. Stu was dabbing at it with a wipe, and I batted his hand away. "Stop! I can do that."

"So can I," he said firmly. "And quit moving. It'll go faster if you quit squirming."

I gritted my teeth while he continued to work. My muscles finally relaxed after the lidocaine kicked in. I pulled myself to my feet and fell into the closest chair.

Augustina's blond head came up. "When the Megazotz transformed, their little bits didn't come up on the heatmap, so we're going to need another way to track them. I've asked Steve and Dria if they can think of anything, so hopefully, they'll have some ideas. And if we're going to name the little Megazotz bits, I have a suggestion. Minizotz!" She smiled broadly.

I nearly laughed out loud. "I love it! Minizotz it is."

Stu reached over and squeezed my knee. "How many of your security cameras are the newer models you ordered when you first started?"

I thought for a moment. "Eighty percent, maybe…"

The cameras were all over Chavez Ravine, and I had upgraded most of them.

"Those can be switched to infrared, which might detect the little things," he said. "That can be done remotely with a software update. I'll take care of that."

What was it with Stu and his sexy technical jargon? The words hit me in a warm rush, starting low at my thighs and surging upward through my body.

Or maybe it was just a sign of perimenopause.

"That's great," I said. "We're going to need to switch gears, though. We need a new plan."

All eyes turned toward me. When I didn't answer right away, Stu tapped my knee.

"You going to share it or keep us in suspense?"

It wasn't that I was playing coy. I just needed a little extra time to think through the tricky bits. The plan wasn't perfect. We might even have to improvise. But we had learned a lot about the Megazotz, and we needed to respond accordingly.

"We need a new trap zone," I finally said. "Reloading killed us today, and the squirt guns are okay for hitting large objects, but not so useful against a cloud of Minizotz. The clay seems to have been effective, but we need a new delivery system and a massive supply of elixir. Which means instead of carrying the red clay elixir to them, we need to draw them to the red clay."

It sounded so simple.

Chapter 33

"Oh, Maddy…Not another plan! How many of your plans must I listen to?"

My mother was being her usual gracious self, but as much as she irritated me, I needed her, so I let her comment slide and explained what we had to do. When I was finished, there was a long silence, and for a moment, I thought the call had been dropped. But when she finally spoke, her attitude had completely changed.

"Madre mia de Dios," she finally said. "I do believe that will work. Can you send that nice Malik boy to come get me? I need to change and fix my hair."

I pressed a finger between my eyes. "Mother," I said sternly. "This is a come-as-you-are-and-as-fast-as-you-can kind of situation. It's not one of your psychic shows."

"Well, you can look like a slob if you want to, but at my age, one can't just roll out of the house looking like something the cat dragged in. And speaking of cats…You need to make sure Sam is there to help us."

"Mother, Sam goes nuts if he even sees a fly buzzing around the house. Plus, he's already been hurt by one of those things. There's no telling what he'll do when he sees them."

My mother gave a dismissive sniff. "Honestly, Madeline, you act like he's an ordinary house cat when it's clear he's not. We need him. To amplify our summons."

That was a bit too much, even for my mother, the psychic. "Yes, he's special, but he's not a...megaphone."

"That's where you're wrong, Madeline," my mother said briskly. "And you know very well I'm not talking about that kind of amplification. I'm talking about the spiritual kind. Based on what I sense in him, he's more effective than any stone or crystal. He can channel and amplify our intentions, both to the Bantacorte spirits and to the Megazotz themselves."

We were at the point in our conversation where I usually started to tune out, but this time, I was inclined to listen. There *was* something special about Sam. Not only had he helped me craft spells that had worked, but he had also guided me toward the right ingredients too. And there was no denying the connection between him and my great-aunt. Sam loved hanging around the Little Lencha figurine, and she glowed more often when he was around.

"Fine," I said reluctantly. "We'll bring him along too."

As painful as it was dealing with my mother, she wouldn't be bothered seeing me perform magic. My team was a different story.

Me, my mother, and a cat acting all woo-woo witchy in full view of everyone was going to be a lot for them to take. I needed to convince them that I wasn't having a breakdown, that it was all strategic, that this was part of a plan and not me finally losing my shit in a big, dramatic way.

The command center had never been so busy. The place stank of sulfur, and my team was smearing neem oil over their necks and faces. Nobody had time for a lengthy discussion, so I presented my plan quickly.

"Here's the drill...You all know about the red clay in the yard in La Loma, right? That's the stuff that works with my...powers. And I don't believe I've mentioned this to all of you yet, but the Megazotz seem to be attracted to my mother and me."

There was no point in talking about ancient brujas or glowing figurines, so I just stuck to the operational parts of my plan.

"My mother and I will be the bait luring the Minizotz to the yard, where we'll have an abundance of weapons and clay in case we need to pivot. We now know the Megazotz can appear as giant bats or as tiny insects, so this time, we'll be ready for both."

"Sounds pretty badass to me," Ron said, wrapping duct tape around his wrists and enough of his hand to protect his skin while keeping his fingers free enough to move.

Bailey had recovered enough to join us. She was drinking coffee while Malik duct-taped her ankles. "I love it when you use your magic!"

I asked Stu to take the Hummer and fetch my mother and Hernan, a teeny bit of defiance on my part since she had asked for Malik.

An hour later, we were all gathered in Lencha's former backyard. The gnomes had reluctantly agreed to allow my team to hide out in their long, low house, and from the grunts and groans coming from behind the wooden planks, it was a tight and uncomfortable fit.

By sheer good luck, the squall had moved north, and we were in a lull before another one moved in. Clouds scuttled across the gray sky, occasionally drizzling on our heads. The wind blew wet leaves into our faces, but the rain stayed away.

My mother had arrived wearing an eccentric mix of the practical and the dramatic: a black matching velour tracksuit, a colorful southwest-style fringed shawl draped around her shoulders, and a red scarf around her head.

Sam swirled around our ankles, meowing.

"Hello, little buddy," I said. "Can we agree that today there will be no chasing? Anything? Let's just stick to the plan, okay?"

His green eyes flickered upward. Could all cats roll their eyes, or was it just Sam?

I turned to my mother. "Should we hold hands?"

Attempting magic with someone else was making me itchy and uncomfortable. I was more of a go-it-alone kind of bruja. But it was time to buck up.

My mother grabbed my hand. "Of course, Madeline."

Sam sat on my foot.

I pulled Little Lencha from a pocket of my trench coat and put her on the ground between us. The effect was almost immediate. The figurine turned black. That was new. And promising. Lencha had turned all sorts of colors, but never black.

My mother's eyes widened, and she bowed her head. "Hello, Tia. Welcome," she said, then turned to me. "Chimalma appeared to you," she whispered. "So, you need to be the one to call her."

I could feel eyes staring at me. The gnome's house had cracks between the planks. I imagined my team, on their knees, faces pressed against the wood, watching.

But that wasn't the time to suffer from a crippling bout of performance anxiety.

I needed to focus. To block everything and everyone out. I pushed back my shoulders and closed my eyes. Sam stood on his hind legs and wrapped his front paws around my shin. He pressed his head into my knee. An electric tingle raced upward, hitting every nerve along the way.

My eyes popped open. The air around Sam seemed to shimmer, and I felt an inexplicable connection to every living thing around me—the grass, the damp earth, the trees, my friends in the gnome house, Stu and Hernan in the shed, and my mother next to me. Sam's touch was enhancing my senses, making me a live wire ready to spark.

Leaves skittered across the ground.

"Chimalma," I cried. "Chimalma, please come!"

The air grew warmer, and the wind picked up, whipping my hair around my face. The scent of earth and spice filled my nostrils. Rosemary. Sage. Chili. The spirit of Chimalma appeared again, as substantial and reassuring as comfort food on a dreary day.

Sam's grip tightened. His claws dug through the fabric of my pants. It was weirdly grounding, keeping me tethered while the world around me began to shift. My mother's hand trembled in mine, and when I glanced over at her, her eyes were open but unseeing. Her lips were moving, chanting words I couldn't hear.

The wind shifted, and a chill gripped the air. The scent of familiar herbs vanished, replaced by cold nothingness. Sam hissed. When I glanced down at him, his green eyes were fixed on the sky. My mother's chanting grew louder, her voice urgent.

Bailey's voice came from the gnomes' house. "I can hear them. The swarm is coming!"

Prickly tendrils crawled down my spine, but I pushed the fear aside. We needed every bit of help we could get. I closed my eyes, reaching out to our ancestral land in Mexico.

"Bantacorte brujas," I called, yelling over the winds. "We need you!"

I meant to say something more commanding and poetic, like in the movies. Something like "Join us now! Lend us your strength!" Instead, it sounded like we needed help making tamales because the masa was drying out.

The wind howled louder, and the Bantacorte brujas stirred in the air. Sam rubbed his head against my shin.

My hands began to tingle. My mother's hand jerked in mine.

"It's working," she whispered.

I was desperate to watch the Minizotz arrive, but I didn't dare open my eyes and break the rhythm of our magic. Many brujas drew closer, their ancient power beginning to intermingle with ours. My hands became so hot it was a wonder my mother hadn't cried out in pain. Instead, her chanting had reached a fever pitch.

Something touched my shoulder, and I yelped. My eyes snapped open, and I whirled around, my heart in my throat. My hand broke loose from my mother's grip.

Chimalma was there, solid and real, with a large group of ghostly figures standing behind her. Women. Nineteen of them. Chimalma turned and beckoned them closer. They floated toward us, and their edges resolved. The details of their beautiful brown faces did too. Their layered garments fluttered in the wind—tunics, embroidered scarves, and homespun skirts.

The Bantacorte brujas. All of them.

Tears blurred my vision, and I wiped them away with the back of my hand. "Thank you," I whispered. "Thank you."

Chimalma's dark eyes slid past me and flicked upward, toward the sky.

A familiar sound, like sand being poured through a funnel, filled my ears. The swarm of Minizotz was fast approaching. The tone changed, deepened, and the vibrating hum rattled the loose gravel at our feet.

To the west, a cloud of black appeared in the steel gray sky.

I turned to the Bantacorte brujas and pointed at the stretch of hard red clay, the same stuff Lencha had brought with her from Mexico, the same stuff used to contain the demon bats in remote Mexican caves until they had found a way to escape. The witches nodded. No words were needed between us. They understood what had to be done.

217

My ancestors lined up on either side of the bed of clay and raised their hands in the air, palms facing outward. Blood roared in my ears. I followed their example, and so did my mother. Sam climbed up my body until he was wrapped around my shoulders like a warm, furry stole.

The clay was changing and turning black, with molten cracks that glowed like magma under the earth. The buzzing hum of the tiny, winged creatures was deafening.

The door to the gnome's house banged open, and my team dashed outside, weapons in hand. Their mouths fell open when they spotted my new companions. They spun around to face the incoming threat.

Just when the black cloud reached the gate, the Minizotz halted midair and hovered in place, as if unsure what to do. Panic bubbled in my gut. Had they sensed the power of the brujas? Would they retreat? We needed them to come closer. Much closer.

The cloud pulsated, growing brighter until it was nearly blinding.

"What's happening?" Ron shouted.

I squinted and raised a hand to shield my eyes.

The hum reached a crescendo, and then, abruptly, the light exploded. When my vision cleared, the tiny creatures were gone, and towering over the gate were the massive figures of the Megazotz.

"Fuckity fuck fuck! They changed back!" Bailey shouted.

We had come locked and loaded for the mini versions but were now facing down their original gigantic forms.

"Back to the shelter! Grab the elixir sprayers!" Liam called.

While my team stampeded toward the gnomes' house, the leathery wings of the Megazotz stretched wide and began flapping so furiously the palm trees swayed in the breeze. They rushed toward us, bodies blotting out the sky. Arcs of red-tinged liquid shot upward, singeing their bellies and wings, but that didn't stop them. They were headed straight for us.

I glanced at the Bantacorte brujas. They were all making the same gesture, arms stretched forward, fingers curling, as though inviting the Megazotz closer.

Sam banged his head against my knee. I took the hint and began beckoning the monsters too. But the moment I curled my fingers, a shimmering white rope appeared in my hands, connecting me to the advancing horde.

The ground beneath us rumbled, and I glanced down. The black clay was beginning to churn and bubble. It liquefied, transforming into an inky pool. The largest Megazotz swooped toward me, but before it reached us, it hesitated, wings flapping frantically, hovering above the liquid. I pulled on the thick rope, and the other creatures quickly flanked their leader. Their fear of the clay and their panic were almost electric while they struggled against the rope.

And the clay's hunger was an unforgiving, ravenous void.

The rope pulsed, and I gritted my teeth, pulling harder.

The creatures resisted, but our combined bruja power was too strong.

I jerked the first enormous Megazotz down into the pool. The liquid churned violently while the creature thrashed, shrieking and trying to escape. But the more it struggled, the faster it was pulled under.

I heaved on the rope once more, yanking as hard as I could. With the strength of twenty-three generations of brujas, I drew the rope toward me, hand over hand, tugging the creatures toward the clay. They began to shriek, fighting against the cord in a panic of noise and movement, but it was all in vain.

One by one, the remaining demon bats disappeared under the surface.

I released the rope, and it dissolved into a million flecks of dust before it fell to the ground.

The quiet, still air around us told me we were alone again. I looked around me but saw only my mother, my cat, and my team. The Bantacorte brujas had gone, their jobs done.

A wave of dizziness knocked me to my knees, and Sam pushed his big furry head into my neck. I was so tired. My hand felt like a ten-pound weight while I stroked his fur.

"Good job, Sam," I said, my voice breaking.

The black pool returned to its normal shade of terra cotta but remained a thick liquid. A moment later, something popped out and landed at my feet with a dull thud. The liquid began to froth and bubble again, like boiling mud.

My mother reached for my hand, and together we watched, transfixed, while the surface began to dull and solidify, hardening from the edges inward, locking the Megazotz within its depths.

Stu pulled me to my feet and hugged me.

My mother bent over with a little grunt, picked up the object from the ground, and pressed it into my hand with a rueful chuckle. "I think this is yours."

It was as heavy as a paperweight and still warm. I looked down at the object in my hand and began to laugh.

"Now, that's one darn tootin' memento," Hernan said.

He was right. It was a crude figure of the Megazotz leader, made from my aunt's magic clay, perfectly capturing the alarmed expression on its squashed face while it disappeared into the earth.

Chapter 34

It was shocking how quickly life returned to normal in Chavez Ravine. I ended the lockdown immediately, and within hours, people were outside cleaning up storm debris, and cars were back on the roads. By the next day, Olga's Cantina and Muertos Café were doing a booming business.

Everyone who had been staying at Stu's place left for home, including me. Augustina had given my little house in La Loma a thorough cleaning and had mopped the floors with lavender-scented Fabuloso. A dozen yellow roses in a vase sat on the kitchen table, along with a freshly baked pound cake.

It felt good to be in my own place. Little Lencha was back on the workbench in the sunroom, resting peacefully. Sam dozed on the striped ottoman, worn out from his work. I blasted some Tito Puente and did a workout, took a long hot soak in the bathtub, stopped for a cafecito at Muertos Café, and then went grocery shopping at Palo Verde Market, where I splurged on skirt steak.

Though I was a little nervous about running into people and getting bombarded with complaints about how long it had taken to get rid of the Megazotz, I was instead greeted with smiles.

Even the checkout clerk was grateful. "Thank goodness for you and your team!"

I ran into Rory Tuck, the hot-headed developer who had built several new homes at the end of my street next to Elysian Park. When he came up behind me in the checkout lane at the market, I cringed, expecting a public lashing for having upset his new homeowners, but he clapped me on the back, congratulated me on a job well done, and said he owed me a drink.

I spent the afternoon and early evening in the kitchen, cooking, with the windows cracked open to let in the fresh air. My neighbors Leo and Toby returned from out of town and stopped by to say hello.

"I'm so glad we missed all that hullabaloo," Leo said. "Come over for G&Ts later?"

Leo made the demon bats from Mexico sound like just another annoying HOA drama.

"Raincheck? Stu's coming over."

Stu had said he had something serious to discuss. He had sounded serious too.

I wondered if all my bruja behavior had bothered him. He seemed to take it in stride, but between the gathering of Bantacorte brujas and my magical cat, it was a lot.

I also felt a little guilty I hadn't spent more time with Clare, who, after all, had been in the house for the entirety of the lockdown. Once it ended, Stu said Clare missed the excitement and the company and was now moping around, complaining about how sad it was to be an only child. I had invited her to dinner, but Clare had declined, saying she was going to stay home to eat pizza and watch movies with her best friend, Iris. And they were having a sleepover. Which was Clare's way of telling me she was fine if her dad stayed the night.

I made a salad and a vegetable casserole, with mushrooms and zucchini flowers, to go along with the grilled skirt steak. Then I set the kitchen table, wishing I had a proper dining room. After spending time in Stu's enormous house, mine felt small.

Stu arrived with two bottles of pinot noir. He was dressed casually in jeans and a soft blue shirt with rolled-up sleeves. The color was a shade lighter than his eyes. When he set the wine on the kitchen counter, I couldn't help but notice his hands trembling slightly. He was giving off a nervous energy.

"Everything okay?" I asked, fighting off a wave of dread and trying to keep my tone light.

Stu hesitated a moment before replying. "Yeah. Fine. But I guess I should say what I need to say and get it over with."

I watched him take a deep breath, clearly steeling himself for whatever news he had to share. Maybe his wife had ditched her new husband and wanted Stu back. Perhaps he had accepted a new job in a foreign country. Maybe he had reconnected with an old girlfriend who had a regular job, a normal life, and bigger boobs.

I cleared my throat and nodded. "Yeah. Sure. Go for it."

Stu walked out of the kitchen and returned a moment later, his hands behind his back, his face red.

I had never seen him so flustered. "Forget something?"

In one giant step, he closed the distance between us and placed a small box next to a flickering candle on the table.

My heart started pounding. It wasn't just any box. It was a jewelry box. A *ring* box. Chartreuse velvet.

"What's this?" I sounded suspicious, like Stu was about to prank me.

He ran his fingers through his sandy hair. "I've been waiting for the right moment, except it never seems to be the right moment." He grimaced. "Just open it."

My fingers trembled slightly while I unlatched the brass clasp and lifted the lid. A square diamond set in a gold band glistened against green velvet. I dragged my eyes away from the ring to Stu, who was pressing his fists against his chin and shifting from foot to foot.

For a successful businessman, he was acting uncharacteristically unsure of himself.

"Is it okay?" he stammered. "Do you like it?"

I jumped to my feet and threw my arms around him. "Of course, I like it. I *love* it. It's beautiful. But I had no idea you…" I ran out of words.

Stu pulled away and grinned. "Have been thinking about asking you to marry me? I wanted to surprise you, but Julia said I should ask you first, and then you'd say yes, and then we'd go pick out rings together. Except I wasn't so sure you'd say yes. So, I thought maybe seeing the ring would help convince you—"

"Convince me! You thought I'd need convincing?"

Stu shrugged. "I was worried you'd prefer just living together. Or that it was too soon, that I was rushing things."

My insides fizzed like champagne. This smart, amazing man had just proposed. To me! And for some crazy reason, he had been nervous about it and thought I might turn him down. As if that would ever happen. I wasn't sure what the future of Chavez Ravine would bring, but I wouldn't have to face it alone. Stu, my husband, would be at my side.

Tears stung my eyes. "As if I'd ever pass up an opportunity to spend the rest of my life with you." My voice wobbled a little.

Stu grabbed my left hand and tapped my ring finger. "So, is that a yes?"

"That's a *hell yes!*" My feet seemed to have lives of their own, and they started to tap out a Latin-style rhythm.

Stu was sexy, supportive, and kind. He wasn't possessive, needy, self-absorbed, or negative. And I loved being around him.

I held out the box. "I love you. As in, I *adore* you. Now, put that on my finger and let's celebrate. In the bedroom."

Stu laughed, and his blue eyes twinkled. "I admire a lady who knows what she wants."

But first, I turned the oven off. There would be plenty of heat upstairs.

———•··•·┊┊┊┊·•··•·———

The next morning, while Stu was showering, Sam sauntered in from the hallway. His green eyes were fixed on the emerald-cut ring sparkling on my finger.

I held out my hand. "Good morning. Stu asked me to marry him. And I said yes, of course. But I just want you to know…you'll always be my cat. My special cat. Nothing can ever change that."

Sam lifted his large head, stretched, and gave an enormous yawn. He couldn't have looked more bored if he had tried.

"I'll get your breakfast, sir." I reached for a can of food from the cupboard, a little annoyed Sam hadn't been more enthusiastic. There was no doubt he had understood me.

Maybe Stu had spent enough time in my house that Sam didn't understand what the big deal was. The guy already walked around with a towel around his waist and occasionally served Sam breakfast. What difference would a ring make to a cat?

Clare, when we told her later that day, had been much more excited. Genuinely so. She had jumped up and down and thrown her arms around my neck.

"This is awesome," she had said. "It's like you two were meant for each other!"

Stu seemed very relieved, and I will admit, I was too. Her mother's affair had wrecked Clare's world. When I finally came on the scene, Clare had greeted me like a threatened porcupine. But between my cooking, attention, and hard-earned brujería, I had won her over.

My mother was a harder sell.

"That's wonderful," she said, her tone carefully neutral.

We were sitting in the living room of Hernan's house. It was only November, but my mother had already decorated for Christmas, complete with a seven-foot fir tree covered in twinkling chili lights.

"Is there a problem?" I asked, keeping my voice light.

Hernan's eyes flicked between us, wary.

My mother gave a little shrug. "No, not a problem for us. But you're marrying someone with a child. Have you given any thought to being a stepmother? What that responsibility entails?"

"She has parents," I said. "I'm not replacing anyone. I'm just an extra set of hands."

"You make it sound so easy." She sipped her hot toddy and studied me over the rim of her mug. "Have you given any thought to when you'll be getting married? We don't want to have our weddings too close together, now do we?"

And there it was. My mother didn't care about stepmotherhood. She just didn't want to share the spotlight.

"No, we don't want that," I agreed.

"Well, it would be nice if we could coordinate the dates. What kind of wedding are you going to have?"

Stu and I hadn't discussed it, but I knew what I wanted and was fairly sure he would see things my way. "A small one. Casual."

She nodded approvingly. "That sounds nice. Given your age."

"Malena!" Hernan looked horrified. "*We're* the old ones, remember?"

My mother bristled. "We're only as old as we feel. What I'm saying is, Maddy won't want a big traditional wedding. She's forty, not twenty-five." She looked at me, and her expression softened. "I'm sorry, hija. You just took me by surprise, that's all. I had no idea you and Stu were even thinking about getting married. But honestly, I am very happy for you. How about a hug?"

She stretched out her arms.

While I was hugging her back, Hernan winked, like we were two old conspirators, and I felt a warm rush of affection for my future stepfather. Tears pricked at the corners of my eyes, and I quickly blinked them away.

I had a busy afternoon ahead of me. Stu and I were meeting with Rory Tuck about building a new house on Great-Aunt Lencha's former property, a plan that would preserve the shed and the magical red clay.

That evening, we took Clare for a birthday dinner at Olga's Cantina. The party for her and Iris was just days away, but that was for their friend group, and we wanted to celebrate her eighteenth too. Olga's was Clare's choice. She had met the restaurant owner during a music video shoot, where she'd had a small part arranged by Stu's most famous client, pop star Bad Pete. To Clare's surprise, and everyone else's too, Olga had invited Pete, and he stopped by to take pictures with the ecstatic birthday girl and give her a present—a stack of books about succeeding in college.

"I wish I'd gone to uni," he said wistfully just before he left.

Becca Tey, the actress, was there too. She had arrived early, and we met for a drink to catch up before everyone else showed up. Her dark hair and eyes set off the white satin of her blouse.

At dinner, I sat between Becca and Stu, across from Hernan and my mother.

When we started our second course of machaca, Becca glanced over at Clare, who was giggling over something with Julia Suarez. "She's such a great girl," Becca said fondly. "I think you've been a good influence on her. She seems a lot more confident since you came on the scene."

I nearly choked on my red wine. "She never had a problem giving me back-off vibes when I first started going out with her father."

Becca rolled her eyes. "That's not what I mean. She was just…insecure. Maybe even a little jealous. I'm talking about the kind of confidence that comes when a kid knows they're safe. Loved. The kind of kid who never has to second-guess their place. After what happened between her father and his ex-wife, that's exactly what she needed, and that's what you gave her."

Becca raised her glass.

"Good job," she said with a wink. "Here's to not being a sucky stepmom." Her eyes fell to the ring on my left hand. "And congratulations. Stu's a great guy. I'm sure your engagement has sent every single cougar within a ten-mile radius into mourning."

We clinked our glasses.

"And congratulations on your new part. That's fantastic. It's the same role that made you famous, right? But now in the new reboot?"

"Yes! Can you believe it?" Becca grinned. Her teeth were very white. "My agent pulled off a miracle because the producers wanted a much younger actor. I actually get to play my own age for once. Haha!"

I was about to reply about the unfairness of it all when Clare called me over. "Maddy! Maddy! Look what Julia gave me!"

I went over to investigate. Clare held up a black T-shirt. There was no mistaking Julia's distinctive artwork. It showed a woman with her face painted like a Day of the Dead skull, hair tied up in a red and white polka-dot scarf, flexing an arm muscle. A wonderful take on Rosie the Riveter. But it was the caption that made me laugh. "Chingonas Can Do It!"

"It's hilarious, right?" Clare said. "And she made one for all of us. Your mom and Becca too. So we can wear them when we're together."

My insides went as soft and gooey as flan straight out of the oven. I planted a kiss on her forehead. "It's better than hilarious," I said, ruffling Julia's auburn hair. "It's perfect."

Clare beamed. "It's a good thing you taught me how to be a chingona because I'm pretty sure I'm going to need to be one at college." She grabbed my hand and pulled me close. "And if that doesn't work, I'll have a bruja stepmom who can help me out. Right?"

I clutched my T-shirt to my chest. Tears stung my eyes, and I nodded. "Chingonas unidas." I flexed my bicep, imitating Rosie's famous pose.

Chapter 35

My mother certainly knew how to reclaim the spotlight.

Just hours after Stu and I told friends about our news, my mother announced *she* planned to marry the weekend before Christmas.

"But that's so soon!" I tried not to sound put out. "Are you sure?"

"Yes, I'm sure. Hernan says at our age and with his health issues, it would be silly to wait."

She dropped the bomb while we were out shopping with Julia at our favorite boutique in Los Angeles. It sold beautiful one-of-a-kind samples and was the same place where I had found the trench coats that became staples of my wardrobe.

My mother held up a knee-length champagne dress. "What do you think about this?"

"For your wedding?"

My mother rolled her eyes. "Where else would I wear something like this? Yes, for my wedding. We've decided on a simple service at Santo Nino church, with the reception at Hernan's. I've already talked to Cora about doing the catering, and I'd like to invite your security team, and Steve and Dria, and that adorable Malik fellow."

Before I could reply, she disappeared into a fitting room.

Julia hurried over with a floor-length cream-colored dress. "And here's one for you! It's fabulous, yeah?"

She wasn't exaggerating. A deep V-neck. Gathered at the waist. Flowing chiffon skirt.

I checked the price tag, and my eyes bulged. "What a deal. If it fits, I'm taking it."

"But you haven't tried on any others!" Julia's shoulders drooped. She loved shopping for beautiful and unusual things, and from the moment she heard Stu and I were engaged, she probably imagined many weekends in boutiques, with breaks at cute little cafés.

I actually felt a little guilty when we walked out of the shop carrying two bags holding our wedding dresses.

"I'm starving," my mother said. "Where should we go for lunch?"

"Philippe's," Julia and I said at the same time, and we laughed.

Sadly, our trip to the French dip restaurant was delayed, thanks to an entity eruption on Olivera Street.

I was remembering my first encounter with chaneques on that same street when my phone buzzed in my pocket. It was Jo from the Occult Affairs command center.

"Mads, you'll never guess what just happened."

My heart went still. "Please don't tell me the Megazotz popped up in LA."

Jo scoffed. "No, of course not. Not after what you ladies did to them. Hah! No, it's the chief. He's gone."

"What? Gone as in dead, or gone as in fired?"

"Fired! Effective immediately. He was just escorted out of the building." Jo paused, and I could hear voices in the background. "Sorry, Mads. I gotta go. We're having an all-hands meeting. I'll fill you in later."

Seconds later, my phone chimed with a text from Steve.

OMG. Chief = FIRED. Just happened. Guess the Mayor went ballistic over how he handled CR situation. Cutting off neighborhoods = political suicide. Will update when I know more.

When we finally got to Philippe's, I was in the mood to celebrate. I ordered a nice, cold beer to go along with my lamb French dip.

⸻ ⋅ꞏ⋅ 🏛 ⋅ꞏ⋅ ⸻

Julia, Clare, and I helped my mother decorate the house for the reception. We made centerpieces out of twinkly fairy lights in mason jars, with sprigs of eucalyptus tied with jute. All three of us were staying the night. Clare had proposed doing my mother's makeup, and to my surprise, my mother agreed.

"Well, she's practically my step-granddaughter, so I couldn't very well say no," she had confided.

The next day, Cora and her catering team set up in the kitchen. My mother and Hernan tied the knot in a late afternoon ceremony at the little church in Palo Verde, and by the time we all trooped into Hernan's house—well, Hernan and my mother's house—it smelled of fresh pine garlands and tamales.

The furniture had been cleared out of the large living room, and the double doors to the side yard opened into a heated tent, transforming the space into one big party room with round tables.

I was wearing a sage-colored dress Julia had picked out, with my mother's approval. Clare wore a similar style in a darker green that flattered her complexion.

My mother had carried through with her invitations to my team, who were delighted to be asked. Steve looked sharp in a dark blue suit. Dria wore a dark blue satin jumpsuit. Julia and Ben disappeared for a while after the ceremony, and when they reappeared, Julia was holding Sam, who wriggled out of her arms and came running straight for me.

Sam jumped onto my lap, which was a very un-Sam-like thing to do.

"What's *he* doing here?"

Julia laughed. "I don't know. Your mother asked us to bring him, so we did."

Sam began to knead my thighs with his paws.

"Take it easy," I said, scratching his head. "You're going to rip my dress."

I scanned the room, searching for my mother, and spotted her near the door to the kitchen, watching me. She arched her eyebrows and cocked her head to one side. I knew that expression well. Her silent announcement that she wanted to talk.

I sighed, picked up my heavy cat, and set him on the ground. My mother beckoned me to follow her down the hall toward Hernan's study. The last time I had been there, it needed a good dusting and smelled like old, moldy books. But that had been before Hurricane Malena. The room had undergone a major upgrade and smelled lemon fresh. Even the antique prints on the walls had been updated and were hanging in matching dark wood frames.

I took it all in. "Nice work in here." I turned to my mother. "What's up?"

"Your cat," she said, patting the top of Hernan's desk.

Sam ran through the door and jumped onto the desk. He landed neatly between a stack of books and a rather scary clay Dia de los Muertos skull.

"What about him?" I was surprised she wanted to talk about Sam while we had a house full of guests and a wedding reception in full swing.

"We're going to settle this once and for all," she said, narrowing her eyes. "And no arguments. I'll explain when we're done."

My curiosity made me keep my mouth shut. If she was willing to interrupt her own wedding day festivities, she must have had a good reason.

She took a large votive candle from a shelf and lit it, opened a desk drawer, and retrieved a small tin medal, the kind they sold in church gift shops.

"Is that a saint?" I asked. "Which one?"

My mother ran the medal over the top of Sam's head, then down his neck and back. "Saint Gertrude. The patron saint of cats, though I don't think she's officially sanctioned by the Vatican."

"I see." Although I didn't really. Why my mother thought it was necessary to drag poor Saint Gertrude into whatever she was doing, I had no idea.

Sam twitched his ears and flicked his tail.

"Behave," I warned in a quiet voice.

"He's fine," my mother said. She had never seen him take a chunk out of Stu, and she would have been furious if Sam made her bleed on her wedding dress.

I collapsed into a chair with a sigh of resignation. Laughter drifted in from the hallway. It sounded like people were doing tequila shots, and I wished I could join them.

My mother leaned over Sam and began whispering in his ear. He appeared to listen intently for a while, and then his green eyes slowly closed. My mother stopped whispering but stayed bent over Sam's head. Her face scrunched up, and she began nodding.

I had seen enough of her performances to know she was deep in psychic conversation, but what she and Sam had to talk about was a mystery.

After a few minutes of this, her eyes popped open, and she straightened.

"Well?"

My mother smiled. "Well, that was interesting. And a very successful reading, if I may say so myself."

"And?"

"It's just as I thought. Sam is no ordinary cat. He's an amplifier. Specifically, for brujas...to help with their magic."

I sat upright in my chair. "An amplifier? I thought you were kidding. Is that an actual thing?"

"Of course, it's a thing. I wouldn't joke about something like that. Just like we come from a line of Bantacorte brujas, he comes from a line of Bengals bred just for this purpose."

I frowned. Rory Tuck, Sam's original owner, had called him Hugo.

"Tuck said Sam cost a small fortune."

"And for good reason." My mother sniffed. "The breeder was a witch, and she specialized in this sort of thing."

"Sam told you that?"

"Now you're just being silly. Rory Tuck told me that. I called him the other day and asked him. You could have asked him too, if you would have troubled yourself. I just wanted to hear it from Sam directly. He says he's very happy to have found you. He says he didn't connect with Rory, not the way you two do."

I had already been misty-eyed at the church when my mother and Hernan exchanged their vows, and now I was definitely going to need to go to the bathroom and fix my eye makeup because I was tearing up again.

"Why did you decide to do this today, of all days?"

"It seemed funny not to have him here with us," she said in a small voice. "He's one of us, you know?"

I *did* know, and I was grateful to my mother for what she had just done. I hugged her and then Sam.

He tolerated it for a moment, then batted my head and ran from the room.

Sure enough, Hernan was in the living room, pouring shots of Añejo tequila. His housekeeper, Marta, bustled around in a black pantsuit, handing out appetizers: taquitos and crab and chipotle cream tostados.

After several mushy toasts, Steve knelt by my chair. "I found out what happened to the chief," he said with a sidelong look at Augustina Paz, who was engaged in a lively conversation with Cora.

"Oh?"

He smiled. "Yeah. So, the story is, Cora was at her restaurant for some big event with the mayor, and apparently, they go way back. She gave him an earful about the way the chief denied you and your team the help you needed. She said the chief ordered the quarantine out of spite, and that put everyone in Chavez Ravine at risk. Apparently, that's all he needed to hear."

It wasn't the first time Cora had surprised me, and I felt a whole new level of respect for the founder of a tamale empire. The grandmotherly HOA president knew very well how to wield soft power when she needed to.

Dria joined us. "Hey, Steve...Did you tell Maddy about the eruption holes?"

That got my attention.

"He did not," I said, frowning.

"Well, there's no sign of them." Dria seemed excited to break the news. "They closed up. That's a very good sign."

"So, what do you two think? Were the Megazotz Entities 2.0s?"

Steve shrugged. "Probably not. Especially after what you told us about the Bantacorte witches."

I shot him a look of warning.

"Which we promise not to share," he added hastily.

Dria's head bobbed up and down. "Never. Ever."

Steve leaned in. "I'm beginning to think there's no such thing as an Entity 2.0. One can never be sure, but I'm beginning to doubt it. It's good for job security, though."

I supposed he was right. At one point, I had thought the future of my security team depended upon uncertainty, that as long as there was the possibility of entities invading Chavez Ravine, the community would support us. But after everything we had been through, the board had assured me the Chavez Ravine HOA had no intention of pulling the plug.

Bailey, tipsy from too many tequila shots, pushed back from her chair, stood up, and lifted her champagne glass. "I know you're not technically family, but it feels like you are. All of you. I'm so glad to be here, celebrating with everyone. Thank you for inviting me, Malena and Hernan." She turned to me and gave me a wobbly smile. "We have a lot to celebrate, don't we, Maddy?"

She sat down abruptly and buried her head in Malik's shoulder.

I was thinking of what to say when Cora stood up. She bowed her head toward the bride and groom, who were sitting at a table for two at the front of the room.

"I hope you don't mind, Malena and Hernan. I know this is your day, but I just wanted to say a quick word about how much Chavez Ravine is indebted to Maddy and her team for everything they've done to keep us safe. And, of course, thanks to you both too." She winked. "I understand you played an important role, and for that, you'll forever have my gratitude."

Hernan brought his hands together and dipped his head in acknowledgment. My mother smiled, misty-eyed.

Clare nudged her chair closer to me and Stu and rested her head on my shoulder.

"How are you doing?" I asked.

She nodded, then yawned. "Fine. I'm just tired. And I was thinking…I might study criminal justice in college. You and your friends have such interesting jobs. I'm considering a career in Occult Affairs."

"No!" Stu and I said at the same time, and Clare burst out laughing.

I looked around the room at all the familiar faces. Sam brushed up against my leg.

Stu leaned forward and peered into my eyes. "Are you okay?"

I took a bite of tamale. "Better than okay," I said, returning Hernan's wave from across the room. "I'm darn tootin' fantastic."

THE END

Author's note

Thank you for coming along on this journey with Maddy Madrigal and her crew.

I'll admit it: My heart hurts a little knowing this is likely my last book set in Chavez Ravine. My mother and her family lived in Palo Verde and were among the evicted residents, and these stories have been my way of keeping their memories alive.

But they've also been something more. I've spent years imagining what Chavez Ravine might look like today if the neighborhoods had been allowed to survive. With its stunning geography and prime Los Angeles location—right where Dodger Stadium now sits—I suspect it would have faced intense gentrification. That "what if" is what led me to reimagine it as a gated community with an HOA. I hope you enjoyed reading about that alternate world as much as I enjoyed building it.

As for what's next, I'm planning a prequel novella about Maddy's early days in Occult Affairs, and after that, a brand new series.

The best way to stay in the loop is to join my newsletter at debracastaneda.com. I hope to see you there!

Debra Castaneda

Keep reading for a preview of *A Dark and Rising Tide*, a novel inspired by real events

Chapter 1

If the man in the small boat didn't sit down, it would tip over.

He had no business being out there—a tourist probably getting his first glimpse of a great white shark circling just below the surface. A storm was coming, and Marty, the owner of Boat & Tackle, should have closed shop. But he liked money as much as he did the whiskey in his stainless steel coffee mug, and he obviously thought he could sneak in a few rentals before calling it a day.

Marty never seemed to learn his lesson, renting his motorized skiffs to anyone over twenty-one with a credit card, including men who'd knocked back too many beermosas in the restaurant at the end of the pier.

Carla scowled and wiped at a stubborn window smudge. The entire back of the restaurant was one plate of glass after another, and she had a clear shot of the action. Marty was hanging over the railing, shouting instructions and probably confusing the hell out of the boater. A small group of onlookers peered over the railing.

Sliding open the glass door, Carla stepped outside on the deck, still clutching the damp rag. The relentless winter surf roared two dozen yards away—a distance that didn't seem nearly far enough during high tide. The damp air was chilly and heavy with the scent of the sea. Cries of seagulls overhead pierced through the rumble of crashing waves.

Carla had weathered many storms since she'd taken over Pancha's Mexican Restaurant from her parents twelve years ago, and she knew the forecasts were often wrong. She remembered the last time meteorologists had predicted a massive storm. Everyone had panicked and evacuated, but the storm had gone off course. Carla closed the restaurant for nothing and had paid to stay in a motel, with no money coming in.

This time, no matter how dire the forecasts, she was determined not to leave. Besides, her apartment was on the second floor. Even if Ocean View Drive flooded, she'd be safe up there.

The small red boat reached the base of the stairs below the pier. Marty was down there, trying to help the man out.

"They're both going to end up in the water."

Carla glanced over in surprise. It was Matt Harmon, her best friend's husband and owner of the fish restaurant next door.

"I thought you decided not to open today."

He pulled a face. "Yuki reminded me we booked a private party for lunch. A bunch of women coming from Stockton or someplace for a bridal shower."

"I guess they haven't been watching the news," Carla said, one eye still on the men stumbling up the ramp.

Matt scraped a hand through what was left of his red hair. "I just hope they have a designated driver. The last shower we had got pretty wild."

"I remember. They came to my place afterwards, and one of them threw up nachos. That shit ended up on the ceiling."

Matt grimaced. "Yuki told me. Sorry." He jerked his head in the direction of the pier. "Think that dude out there got bumped by a shark?"

Carla laughed. "Maybe he just lost his phone."

The smile quickly vanished. A blank look spread over her face as she recalled her son's panic when his phone fell into the creek while they were kayaking together.

Days later, she'd lost him.

Her throat tightened.

Breathe. Just breathe. Like the therapist said.

Matt swiveled to face her. "You okay?"

As okay as I'll ever be. She didn't need to tell Matt that. He knew. Knew all about it. Most people did, even if they didn't say anything.

Inside, the phone rang. Carla wished Matt good luck with the bridal shower lunch, then ran in to answer it. It was an old-fashioned land line, an ugly beige box stuck to the wall next to the bar, with a long cord that tended to tangle. She only kept it because some of the locals still used it, and they constituted most of her clientele during the off-season.

"You're probably wondering what the hell is going on over here," Sue said without preamble. Carla had known the woman since her parents opened the restaurant forty years ago. Sue was the sensible half of Boat & Tackle.

"The guy on the boat saw a shark?" Carla guessed.

"No, no sharks. Said he was fishing, caught something, and was pulling it in, but when he saw what it was, it scared the bejeesus out of him, and he couldn't figure out how to get it off the line, so he dropped the darn rod. It was one of our nicer rentals, of course."

Carla nudged open the swinging door into the kitchen and peered through the gap. Gilbert was dropping sprigs of cilantro into a steel pot bubbling on the stove. The skull tattoos on his arms were so old, the lines had grown blurry, and they now looked like green blobs against his brown skin.

In the distance, a siren wailed.

"You called an ambulance?" The man appeared to have made it off the skiff just fine.

"We did," Sue said, voice rising with excitement. "Whatever it was, stung him. Real bad."

"A jellyfish?"

"Nope. Said it was big and ugly and got him with the end of a long tentacle or something."

Carla frowned. She was no expert on fish, but she'd never heard of anything like that in the Monterey Bay.

"Did you call Amalia?"

Amalia owned San Refugio Charters, Whale Watching & Cruises. She ran her business out of an office on the other side of the fish restaurant, next to the swollen creek. Amalia could name most of the species out there.

"Yup. She's coming over now, as a matter of fact." Sue paused. "You should see the guy's arm where it got him. It's got a hole in it, and it's all purple and gross-looking, and he's acting real out of it. I hope he doesn't have a fit or something before the paramedics get here."

The wailing siren drew closer.

"That's terrible," Carla muttered. If the restaurant weren't opening soon, she'd run over there and look for herself.

"I tried calling Peter, but he didn't answer," Sue said, sounding offended.

Peter was a former park ranger and state lifeguard. He lived in the San Refugio Ocean Condominiums, the unit closest to the water. On many a night, Carla helped keep his bed warm and, in the morning, cooked chilaquiles in a tiny kitchen with chipped turquoise tiles. The place had to be worth two million dollars.

"Peter went to the East Bay to see his nephews," she explained.

"He's a good guy. You should make him put a ring on it."

Sue hung up before Carla could think of a snappy comeback.

Carla went out on the deck, just in time to see the paramedics and an ambulance roll past the condos, red lights flashing.

She watched the vehicles make their way toward the far end of the rickety pier. It was a miracle the thing was still standing. In her four decades in the seaside village, several storms had come through and done their best to knock it down, but it still stood.

Her gaze drifted to the sea. The sky was darkening—gray clouds rolling over the bay.

The bay where her only child rested in a watery grave.

Books by Debra Castaneda

Maddy Madrigal Mysteries
Monsters, mayhem, and Mexican food

Barely Magic (Maddy Madrigal Mysteries Book 1)
Maddy lands a cushy security job in a gated community but must confront a supernatural threat and come to terms with her magical heritage.

Somewhat Magic (Maddy Madrigal Mysteries Book 2)
In the heart of Los Angeles, Maddy Madrigal battles legendary creatures and unscrupulous developers as an old protective spell begins to fail.

Desperate Magic (Maddy Madrigal Mysteries Book 3)
Maddy Madrigal must unravel a web of supernatural clues and confront ancient predators to stop a string of brutal murders.

Mortal Magic (Maddy Madrigal Mysteries Book 4)
Something ancient and deadly is roosting outside Chavez Ravine, and Maddy's weapons, magic, and extremely agitated cat aren't enough to fight it off.

Tangled Magic (Maddy Madrigal Mysteries Book 5)
Maddy must combine her magic and detective skills to put an end to a dangerous and powerful legacy. But HOA politics and a dangerous romance get in the way.

Major Magic (Maddy Madrigal Mysteries Book 6)
The moment Maddy's been dreading finally arrives: New and dangerous creatures appear in Chavez Ravine. The epic conclusion!

Dark Earth Rising
Themed novels that can be read in any order

A Dark and Rising Tide
When a massive storm surge hits the central coast of California, the ferocious surf destroys buildings, floods streets, and washes up something sinister from the depths of the Monterey Bay.

The Devil's Shallows
Eight miles of mystery. One night of terror. Residents trapped in a remote neighborhood confront the unimaginable.

The Copper Man
Haunted tunnels. Unexplained deaths. Eerie sightings. Decades after The Copper Man killed her brother, Leah Shaw returns to the remote mining town of Tribulation Gulch where a lethal mystery awaits.

The Root Witch
A beautiful forest. A terrifying legend. It's 1986. Two strangers, hundreds of miles apart, grapple with disturbing incidents in a one-of-a-kind quaking aspen forest.

Circus at Devil's Landing
Creatures that howl in the night, a mysterious circus, and a clash between a ringmaster and a woman determined to rescue her captured lover.

The Spore Queen
A charming reporter, an ailing tech mogul, and two strangers hiding secrets are brought together by a mysterious fungus, one that will either save them or destroy them.

Chavez Ravine Novels
Stand-alone novels set in Chavez Ravine, Los Angeles during turbulent times

The Monsters of Chavez Ravine
A 2021 International Latino Book Awards Gold Medal Winner! Before Dodger Stadium, dark forces terrorized Chavez Ravine.

The Night Lady
A rebel curandera, a plucky seamstress, and a young reporter are pulled into the investigation of a killer terrorizing Chavez Ravine.

The Haunting of Chavez Ravine
La Llorona is terrorizing people in the hills of Chavez Ravine, and a sassy curandera and her clever young niece must stop her.

The Christmas Cucuy
It's Christmas Eve, 1949, and Kiki's dreams are about to come true: she'll be singing at Palladium with her old bandmates. But when she threatens her rambunctious son with El Cucuy, her plans change.